THE PRAYER BOX

BY HARVEY S. CARAS

To Joanne, the love of my life,
whose incredible love and kindness
inspired me to write this book.

CHAPTER 1

Susan Gold was sound asleep in the bedroom of her Florida home around midnight when she was startled awake by the sound of her door-bell. It wasn't just one ring but over and over until she was able to get out of bed, grab her robe, and hustle to the front door, where she was met by her best friend, Carla Rintone, in full panic mode. The headlights of Carla's car blinded Susan as she opened the door.

"Where is it? I gotta have it now!" Carla screamed in anguish.

"What are you talking about, honey?"

"The box, the box. I need the box!" Carla burst into the house and began to search frantically. "Where is the box? Please Susie, I need it right now!"

"Okay, okay Carla I'll get it for you but please tell me why you need it." Susan walked straight to the bookcase, removed the little wooden box from its perch and handed it to her friend.

"Danny was in an accident. I'll explain later. I gotta run. I'll call you later." Carla ran out the door.

Susan watched as Carla ran to her waiting car clutching the little box, backed out of the driveway, and sped away. She tried to go back to sleep but her mind raced with the fear of what might have happened to Daniel.

Danny was Carla's only son. He had just turned thirty. For the past three years, since his divorce, he had been living in Carla's house. But what was wrong with him tonight? What kind of accident did he have? How badly was he injured? What could be so bad that Carla needed the prayer box? And would the prayer box really do any good? It had never been tested before, at least not since it had showed up in Susan's house two weeks ago. What if it really works? Oh my God, what if it fails? Do we even know how to use it?

For two hours she sat waiting for the phone to ring with news from Carla. But nothing. At two in the morning she took a sleeping pill and jumped into bed.

The pill kept Susan in a heavy sleep until she was awakened by a phone call at nine AM. She eagerly grabbed the phone, hoping to hear Carla's voice.

"Hello," she said.

"Susie, where are you?" came the booming voice of her neighbor Patty Eagan. "We're next on the tee."

Susan had completely forgotten about her golf game today.

"Sorry Patty, go ahead without me this morning. Something happened last night and I have to wait here until it gets resolved."

"Anything I can do to help?"

"Uh no, but thanks. I just have to wait for a phone call. Maybe I'll catch up with you on the course later."

"Okay, honey. We'll miss ya."

Susan got out of bed, washed her face and walked to the kitchen to make a cup of coffee. Just as she put the cup to her lips the front door opened and in walked Carla. It was obvious she had been up all night and she was holding the little box. Tears filled her eyes.

"It worked Suze, it worked!"

"Come sit and tell me all about it." She poured a second cup of coffee and the two friends sat down in the lanai by the pool.

Carla blew on her coffee and began.

"I got a call last night from the emergency room at Martin Memorial. They said Danny was in a motor cycle accident and they needed me to get there as soon as possible."

Susan took a sip of coffee. "Oh my God," she said.

Carla was shaking as she spoke. "That's why I came here first to get the box."

Susan offered her friend a muffin. "So what happened when you got there?"

"They took me into the ER and they said Danny was in surgery. They said he had multiple injuries and that a doctor would come and talk to me as soon as he was out of surgery."

"Oh, God."

"I waited for what seemed like hours before a doctor finally came to talk to me. He said Daniel had suffered a serious brain injury. The surgery was done to control the swelling of the brain. I asked if Danny was going to make it and he shook his head."

"He shook his head no?"

"He said he had seen many head injuries but this was one of the worst he had ever seen. Danny was thrown off his bike and , even though he was wearing a helmet, his head smashed into the pavement at about thirty miles an hour."

"So what happened next?"

"Then the doctor asked me if Danny was an organ donor. That's when I freaked out. I said 'take me to him now!'"

"Did they let you see him?"

"I wasn't taking no for an answer so they took me to him. I could barely recognize him. His head was all swollen and bandaged and he was hooked up to machines. It was the most horrible sight I ever saw. That's when I opened the prayer box."

"You opened it?"

"Well, I figured if I was gonna pray for Danny I would use the box to pray too, so I opened it and set it down next him in his bed."

Both women paused to drink and eat as Carla continued.

"I sat there for hours just watching Danny. At one point a woman came in and asked if I would sign papers to donate Danny's organs. She said he could save many lives with his organs and they had a team on call to take care of it."

"What did you say to the lady?"

"You don't want to hear what I said," Carla smiled for the first time. "Let's just say I told her no."

"But did they tell you he had no hope to survive?"

"They said he was brain dead. Brain dead. They said my Danny was brain dead! I told her to get the hell out of the room 'cause I wasn't buying that. I told her to go find another body to cut open."

"So what happened next?"

"Not much really. I sat in the room holding his hand. I talked to him and told him he was gonna be okay. I told him about the prayer box and I talked about his kids and how they were looking forward to seeing him next weekend. I just kept talking."

"Did he give any response?"

"Nothing. Then a priest came into the room and asked if I wanted him to administer the last rights. I told him my son was still alive and he said that the last rights was just a precaution and in no way meant that Danny would die. So I let him do it."

"Then what happened?"

"Then I waited and waited. Nurses and doctors kept coming into the room and checking him. None of them said anything to me except one nurse tried to remove the prayer box from his bed and I told her to leave it there. She asked what it was and I told her a prayer box. I could see she was amused by it, like it was a desperate attempt by a desperate mother to save her son."

"And that's exactly what it was," Susan said as she poured Carla a second cup.

"That's true, but I didn't need her smirk at that moment. But I kept my mouth shut and waited and waited, until…." Carla stopped to sip her coffee.

"Until what? Until what?" Susan could hardly control her emotions.

"Until five in the morning. I was struggling to stay awake, but I wouldn't let myself fall asleep. I was staring at Danny when all of a sudden he opened his eyes."

"He opened his eyes?"

"He opened his eyes, Susie. He opened his eyes!" Carla's face lit up.

"Then what?"

"I called the nurse and the next thing you know the room was filled with people in white coats. They were doing all kinds of tests, checking all kinds of machines, and then one nurse looked at me and gave me the thumbs up sign."

"She did that?"

"Yep, she gave me the thumbs up. A few minutes later a doctor told me that this was a miracle. In all his years he had never seen anything like it."

"So Danny's gonna be alright?"

"They told me he has a fractured skull and several broken bones and he's gonna need a lot of physical therapy but his brain swelling went down and he should make a full recovery." Carla broke down crying as the emotion of the night finally caught up with her. She and Susan hugged as they both remained silent.

A few minutes later as they sipped their coffee Susan softly said "It was the prayer box wasn't it, Carla?"

"It sure as hell was."

"Sure as hell?" Susan replied with a grin, "Sure as hell? I think you got that all wrong, honey."

The two friends laughed, and when the laughter stopped they looked at each other as reality sunk in. The prayer box was real.

CHAPTER 2

Two Weeks Earlier

Susan always knew that she would be doing this someday. For years she and her beloved Steven had talked about selling their Lexington, Massachusetts home and moving permanently to Florida. Today was the day that dream came true.

But she never expected to be doing it without Steven. His sudden death a little over a year ago had robbed her of her life partner and forced her to make decisions she had never planned to make alone.

Susan and Steven had gone from high school sweethearts, to college roommates, to husband and wife, parents, and grandparents. And through it all they had remained the best of friends. Now, at sixty-one, facing the rest of her life without Steven was almost unbearable.

It had taken more than a year for Susan to get over the shock of the heart attack, to pull herself together, sell the house, and make the move to Florida. At first she was reluctant to go but her daughter Jennifer had convinced her to do it. Jennifer said "Mom you need to make a change in your life. You don't have to stay here and put up with these cold winters any more. You have a lot of good friends in Florida and daddy would have wanted you to do this." That is what gave Susan the impetus she needed to head south.

She was fortunate to have a lot of friends in Stuart, Florida. She and Steven had been coming to their house in Stuart for several years and along the way they had met some wonderful people, but none more important to her than Carla Rintone.

Carla was the rock in Susan's life. When she needed a shoulder to cry on Carla was there. Whenever she needed a friend to rely on Carla was there. And most of all, when she needed a good laugh Carla could always be counted on to say or do something ridiculous.

Two friends could not be more different. Susan, the Jewish girl from Boston, was short, dark, conservative in her dress, shy with strangers, and married for thirty eight years to one man. Carla, the flamboyant Italian from New York, was tall, bleached blond, flashy, outgoing, funny, married and divorced four times, twice with the same guy. She once told Susan, "I'm sixty-one but when I go shopping I have dyslexia. I buy clothes for a sixteen year old."

But dear friends they were. It was Carla who had dropped everything and flown to Boston to be with Susan right after Steven died. For three weeks she had stayed with Susan, helping her make the funeral arrangements, handling the memorial week, and, most importantly, helping her to deal with the grief that had overwhelmed her.

It was Carla who watched over Susan's Florida home for a full year before Susan returned. Twice a week she would drive from her condo on Hutchinson Island to check on her friend's house. And it was Carla who was here with her now, helping to unpack all of the special things that had been shipped from Lexington.

Susan and Jennifer had managed to sell most of the furniture in the old house and Jennifer took a few things for her summer cottage on Miracle Lake in New Hampshire. A few yard sales and a visit from Goodwill took care of the rest, and all that remained to be shipped to Florida were the photos, special dishes, and other mementos of a life that would forever be changed.

Five large cartons had arrived by UPS and the two friends were reminiscing over each item as Susan determined where to place it in the Stuart house. It was a small house, two bedrooms and a den, just the right size for a couple entering their golden years. It was half the size of their Lexington home, but just perfect for them.

Each UPS box was carried into the house and opened. Slowly the contents were removed, piece by piece. Each artifact would be granted a special place in the Florida home.

The collage of family photos was mounted prominently in the family room. The set of carving and steak knives given to her by her mother was set lovingly on the kitchen countertop. The ugly portrait that Steven had painted of Susan in their art class was placed in the garage.

It was then that Carla showed the box to Susan.

"Where do you want to put this?" she said, holding the box aloft so Susan could get a good look at it.

The box was wooden and very old, about four inches long and two inches wide. It looked like a mini treasure chest.

"What box?" Susan responded quickly. She walked over and took the box from Carla and examined it briefly. "I've never seen this box in my life. Where did you get it?"

"It was right in this carton, wrapped in paper."

"I don't know what it is. Maybe Jenny packed it for me up north. Maybe it belonged to her."

Carla grabbed the box, opened the top, and looked inside. "It's empty," she said.

"Why would someone send me an empty old box?" Susan pondered.

A few hours later the friends had unpacked everything and were eating lunch at the local Ale House. Susan was still perplexed by that strange box, now staring at her from the restaurant table top. It was really ugly, she thought, but there must be a reason it was delivered to my house.

"Why don't you call Jenny and see what she knows?" Carla suggested.

Susan hit the speed button on her cell phone and in an instant she was connected to her daughter in New Hampshire.

"Hi, honey. We unpacked everything but we found a little wooden box that I have never seen before. It's very small and very ugly. Do you know anything about it?"

"No idea what your talking about, mom," came the quick reply.

"Could it have been daddy's?"

"Mom, you know daddy kept no secrets from you. If he had a box like that we both would have seen it."

"Then how did it get into my carton?"

"Don't know and don't care, mom. I gotta go. Just throw it away." Jennifer ended the call abruptly.

This was not a surprising response from her daughter. Jennifer was always the practical one in the family, a type A personality who was always on the go. She simply had no time to solve a mystery.

But Susan was not going to throw the box away. She was intrigued by how it had arrived in her house and she wanted to know what it was. Carla grabbed the box from the table and examined it carefully.

"Looks like Chinese letters on the box. Probably made in China just like everything else," she laughed.

Susan looked at the letters.

"This isn't Chinese, it's Hebrew."

"Hebrew? How do you know that?"

"I still remember from my Bat Mitzvah," Susan replied proudly. "That's about all I remember. That, and making out with Barry Littenberg in the coat room that day." She paused for a second and continued. "It was fun until our braces locked."

"So, you kissed a lot of boys?"

"I guess," she giggled, "but only until I met Steven two years later."

"Okay, you're sure it's Hebrew. So what does it say?"

Susan laughed. "You're kidding, right? I took Bat Mitzvah lessons almost fifty years ago and you think that makes me a Hebrew scholar?"

"Obviously not. I thought all Jews spoke Hebrew."

"My Hebrew is about as good as your Italian."

"Okay, so we're in big trouble. Do you know anybody who can translate for us?"

"A Rabbi, I guess."

"And do you know a Rabbi or should we call Rabbis-R-Us?"

"I know where there's a synagogue, and I assume that wherever you find a synagogue you'll find a Rabbi."

The two friends finished lunch. As they were walking out of the Ale House, Carla suddenly ran over to a man, grabbed him from behind, and squeezed him repeatedly until a piece of food was projected out of his mouth. The man had been choking and Carla saved him. People in the restaurant began to applaud as the man thanked Carla repeatedly for what she had done. He tried to give her money but she refused to take it. Carla stayed and talked to the man and his wife for a few minutes and then walked towards her friend at the front door of the restaurant.

"Holy smokes, Carla! How did do you do that?" Susan shouted.

"When I was a waitress at Rusty's they made us all learn how to do the Heimlich Maneuver. I guess they were expecting people to choke on the crappy food they served," Carla said calmly. "Never used it there but this is the second time I've used it since I left Rusty's."

"I am impressed, girlfriend." Susan said, as they started walking out of the restaurant. As they approached the restaurant door another round of applause began. Carla turned, waived, smiled, and bowed to acknowledge her admirers.

"You are a piece of work," Susan said.

"And don't ever forget that, Susie Q." Carla quipped.

The women drove south on Federal Highway towards the synagogue in Hobe Sound. After a fifteen minute ride they arrived at a strip shopping center. Prominently displayed on one of the store fronts were the words CHABAD JEWISH CENTER.

They parked the car, grabbed the box, and walked in the front door. To their right was a small unoccupied office and directly ahead was a large room. A young woman was sitting on the floor reading to a group of six small children. She noticed as Susan and Carla entered, stood up and walked over to greet them. She was wearing a long gray skirt and black sweater. Her head was covered in a dark scarf that completely hid her hair from view.

"May I help you?" the woman asked.

Susan spoke first. "Hello, my name is Susan Gold and this is my friend Carla. I have this box with Hebrew writing and I was hoping that the Rabbi could tell us what it says."

Susan handed the box to the woman, who held it up towards her eyes.

"My name is Rivka Rosenberg," she said softly. "I am the Rabbi's wife."

"Can you read Hebrew?" Carla asked.

Rivka grinned. "But of course I can," she laughed, "women are allowed to learn Hebrew too."

"So what does it say?" Susan asked, trying to hide her embarrassment about Carla's question.

"The words on the box are *Mi Sheberakh*," Rivka announced.

"And that means…?"

"*Mi Sheberakh* are the first two words of a prayer that is said every Sabbath to ask *Hashem* to heal the sick and injured."

"*Hashem*?" Carla asked.

"*Hashem* is our word for God," Rivka replied. "The prayer says, 'May he who blessed our fathers Abraham, Isaac, and Jacob, bless the one who is ill.' We believe that this prayer can give comfort and healing to those in need of both. It is an important part of our service."

"It's got a lot of letters on the back, too," Susan said as she turned the box over.

"I don't know," Rivka replied, as she looked at the back. "They just look like English letters to me."

In a few minutes the front door opened and in walked a very tall man dressed in a black suit, white shirt, no tie, with a black hat and a long scraggly beard.

"This is my husband, Mendel Rosenberg," Rivka announced. "He is the Rabbi you are looking for."

Susan held out her hand to shake but the Rabbi quickly placed his hand in his pocket.

"I'm very happy to meet you," he said sternly, "but our custom is that the only physical contact between a man and a woman should be between husband and wife."

"I wish somebody had taught that custom to my third husband!" Carla said.

Susan was mortified and looked at Carla with a stare of derision. Rivka smiled and suppressed a laugh.

The Rabbi was oblivious. He was busy staring at the box. He took it from his wife and examined it carefully.

"Where did you get this box?" he asked.

"I don't really know," Susan responded quickly. "It just appeared in my house. Do you know anything about it?"

"I am not an expert on these things but I have heard stories about prayer boxes that are used to heal the sick and injured. This looks like it could be one of them."

"Does it have magical powers?" Carla asked.

"Again, I am not the expert here, but there's a Rabbi in New York that you should see. His name is Shlomo Glickstein. Rabbi Glickstein is one of the world's leading scholars in *Kabbalah*. He may know about this box."

"*Kabbalah*?" the friends both asked at the same time.

"*Kabbalah* is the study of Jewish mysticism that dates back hundreds of years. Only a few select Rabbis are true scholars of *Kabbalah*."

Carla whispered to Susan, "I think that's what Madonna does." But the whisper was a little too loud.

"Yes, that is what Madonna does," Rivka said with a grin, "but believe me when I tell you she is not a scholar on the subject."

"Would you like me to make arrangements for you to meet Rabbi Glickstein?" the rabbi asked.

"Sure," said Carla.

"Maybe," said Susan. "Let me think about it and get back to you on that."

"Okay, here is my card," the rabbi said. "Please call me if you want me to set up that meeting."

"Thank you both." Susan replied as she turned and walked out the door.

Carla held out her hand to the Rabbi and quickly remembered the faux pas. With a quick "oops," she did a pirouette and shook hands with Rivka.

As they sat in the car Carla was excited. "We have to visit that guy in New York."

"I'm not so sure."

"Not sure? Why in the world are you not sure?"

"I don't know Carla. Maybe this is not what I want to spend my time on right now. Let me think about it, okay?"

They drove home in silence, unaware of the perilous journey that awaited them.

CHAPTER 3

This was a bittersweet day for Jeff Morton.

As he drove into the parking lot of the building that had housed his dental practice for the past thirty years, he felt tears well up in his eyes. By the end of the day the sign JEFFREY MORTON D.D.S would be removed forever and only the name MICHAEL MORTON would remain. Jeff was so proud to be turning over the practice to his only son, but the thought of giving up the practice was in many ways very depressing.

Ever since he was a little boy, Jeff's dream was to practice dentistry with his dad, Donald Morton. While other boys growing up in the fifties worshiped cowboy stars and athletes, Jeff's one and only hero was his dad. The day after he graduated from Tufts Dental school he joined the Morton dental practice on Salem Street in Malden, Massachusetts.

Father and son had made a great team until Parkinson's Disease robbed Donald of his ability, leaving Jeff to run the practice alone until Michael was ready to join him. Dentistry had been in the Morton family for five generations, dating all the way back to their relatives in Scotland over one hundred years ago. And now it would be Michael's job to keep the legacy alive.

"Good morning, Doctor J," said the receptionist Wanda Davis. Wanda was an attractive woman in her mid forties. Tall, friendly, and always conservatively dressed, with sparkling white teeth she was the perfect receptionist for a dental office. She had been with the Morton dental practice for over ten years.

"Hello Wanda, how are you today?"

"Just fine sir, but more importantly how are you?"

"I'm doing okay. A little sad but excited to start the next phase of my life."

"I'm gonna miss you, Doctor J."

"And I'm gonna miss you too. Especially I'll miss being called Doctor J."

"You have a patient waiting for you in your office," Wanda said in a matter of fact tone.

"In my office? Okay." Jeff replied as he sauntered past Wanda towards his office. Wanda followed behind.

When he open the door Jeff was greeted by a large gathering of people who yelled "surprise!"

There was the entire team of dental hygienists and eight of Jeff's longest running patients. And of course there was Michael holding a cake in the shape of a tooth that said "Good Luck Doctor J".

Jeff couldn't hold back the tears. "Oh my God," he said, "I love you all. Every one of you. And I thank you for all you have done to make my life here so special. I will always be grateful."

"And we all love you too, Dad," Michael replied. "We're gonna miss you around here but we know that our loss is World Health Teams' gain."

Jeff had volunteered to work for World Health Teams, a group that provides health care to some of the poorest and most remote people in the world. As part of a team Jeff would be traveling to those countries to deliver free dental care to those who need it most. It was his way of giving back to the world for all the good the world had given him. As a divorced man with no family obligations he figured this was the time for an adventure like this.

"Where will you be going, Doc?" asked hygienist Megan Cary, a young twenty something who was new to the practice.

"My first assignment will be somewhere in South America or Africa this fall. They haven't got the details worked out yet but I'm very excited to be going. But I'll be back and you'll see me around here probably more than you want to."

Michael walked up to his dad and handed him a large UPS box.

"This came from Florida, dad."

Jeff examined the box and the mailing label. "It's from Ernie," he yelled.

Ernie Pantaloni was Jeff's roommate in dental school. They were as different as night and day. Jeff, the reserved Bostonian and Ernie, the loud New Yorker. But they were best of friends and had remained so for over forty years.

Jeff immediately opened the box and laughed. It was a blow up female doll with, as the label described, "real working parts." Jeff was reluctant to show the ladies but eventually he did. He read the gift card inside the box, "Now that you are retired it's time to get a new girlfriend. Love, Ernie Pants."

"Leave it to Ernie Pants," he said with a laugh.

As everyone laughed and began eating the cake. Michael walked up close to his dad and whispered, "What about grandma, dad?"

Together they walked outside the small office so they could be alone.

Jeff sighed. "I don't know, Mickey. She's going downhill very fast. I'm heading up to the lake next week to stay with her." The sadness in his eyes was evident. "I don't think grandma will make it though the summer, Mick. That's why I delayed my new assignment until fall."

"Pancreatic is the worst kind."

"I know, Mickey. All we're doing now is keeping her out of pain. She's a strong woman, your grandmother, but I'm afraid this is a battle she has to lose."

"I wanted to ask you something." Michael hesitated. "Should I tell mom about grandma, Dad?"

Jeff pondered the question for a moment.

"Do what you think is best, Mickey. You know grandma always liked your mom."

"Until she walked out on you."

"That was a long time ago, Mickey. I'm over that and over her too. But she might want to at least send a card to grandma. So yeah, let her know what's going on."

Jeff's divorce had been very painful. His wife Pam had an affair with her fitness coach, and when that ended she took up with her tennis coach. Jeff always believed that he was a devoted husband who deserved better. Now Pam was living with a man twenty-five years her junior. Certainly she looked good for a sixty-five year old woman but Jeff was pretty sure that her new boyfriend was more interested in the alimony payments she received from him than he was in having Pam as a life partner.

"You know, Dad," Michael said, "It's been four years since you and mom got divorced. Maybe its time for you to find someone else."

Even now at sixty-eight Jeff was a very handsome man. Standing six-foot-four he towered over most people, and through hard work at the gym and daily walks he had managed to keep his weight at the same two hundred twenty-five pounds for the past twenty years. Only his silver gray hair gave away his age.

"Mickey, I'm sixty-eight years old without a job. Who's gonna want me now?"

"You're free as a bird now, Dad, all your life you have been doing things for others, most of all me. I just want you to be happy."

"I am happy, Mickey, and I want you to know that you and your beautiful family give me more joy than anything else in my life. I'm so proud of you, the son, the husband, the father, and the dentist you have become. I feel so good now that I am leaving the Morton family dentistry legacy to you."

"I love you, Dad." Mickey said as he hugged Jeff. "I promise I won't let you down."

They both cried.

CHAPTER 4

Jeff said his final goodbyes to the staff and patients, packed up his personal belongings, including his new "blow up girlfriend" and drove the six miles to his home in Medford. When he arrived he poured himself a Hendricks and tonic and sat on the back porch to enjoy the sunset.

Just as he took his first sip his cell phone rang. The word MOM appeared on the screen.

"Hi mom. Is everything alright?"

A weak voice came over the phone. "No, honey, I'm afraid not." Then she coughed a few times. "How soon can you get up here to the lake?"

Beverly Morton was always a strong woman. While Jeff's dad was a very successful dentist, it was mom who ruled the family. Even at ninety-one and suffering from pancreatic cancer she was still the matriarch of the Morton family.

"On my way, mom. Do you need anything?"

"Just you honey."

Thirty minutes later Jeff was driving on route 93 for the hour and a half trip to Miracle Lake. He enjoyed the tranquility of the lake and he went there as often as he could. But this time he was packed for a long stay. This would probably be the last time he would see his mother alive.

As he drove north on route 93 Jeff conjured memories of his mom and dad. They were high school sweethearts, and when dad joined the Navy in 1942 mom waited for him. They were married in 1945. Michael was born in 1947 and Jeff was born two years later.

Jeff remembered that his parents were the most loving couple he had ever seen. Even in their later years they would hold hands, kiss, and hug openly. They were truly an odd couple, with dad towering over mom. He was six foot three and she was barely five feet. But dad always said that mom was "just the right size for me." He always called her "gorgeous" and she called him "adorable". Their's was a match made in heaven. In fact, their marriage was exactly what Jeff once had with Pam, until Pam threw it all away.

His brother Michael's death in 1967 was a devastating blow to both of his parents, but somehow they came through the tragedy with their love and faith still intact. They grieved but found the strength to move on and live a happy life. In her later years, however, mom was more openly talking about Michael, often blaming herself for his death.

Dad's passing two years ago was a blessing, as Parkinson's had made it impossible for him to care for himself. Mom was his one and only care giver and she devoted herself to the man she loved. The strain of the constant care he needed aged mom rapidly.

As Jeff pulled up to the little yellow Victorian house at Miracle Lake he was filled with emotion. But he was determined to put on a brave face for his mom. He parked the car and walked up the steps to the front door.

Jeff walked in and saw his mother sitting in a wheelchair in the living room. When Beverly saw her son she rose out of the chair to greet him.

"Mom." He grabbed her and held her close to him. Then he helped her sit back down in her wheelchair. He bent down so she could kiss his forehead, which she did several times before letting him go.

"It's so good to see you, Jeffy."

"I was worried when you called, mom. How are you doing?"

"Not good, honey. I think it's time. My nurse stops by every day and they keep giving me stronger medicine for the pain but I can't take too much more of this."

"Mom."

"I'm ready to be with daddy and Michael."

"I understand, mom," Jeff said. "What can I do for you today?"

"Just stay with me, Jeffy. You're all I have left in the world."

"Yes mom I will stay with you, and Mickey will come up this weekend with Lauren and the kids."

"I hate for my great grandchildren to see me like this, Jeffy."

"They really want to see you, mom. Please don't say no to them."

"Okay, honey. I really want to say goodbye and to let them know how much I love them."

"Good, mom. Can I fix you a cup of tea?"

"Yes, I have green tea in the cupboard."

Quickly Jeff found the tea and filled a cup from the instant hot water tap. He added the tea bag and a little lemon juice and handed it to Beverly. She sipped and spoke.

"I've had a great life, Jeffy. More than any girl could ever ask for. I married the man of my dreams and he was my best friend for almost seventy years. He gave me two beautiful sons…"

She began to cry.

"I still can't believe that Michael killed himself, Jeffy. He had every reason to live."

Jeff held his mother's trembling hand.

"Mom, Michael didn't kill himself."

"He jumped off a building!"

"I know, mom, but we've been over this many times. He was in college in the sixties. He was fooling around with LSD and the kids told him he could fly. He was too stoned to understand what he was doing when he jumped. It was an accident."

"I should never have let him go to school in Vermont. People told me it was a druggie school."

"Please, mom, don't blame yourself. This could have happened anywhere. Please let it go."

"I try, Jeffy. I try."

"Hey," Jeff said as he sat on the floor next to his mom, still holding her hand. "Do you remember when Michael and I played on the same Little League team and dad was our coach?"

Beverly's face lit up.

"I sure do. I went to every game and even every practice."

"Mom, dad told Michael and me something one day after we had lost a tough game. I was saying that the umpire cheated for the other team. Do you remember what dad said?"

"I sure do."

"He said 'Guys, long after people forget the score of the game they will remember the kind of person you are.'"

"Yes he did."

"I never forgot those words mom and I said them quite often to my Mickey as he was growing up."

"Yes you did."

"So, mom, I want you and me to remember the kind of person Michael was."

Beverly smiled. "He was a sweet, sweet boy," she gushed. "He was always trying to take care of his little brother, too."

"Yes, mom. He whacked me a few times but I always knew he had my back."

"Jeffy?"

"Yes, mom."

"Promise me that you'll bury me right between Michael and daddy."

"I promise, mom."

With that Beverly fell sound asleep in her wheelchair.

CHAPTER 5

Carolyn Johnson was more than just a next door neighbor to Susan. The two had lost their husbands only weeks apart last year. While Steven's death from a heart attack was a shock to Susan, things were much different for Carolyn. Her husband had been suffering from Alzheimer's disease for years and by the time he passed it was a blessing. He could no longer even recognize his wife or daughters and was living in a nursing home.

Carolyn offered great comfort to Susan after Steven's death and the two became much closer than just neighbors.

Susan remembered that Carolyn's daughter Andrea was scheduled for surgery within the next day or so. Andrea was pregnant with twins and there was a complication that required her to have a c-section and deliver the babies four weeks early. She called Carolyn for an update.

"She's at Lawnwood hospital right now," Carolyn replied. "I'm about to call an Uber driver to take me there."

Susan looked at the prayer box on the table. She wanted Carolyn to have it for her daughter.

"Uber driver?" She barked. "No way, honey, I'm gonna drive you to the hospital. I'll be there in two minutes."

Within a few minutes Carolyn was in the passenger seat of Susan's Toyota as they made their way to the hospital. She was crying as she spoke to Susan.

"You know, Sue," she began, "when I was pregnant with Andrea forty years ago I was carrying her identical twin as well."

"Wow," Susan responded, "I never knew that."

"I haven't talked about it with you or anyone else for that matter. It was very painful."

"What happened?"

"All along they were monitoring me and listening to the two heartbeats," she said as she grasped for the right words to say. "But then in my last month one of the hearts stopped beating."

"Oh my God."

"It took me several days to accept the fact that one of my babies was dead," she continued, wiping tears from her eyes as she spoke. "And the worst part was that I had to carry both babies to term, knowing that only one would come home with me."

"I'm so sorry, Carolyn."

"When I delivered the two babies, we named them Andrea and Angela. Andrea came home with us and we had to bury my little angle Angela."

By now both women were sobbing.

"There has been a hole in my heart for forty years, Sue, and Andi has always missed having her twin sister. We visit the gravesite every year on their birthday."

"I wish I could think of words to say, Carolyn."

"Thanks, Sue. No words are necessary. But now what we need are prayers for Andi."

"So what's going on with Andi?"

Carolyn took a deep breath.

"You know Andi and Jake have been trying to have kids for ten years. And when she finally got pregnant she was thirty-nine years old."

"So, what's the problem?"

"You won't believe it, Sue," Carolyn replied. "It was a replay of my pregnancy."

"A replay? How?"

"Andi is carrying twins, just like I was."

"Yes."

"And last week they found that one of the twin's heart is not beating normally."

"Oh, so what does that mean?"

"They decided that the baby will need open heart surgery."

"Open heart?"

"Nowadays they can do it in the womb, but since Andi is at 35 weeks they decided to take the babies and do the surgery outside the womb where the success rate is much higher."

"So that's all happening today?"

"Yes, they are setting up for a c-section at eleven followed immediately by the heart surgery on the baby."

"They have great doctors at Lawnwood," Susan said in an effort to reassure her friend.

"I know, Sue. I truly believe that. Everyone told us that Lawnwood is one of the best heart hospitals in the country."

"I've heard that, too."

"But the doctors have been very realistic with us. They say that there is only about one chance in ten that the baby will survive."

"Oh no!" Susan yelled. She peeked into her handbag to see if the prayer box was there. "I want to sit with you until after they're finished, okay?'

"Thank you, Sue, but it could be a long day. You don't have to stay. My son-law can drive me home."

"I want to stay," Sue said firmly.

"Okay."

They arrived at the hospital at 10:45 and sat in the waiting room. At 11:30 a doctor came out and asked if they were relatives.

"I'm her mother," Carolyn replied.

"Just wanted you to know that the c-section went fine. Your daughter is holding one of the babies and the other is getting prepped for surgery."

"Is she gonna make it, doc?"

The doctor was stoic. "We're gonna need a lot of help on this one, but I can assure you we have some of the best doctors in the world working on your granddaughter."

"Can I see my daughter now?"

"Yes, as a matter of fact she was asking for you."

"This is my friend, can she come in too?"

"I'm sorry, but hospital rules are that only immediate family can see her now. Probably tomorrow your friend can come."

As Carolyn got up to go with the doctor, Susan grabbed her arm. She reached into her handbag, removed the prayer box, and placed it firmly in Carolyn's hand.

"What is this?" Carolyn said as she glanced at the box in her hand.

"It's called a prayer box, honey. I'll tell you all about it later," Susan replied. "Please take this into Andi's room and keep it there until the surgery is over."

Carolyn looked at the box and started to hand it back to Susan. Susan held up her hands and said "No, please take it with you."

Carolyn nodded and grasped the box firmly as she walked out of the waiting room. Susan stayed behind as instructed.

Time dragged on and on as Susan sat quietly in the waiting room. Minutes turned into hours, until finally she saw her friend enter the waiting room. She was holding the prayer box.

"How did it go?" Susan asked apprehensively.

"She's gonna make it, Sue," Carolyn shouted. "She's okay!"

"What happened?"

"I'm not sure but the doctor said the problem turned out to be a lot less complicated than they thought. They couldn't understand how that was possible."

Susan smiled and glanced at the prayer box, which was firmly in Carolyn's grasp. Her friend lifted the box and examined it.

"Do you think this box...?"

"I don't know, Carolyn, but I'm so happy to hear the good news."

Carolyn paused for a moment. "And here's the best news of all."

"What could be better than this?"

Carolyn took a deep breath. "Andi had names picked out for the babies. She planned to call them Megan and Miley."

"Oh, that's cute." Susan replied.

"But now she's changed her mind. The new names will be Megan and Angela."

"Angela?"

Carolyn was overcome with emotion. Tears streamed down her face. "Yes, Angela!" she whispered, clasping her hands. "My little angel has come home to me."

The two friends held each other tightly and cried together, tears of joy.

CHAPTER 6

The next three weeks were filled with excitement for Susan and Carla. Danny's condition got better and better and soon he was able to come home and resume a normal life. He eventually went back to his job at the local Hilton hotel. Carolyn's two new granddaughters were home with their parents and little Angela was doing fine.

The prayer box had worked its miracles on Danny and Andi, but they were not the only ones. Susan found many uses for the box and each time it performed its miracles.

Bill Scanlon was a neighbor in desperate need of a liver transplant. At sixty-five he was considered too old and too sick for the transplant list. He had only weeks to live. Susan learned about Bill's condition and brought the prayer box to his house. She told him about the Danny and Carolyn miracles and asked him to keep the box in a safe place in his house until it worked for him too.

Bill was a joker, and, even with death staring him in the face, he had a crack to make when he saw the prayer box.

"This thing better work," he said. "because I'm much too handsome to die."

Three days later, Bill and his wife Janet drove four hours north to the Mayo Clinic in Jacksonville for a routine visit to monitor his condition. At the last minute, Bill grabbed the prayer box from its shelf and put it in his car.

As expected, the Mayo Clinic doctors told Bill that, without a transplant, he would not last through the end of the month. And since he was not on the donor list there was no chance he would ever get a transplant. They were advised to put things in order and plan for the inevitable end of his life.

They were too tired and too upset to make the long drive back home so they checked into the local hotel right next to the Mayo Clinic. Both husband and wife were in tears as they tried to rest before the expected drive home the next day. Neither of them could sleep.

That night at three AM they received a call from the clinic on Bill's cell phone. A donor liver that matched Bill had arrived at the clinic and since he was there on site he was chosen to get it! Within an hour Bill was prepped and rushed into surgery for the life saving transplant. Had the liver arrived one day earlier or one day later Bill would not have received it.

This was a miracle.

Janet could hardly wait to call Susan with the news. As soon as she returned home she brought the prayer box back to Susan. "You know," she said candidly. "When you first brought this ugly little box to our house I was angry. We needed a liver, not a little box, I thought. But now I believe in the power of this box, and Bill and I will be grateful to you forever."

* * *

A few days later Susan got a call from her golf partner Patty Egan. She was in tears.

"Eddie just got his orders and he's going to Afghanistan." she cried. "We always knew this could happen but now that he's a new dad we didn't expect this. Not now."

Eddie, Patty's only child, was a career military man like his dad. He had already done one tour of duty in Iraq and so they never expected him to be sent overseas again. His young son Dustin was only four months old.

Susan brought the prayer box to Patty's house. She explained the power of the box and reassured Patty that the box would keep her son safe while he was in Afghanistan. Patty's husband Gil was not impressed. "Unless that box contains a new set of orders it won't do a damned thing for Eddie."

Gil was an old Army colonel who refused to believe in luck. He had seen too many men die during his Vietnam tours and there was no magic to save them. Against Gil's wishes Patty took the prayer box and hid it in her nightstand drawer.

It only took two days for the miracle. Patty was on the golf course when she got a call from her daughter-in-law April.

"Mom? Guess what?"

"What happened, April? Is the baby okay?"

"Oh, he's doing fine mom. But I wanted to tell you about Eddie's new orders."

"New orders? What new orders?"

"His deployment was canceled, mom. Instead of going to Afghanistan he's staying right here in Ohio."

Patty burst into tears. "Oh, thank God!"

Another miracle.

* * *

Donna Weiner's daughter Joy was pregnant with her first child when the doctors told her that she had tested positive as a carrier of Tay Sachs disease. Joy's husband Barry was also tested and he too was found to be a carrier.

Donna was at lunch with Susan and Carla as she explained that the odds of her new grandchild being born with Tay Sachs were pretty high, at least one out of four.

"They are now testing the baby with amnio," she explained, "and if the baby has Tay Sachs my daughter will face the tragic choice of having an abortion or raising a child that will die by age four!"

"Were they tested before they got married?" Susan asked. "I remember Steven and I were tested and so were my daughter and her husband."

"I guess because they were so much older and both had been married before they just didn't do it this time."

Later that day Susan stopped by Donna's house with the prayer box. She explained what it was, the results that they had seen from it, and asked Donna to bring it to her daughter.

Donna was happy to have anything that might save her future grandson from death. It took only three days for the tests to come back negative. The baby was fine!

* * *

Sandy Waters was beside herself with grief. She and her husband Richard had just returned from his niece Jackie's wedding in South Carolina.

"She was the most beautiful and happy bride I ever saw," Sandy told Susan. "But just before they left on their honeymoon she was not feeling well so she went to the doctor. They told her she had cancer."

"Instead of a honeymoon," Sandy continued, "she had chemotherapy."

Susan gave the prayer box to Sandy.

"If you can find a way to get this to her in South Carolina it may help." she said.

"We'll try anything," Sandy replied. "My sister is leaving for Columbia tomorrow and I will see that she brings it to Jackie."

One week later the prayer box was returned with a note from Jackie.

"Dear Susan: I want to thank you for sending the prayer box to me. I cannot say for sure if the prayer box was the reason but I am now cancer free. And here's the best news. I'm going to have a baby! I will forever be in your debt."

That was the final straw for Susan. She had to learn more about the prayer box. This would be the beginning of a journey that would change her life forever.

CHAPTER 7

For three weeks Jeff stayed by his ailing mother's side. He slept in the guest room, cooked meals, watched TV at night with her, and ran errands whenever she asked. The visiting nurse had been replaced by a hospice nurse as Beverly's health deteriorated. Each day the hospice nurse arrived at nine and Jeff used that hour for his morning walk around the lake. The lake walk was his favorite thing about being there. It was almost exactly two miles around and, at a brisk pace, he could make the journey in about thirty minutes. More often than not, however, he would stop to chat with some of the neighbors, giving them frequent updates on Beverly's condition.

On this day Jeff stopped several times, first meeting Mr. & Mrs. Adams, a mid-fifties couple who owned the local gas station. James Adams was, as usual, dressed in blue jeans and a white tee shot. His wife Ann was wearing what appeared to be a simple housecoat. They were clearly a humble couple.

"How are things you guys?"

"Couldn't be worse, Doc." Mrs. Adams replied. "Looks like we're gonna lose the station."

"Really? But you've had it for years."

"Yep," Mr. Adams replied. "My daddy built it with his own two hands."

"So what happened?"

"The city council approved a permit for another station right next door to ours."

"That's insane! Why would they do that? There can't be enough customers for two stations."

Mr. Adams held out is hand and rubbed his thumb and fingers together. "Money talks," he said.

"Is it a done deal?"

"Almost," Mrs. Adams replied. "The official vote comes next week but we heard they have the votes all sewn up."

"I'm so sorry folks. I wish there was something I could do."

"Maybe you can come to the meeting and speak up about it."

"I'll be there. Just send the time and place."

"Will do," Mrs. Adams replied. "By the way, how's your mom?"

"Not good I'm afraid."

Mrs. Adams walked closer to Jeff and whispered, "Have you thought about taking her into the lake?"

Jeff was taken aback by that comment. He frequently saw people bathing in the lake and heard the stories about how Miracle Lake could heal the sick. Of course as a medical man he put absolutely no stock in those stories.

"I don't think so," he replied. "I'm afraid it's too late for that."

"Please send her our love." Mr. Adams replied.

Jeff smiled, nodded, and continued his walk. Next he ran into Janice Hanley, a mid-sixties widow who always flirted with him. She was wearing a tight fitting spandex running suit.

"How's my favorite handsome dentist doing? You're looking mighty good today!" Janice said as she batted her eyes and stroked her hair.

"Doing just fine, Jan. Sorry I can't talk right now. My mom's waiting for me."

"Send her my best."

Just as he was about to finish his walk he spotted Jenny Cohen. She was a very attractive young woman who walked around the lake every day.

"Hi Jenny!"

"Hi Jeff," Jenny replied.

"Haven't seen your mom recently," Jeff said. "How is she?"

"She's doing great, thanks."

"I was sorry to hear about your dad."

"Thanks," Jennifer replied, "It was a shock to all of us."

"Heart attack?"

Jennifer nodded. "He had no signs or symptoms."

"So sad. How long has it been now?"

"Just a little over a year, fourteen months." She replied. "Seems like yesterday though."

"I understand."

"And how is Beverly?"

"She's holding her own but I'm afraid it won't be long now."

"I'm sorry, Doc. Please tell her I was asking about her."

"Okay, Jen. Have a nice day."

He arrived back at the house at 11:00 AM. The hospice worker had left. As he opened the door he heard talking. He walked into the living room and was surprised to see his ex-wife Pam sitting in the living room with his mother.

She was a beautiful woman who looked much younger than her sixty-five years. She always spent hours at the gym and on the tennis courts and she bragged about the fact that she weighed the same today as she did when she first got married. She was wearing a long gray skirt and blue sweater. Her hair was pulled back in a pony tail.

"Oh, I'm sorry." Jeff began.

"Hi Jeff, look who's here," Beverly said.

"Hello Jeffrey," Pam responded, "Mickey told me this might be a good time to visit Beverly. I hope you don't mind."

"Of course not. Why should I mind? I'll just leave you two alone."

Pam stood up from her chair. "I also wanted to talk to you today if that's alright, Jeff."

Jeff was taken aback by that request. Could she want more money? Why after four years did she want to talk to him?

"Ah okay. I'm gonna shower. You finish up with Mom and then I'll come down and chat."

All during his shower Jeff thought about ways to say no to Pam. He knew he wasn't very good at that, but now with his retirement he certainly was in no position to give her any more money. Pam had been his college sweetheart, the only woman he had ever truly loved. But her betrayal of him with two other men left a deep scar that had never healed.

He finished his shower, dressed and started downstairs to the living room. But then he walked into the bathroom to add a touch of cologne to his neck.

As he arrived downstairs he could see that Pam was about to leave.

"Would you walk me to my car, Jeff?" She asked as she moved towards the front door.

Jeff followed his ex out the door and into the street. As she approached her car she turned to Jeff. "I really need to talk to you, Jeff, but this is not a good place. Will you meet me at Starbucks?"

Jeff nodded. "Let me get my keys and I'll meet you there in ten minutes."

As he drove the three blocks to Starbucks, Jeff practiced in his mind how he was going to reject Pam's request for more money.

He pulled up to Starbucks and walked in. Pam was sitting at a corner table waiting for him. She had two cups of coffee on the table. Jeff sat across from Pam and she handed him one of the cups.

"Black with two sweeteners, right?"

Jeff nodded and smiled. "It's been a long time since we did this."

Pam set her cup on the table and placed her hand on top of Jeff's. She held his hand as she said, "Jeff, I miss you."

Jeff was startled by the hand holding and the words he heard. He pulled his hand away. "I'm surprised to hear that, Pam."

"Remember when you called me Pammy? I miss that."

"Okay, so what did you want to tell me?"

"Jeffy, I screwed up. I never should have left you!" Tears began rolling down her cheeks.

"What happened to tennis boy?"

"That's been over for a long time. I'm alone now and all I can think about is what a fool I was for leaving you."

"Yes you were."

"I remember all of the good times we had together, Jeff. The vacations we took. Remember our Hawaii trip? And how about when Mickey was born? That was the happiest day of our lives."

"Uh huh."

"We were the happiest people on earth, and we were so much in love!"

"That was a long time ago, Pam."

"Yes it was and I threw it all away, Jeff. I wish there were words that could explain how sorry I am for what I put you through. You are such a good man and you deserved so much better than what I did to you."

Jeff nodded.

"Jeffy?"

Another nod.

"Do you believe in second chances?"

Jeff was startled. He took a sip from his coffee and spoke. "Pam, are you asking for us to get back together?"

Pam reached out for Jeff's hand again. "That's exactly what I am asking, Jeff. I know I don't deserve a second chance but I can only hope that you will think about all the good times we had together and that you will agree that we can have those good times again." She wiped her tears with a napkin. "We were great together once Jeff and we can be again."

Jeff sat stoic and did not respond.

"I want us to be a family again, Jeff! What do you say?"

Jeff could see that Pam was serious. She was pleading with him for a second chance.

"I-I just don't know, Pam. It's been four years and I've moved on."

"Oh…I'm sorry. Is there someone else?"

"Well, no. No there isn't anyone else. It's just that it took me a long time to get over the pain you caused me."

"I understand and I don't blame you if you say no. I realize I'll have to earn back your trust but I'm willing to do whatever it takes if you give me a chance."

Jeff sipped his coffee again. "Pam, I wasn't prepared to hear this from you."

"I suppose you need time to think about it."

"I suppose I do."

"Look, I'm staying at the Hilton near the Manchester airport. I'm in room 239. I will wait there for you all night if that's what it takes. If you come then we can move forward. If not I will never bother you again."

"Okay Pam."

"I'll be waiting."

She stood and walked towards the door. Just before she walked through the door she looked back at Jeff, placed her hand over her heart and said "I love you!".

Jeff stared at the ceiling and finished his coffee.

CHAPTER 8

Susan loved New York. She and Steven would take the train from Boston to New York two or three times each year, stay in a fancy hotel, have a great dinner, and see a Broadway show. It was a guilty pleasure that they shared and one of the many things that made their marriage so good.

This was Susan's first trip to the city since Steven's death and even though she was with Carla, not Steven, and even though they were going to Brooklyn, not Manhattan, it still brought back fond memories of days past.

She double checked her large handbag to make sure that the prayer box was safely inside.

As she pulled up in front of Carla's house for the drive to the airport she was met by her girlfriend and a huge suitcase. Carla could barely lift it to place it in Susan's trunk. And in addition she had two carry on bags.

"Are you nuts?" Susan said. "We're going to New York for two days and it looks like you packed for a month."

"Is this all you got?" Carla asked, as she eyed Susan's tiny overnight bag.

"Two days, Carla!"

"Hell, I couldn't fit my makeup in that little bag."

Susan shrugged. Why argue. This was classic Carla. Three complete outfits for each day, and a hat to match each outfit. And God forbid she should wear the same thing twice. But this was also part of the character that made Carla so interesting. And in no way did it detract from the loving kindness that was in her heart.

The plane ride from West Palm Beach to JFK was uneventful, except for the fact that they had to wait twenty minutes for Carla's suitcase to arrive at baggage claim. Once they grabbed the bag they jumped in a taxi and headed for Brooklyn.

"I guess I was one of the few Bostonians who could say I love New York." she said as the taxi pulled away from JFK airport. She told the driver to take them to the Marriott in Brooklyn.

"Funny," Carla laughed, "us New Yorkers never gave Boston a second thought."

"Yes, I know. To New Yorkers the only thing north of Westchester County is Canada."

"So you got the Rabbi's name?"

"Uh huh. It's Rabbi Glickstein. Shlomo Glickstein. We're supposed to meet him at 770 Eastern Parkway."

"Oh, that's Crown Heights. I remember we drove by there once when I was a kid. It's quite a sight to see."

"Rabbi Rosenberg said that 770 is a big synagogue where all the Rabbis go to pray every day. He said Rabbi Glickstein never misses."

"Does he know we're coming?"

"Rabbi Rosenberg said he texted him and the guy was happy to meet us."

"Rabbis use text messaging? I'm impressed."

"These Rabbis are old fashioned in many ways, but they are apparently very tech savvy. They're not old fashion when it comes to technology. They're very modern."

"But they don't touch women. I remember that!"

"Rabbi Rosenberg told us we should wait outside of 770 until the evening prayer ends around eight o'clock."

They checked into the hotel. Susan carefully hung her clothes in the closet while Carla simply dropped her suitcase on the floor and left everything in it. Susan went into the bathroom and when she returned Carla had changed into a new outfit. She was wearing a long black skirt with sequins down the side, a white silky top with ruffles, and a huge floppy black hat.

"That's what you're wearing?" Susan asked.

"Well, I figured they all wear black and white so I wanted to fit in."

"Oh yeah, you blend!"

"Yeah, just like my cousin Vinny!" They both laughed as they headed out of the room and down the hall to the elevator.

"Did you bring the box?"

Susan checked her bag again. "Yep, I got it."

They went to the lobby and hopped in a taxi. It was 7:30 PM and they didn't want to miss the end of the prayers at 8 PM.

"Do you know what the guy looks like?" Carla asked as the taxi pulled away from the hotel.

"I know he's a short man in his sixties. He has a beard and he'll be wearing a black hat," Susan laughed.

"Yeah, him and a thousand other guys I bet."

The taxi pulled up in front of 770 Eastern Parkway and Susan paid the driver.

The red brick building looked surprisingly new among much older buildings. There were only a few men lingering in front. Susan walked up to a tall young man in a black suit and hat who looked no more than twenty.

"Excuse me. Do you know Rabbi Glickstein?"

At first the young man seemed hesitant to respond. He looked at the two ladies with bewilderment.

"Shlomo Glickstein," Susan said. "We're looking for him. We were hoping you could help us find him. Do you know him?"

The young man paused and then responded. "Yes, he is a teacher at my Yeshiva."

Carla could not resist. "So what does he teach, phys ed?"

Susan grabbed Carla but the young man laughed. "No, he teaches *Kabbalah*."

"Is he in this building now?" Susan asked, pointing to the 770 building in front of them.

"Yes, I would think so. He is *davening maariv*." After looking at the puzzled faces of the two women, he clarified. "He is saying the evening prayers. They should be finished any minute now."

"Can we ask a favor of you?" Susan responded. "Can you point him out to us when he comes out?"

"Is he expecting you?" The young man asked.

"I'm pretty sure he is," Susan replied. " Rabbi Mendel Rosenberg from Florida contacted him about us."

The young man's face lit up. "Mendy Rosenberg? I know him. He was my camp counselor many years ago."

"You went to camp?" Carla asked with a grin. Susan could see that she was about to say something inappropriate so she interrupted.

"So you'll help us find Rabbi Glickstein?"

"Sure, I'll point him out to you."

In less than a minute the service ended and a sea of men began to exit the building. Soon the number swelled to over a hundred. Each was dressed in a black suit, white shirt, and black hat. The older men all had beards. Among the men was a very small man with a full white beard.

"Rabbi Glickstein!" the young man shouted.

Rabbi Glickstein heard his name and came walking towards them.

"These two ladies are here to meet you."

Susan and Carla smiled. Susan held onto Carla's hand to keep her from thrusting it towards the man.

"Oh yes," the rabbi said. "Mendel Rosenberg told me about you."

"I have the prayer box." Susan began eagerly and reached into her handbag to retrieve the box.

"No, not here," the Rabbi shouted, holding up his hands in a defensive posture. He lowered his voice to a whisper. "Not here." He gave a look to the young man that convinced him to walk away.

"We were hoping you could look at it and tell us where it came from." Susan asked.

"Yes and I will do that," the little man replied. "But not here, not now."

"Okay, then where and when?" Carla asked.

"Tomorrow morning at 10 AM in my office." He reached in his pocket and pulled out a business card. He handed the card to Susan and quickly joined the wave of men walking along Eastern Parkway.

"Nice to meet you too," Carla whispered as the Rabbi waked away.

The ladies hailed a cab and rode back to the hotel. In the taxi Carla could not resist a comment.

"Can you believe how tiny that guy is?'

"Yes, he's a little guy."

"Little? Carla grinned. "I wanted to pick him up and burp him."

"I need a glass of wine!" Susan said.

"Me too," Carla replied as the taxi pulled up in front of the hotel. The two friends walked through the hotel lobby to the lounge.

The first thing they noticed were dozens of young men in their black suits and hats, each sitting in the lobby and talking to a young woman. Each man was sitting opposite his lady, talking and sipping from a glass. Some were laughing but most were very serious.

"Holy shit," Carla said. "They're everywhere!"

They sat at the bar and ordered wine. The bar tender, a handsome young man with a vest and bowtie, was amused by their bewilderment. His wore a name tag that said "Lenny."

"Never seen this before?" he asked.

"What is this?" Susan asked.

The bartender filled their wine glasses. "These are called *shitticks*," he said.

"*Shitticks*?" Carla mused. "It looks like a bunch of guys trying to pick up chicks."

Lenny laughed. "In a way you're right about that," he said, "but this is much more formal. These dates are arranged by a matchmaker."

"I heard about these arranged marriages." Susan replied.

"That's a misconception," he responded. "These are not arranged marriages where the bride and groom have no choice."

"So how does it work?" Carla asked.

"When the girls and boys feel that they are ready for marriage they each visit a matchmaker. The matchmaker then tries to find someone suitable for them to marry."

"And when they find someone?"

"And when they find someone they set up a *shittick* like you see here. It's nothing more than a blind date that takes place in a public place like this."

"But what if they don't like each other?" Carla asked.

"If they don't like each other they ask the matchmaker to find them another *shittick*. That's all."

"And if they do hit it off?"

"Ah, that's the best thing, when they like each other. Then they each tell their matchmaker to set up a second *shittick*."

"So the boy can't ask the girl out on a second date?"

"He's not supposed to ask her because that might put pressure on her to go when she doesn't really want to. So instead each one is supposed to contact their matchmaker and only if both ask for a second date does it happen."

At this point Carla could not control herself any longer. "Do any of them say the heck with all that and just head upstairs to a room?"

Lenny laughed. "I've never seen that happen. And I doubt that I ever will. These kids are brought up to believe that sex is reserved for marriage."

Carla sipped her wine and surveyed the room. "Let's see if we can figure out who likes who."

"Carla, let's not." Susan whispered, to no avail.

"See that couple over there?" Carla said, ignoring her friend's plea. "On a scale of one to ten she's about an eight and he's about a three. Unless he's filthy rich he has no chance with her."

Lenny laughed. "I think you're right."

Carla continued, "And see that guy over there? He's looked at his watch three times. He can't wait to get out of here."

"And no goodnight kisses for these kids." Lenny added. "They can't touch each other until they're married."

Carla thought for a minute. "Let me ask you this. If one of those boys was choking on his food would he let me do the Heimlich on him?"

"Carla's a Heimlich expert," Susan added.

Lenny quickly answered, "Oh sure, touching is allowed to save lives. Just not for affection!"

Susan took a final swig of her wine. "I think it's time to go. I'm tired."

"Okay, honey," Carla replied. "Go ahead up. I'm just gonna sit here with my friend Lenny for one more drink and maybe he can find me a shitter too."

"*Shittick.*" both Lenny and Susan shouted at the same time.

Susan went up to the room and fell asleep as soon as her head hit the pillow. Carla joined her in the room two hours later. She had a big smile on her face.

"Where have you been?" Susan asked.

"Oh me? I was just hanging out with my new friend Lenny."

CHAPTER 9

Susan and Carla arrived at Rabbi Glickstein's office a few minutes before ten. They were both overflowing with excitement about what they might learn.

As they entered the building they were met by a young man who told them that the Rabbi was expecting them. He led them into a small office cluttered with books and papers. Within minutes the rabbi entered the room, sat down behind his desk and offered them seats on the other side of the desk.

"Now you can show me the box," he said, motioning for Susan to place the box on the desk.

Susan fumbled through her handbag, retrieved the prayer box, and nervously set it down on the desk. The rabbi picked up the box. He changed glasses and examined it from all sides and all angles. At one point he brought his desk lamp close to the box and turned it on so that he could get a closer look at the box. Then he opened the top drawer of his desk and removed what looked like a jeweler's magnifying glass. He looked at the Hebrew letters on the front and the English letters on the back. The examination lasted for several minutes, and was occasionally punctuated by a "hmmm" sound from the rabbi's lips.

Susan waited with anticipation to hear what he would say. Finally he placed the box on the table and said, "So where did you say you got this box?"

"That's the point, Rabbi, I don't know where it came from. It just appeared one day in a carton that was delivered to my house."

"And that was the first time you'd seen the box?"

"Uh huh."

"My son was in a terrible accident," Carla added, "and the prayer box saved his life."

"And we have seen several more miracles since then." Susan added.

"Hmm," was the rabbi's response.

"Do you know anything about the box?" Susan asked.

The rabbi adjusted his seat, cleared his throat, and began. "First, let me tell you that there is no religious significance to this box other than the fact that it has Hebrew letters on it."

Susan was surprised to hear that. "Okay…"

"But that doesn't mean that it is not real."

"Okay"

"For many years there have been stories about boxes with mystical powers to heal the sick," the rabbi continued. "Most scholars dismiss these stories as just that, stories."

"What do you think?" Carla asked.

"Up until today I would have told you that such prayer boxes do not exist."

"Until today?"

"That's right. As I examine this box it is clear to me that it is very old."

"How old?" Susan asked.

"I'm not an expert on that but I would guess that it is a few hundred years old."

"Wow!" said Carla. "Do you also believe that it has the power to heal?"

The rabbi hesitated for a few seconds. "That I am not sure of," he answered, "but I would never rule it out."

"Is this part of *Kabbalah*?" Susan asked.

Again the rabbi thought for a moment, choosing his words carefully. "That I cannot say for sure," he answered. "I am considered by many to be a *Kabbalah* scholar. If you have a few months to learn with me I could teach you all about *Kabbalah*, but in a nutshell it is the study of the mystical aspects of the Torah."

"That's the Jewish bible." Susan said to Carla.

"I know that, honey," Carla replied tersely. "I grew up in Queens and my neighborhood was half Italian and half Jewish. My mother always said the only difference between us and them was the gravy we used."

The rabbi paused to ponder what he had just heard, decided to ignore it, and continued. "There is no mention of magical prayer boxes anywhere in the *Zohar*, which is a group of books that first defined *Kabbalah*, but there are many who believe that such magical things do exist."

"So how does it work?" Susan asked.

"Nobody knows for sure. But the legend is that these boxes contain all of the *mi sheberakh* prayers for healing that have been said by every Jew in history. This makes these boxes very powerful."

"I see," said Susan, "but where do the boxes come from?"

"Nobody knows that, but supposedly there are only thirty-six of these prayer boxes in the world. They belong to people who are known as the *Lamed Vov*."

"*Lamed Vov*?"

"Yes, those are the Hebrew words for thirty-six. *Kabbalah* teaches that in every generation there must be thirty-six righteous people in the world in order for mankind to exist."

Susan was shocked. "Are you saying that I'm one of those thirty-six righteous people?"

"Well," The rabbi responded, "It appears so."

"But it can't be me," Susan replied. "I haven't been to the synagogue in years!"

The rabbi stood up. "Righteous and religious are two completely different things," he said. "In fact, some of the *lamed vov* may not even be Jewish."

"Who are these llamas?" Carla asked.

The rabbi chuckled. "It's *lamed vov*," he answered, "and only one person knows who they are."

"Who's that?"

"It is a woman named Dina Eliezer. It is said that she is a direct descendant of the *Baal Shem Tov*."

"The what?" Carla asked.

"*The Baal Shem Tov*. His name was Israel Ben Eliezer and he was a *Kabbalah* rabbi back in the 1700's who is credited with starting the Hassidic movement that we know today. He is believed to have performed many miracles."

"Like healing the sick?"

"Some might say that. Others will disagree."

"So where can I find this lady, Dina?"

"Dina Eliezer. She sits every day by the Western Wall."

"The Western Wall of what?" Carla asked

"The Western Wall of the great Temple in Jerusalem." The rabbi said.

"And it's in Jerusalem? " Carla asked. "Like Israel, Jerusalem?"

"Yes. The great Temple was destroyed by the Romans in the first century of the common era. All that remains is the Western Wall. Jews go there from all parts of the world to pray. Some people refer to it as the Wailing Wall."

"Steven, my late husband, always wanted to go there." Susan said softly.

"Many believe that the wall also has magical powers to heal, and so they place notes in the wall asking for healing."

"How will we find this Dina?"

"Oh, you will find her, trust me. She sits in a chair by the women's area of the wall every day. She is very old. You will find her with no difficulty."

"Okay then," Susan said. "We are going to Israel!"

"I think that is a wise thing to do," Rabbi Glickstein added, "but I want you to promise me one thing."

"What's that?"

"Please be very careful with this prayer box." He held it in his hand as he spoke very sternly. "There are people who will stop at nothing to get their hands on something like this."

"Oh my!"

"Whatever you do you should keep this in your possession at all times and don't tell anyone but Dina that you have it. This is very important."

"I understand, Rabbi, and thank you so much for your help and guidance," Susan said as she rose to leave.

"You're very welcome."

Susan placed the prayer box back into her handbag as the two ladies walked out of the office and downstairs to hail a taxi.

Immediately after they left his office Rabbi Glickstein picked up his cell phone and punched in a speed dial number.

"Moishe," he said softly, "You won't believe what I just saw!"

CHAPTER 10

Jeff awoke the next morning with mixed emotions running through his head. He had chosen not to join his ex-wife at the Marriott. Instead he had driven to the hotel and left a hand written note to be delivered to her this morning.

The note wished her well but made it clear that he had moved on. He told her that their common son and grandchildren would always keep them connected and he hoped that they could always have a cordial relationship. But in no uncertain terms he let her know that there would be no reconciliation.

As he dressed he assumed that Pam would be reading the note at that very minute. He wondered what her reaction would be. He stared at his cell phone for a moment to see if she was going to call.

No call came.

Jeff walked down to his mother's room to see how she was doing. The hospice nurse had told him that she probably only had a couple of days left to live so he wanted to be there with her every possible moment.

As he entered her room, Beverly was sleeping. He moved close to her to check to see if she was still breathing. He was startled when her eyes opened and she said "Nope, not dead yet!"

They both smiled. Jeff held his mother's hand. "I love you mom." He whispered.

"Jeffy, I need you to do something for me."

"Anything, mom. Just name it."

"I want you to go to the kitchen and look in the window sill above the sink. There's a small wooden box. I want you to bring it to me."

That seemed like a strange request but Jeff had been told by the hospice nurse that his mother might become very nostalgic as the end approached. He quickly walked to the kitchen and retrieved the box. It was a wooden box about four inches long and two inches wide. It looked very old and worn.

As requested he carried the box into the bedroom and handed it to his frail mother.

Beverly examined the box and began to speak.

"Jeffy."

"Yes, mom."

"What I am about to tell you can never be repeated."

"Okay, mom."

"You are not going to believe what I am about to tell you."

"Really, mom?"

"Yes. You're gonna think this is nothing more that the mumblings of a dying old woman."

"No, I would never…"

"This box has magical powers!"

Suddenly, Jeff understood what Beverly meant about not believing, but he chose to humor his mother."

"How is that possible, mom?"

"It's called a prayer box, Jeffy." She handed him the box.

"You see those words on the box? Those are written in Hebrew."

"Hebrew? Mom, we're Christians. Where did you get a box that has Hebrew words?"

"I don't know."

"You don't know? What do you mean you don't know?" Jeff was losing his patience.

Beverly patted her hand on the bed and said, "Sit down my son, I have a long story to tell you."

Jeff's head was spinning. He sat motionless on his mother's bed as she told him about the prayer box. At first the story was impossible to believe but, the more his mother spoke, the stronger and more coherent she became.

"It all started just after we moved to this house in 1995. Your dad had just retired and we planned to live out our remaining years here." Beverly sat up in her bed. "Jeff, do you remember what this lake was called when we moved here?"

Jeff pondered for a moment. "Wasn't it Milford Lake or something like that?"

"Lake Milton," she corrected him. "It was named after a world war one soldier named James Milton who lived near the lake and died in action in Europe."

"But now it's called Miracle Lake," Jeff replied.

"Yes it is. And this box is the reason why!"

"Oh, wow!"

"When we moved in we had some things shipped from the Malden house. It was just our personal stuff."

"I remember that, mom."

"But when we unpacked our things this box was among them. Neither daddy nor I knew what it was so I threw it in the trash."

"In the trash?"

"Uh huh. But when daddy was taking out the trash the next day the box fell out of the trash bag and landed on his foot."

"You're kidding."

"Nope, that's exactly what happened. So daddy brought it back in and we examined it. That's when we saw the Hebrew letters on it."

"So what did you do then?"

"Do you remember Rabbi Salmon? He was a long time patient of daddy's."

"Of course I do. I took care of him after dad retired."

"Well, daddy showed the box to the rabbi and he contacted some people and the next thing you know we got a visit from two men who were Jewish scholars."

"They came here?"

"Yes, they wanted to see the box. And when they looked at it they were in shock."

"What did they say about it?"

"They told us that there are only thirty-six of these boxes in the world."

"Thirty-six? How did they know that?"

"They said the ancient Jewish teachings were that there are thirty-six righteous people in the world at any one time and that those people were the ones who had these boxes."

"And they said the box has magical powers?"

"Yes, honey. They told us that each box contains all of the prayers of all the people who have ever lived, and that the box has the power to heal the sick."

"So how did you know which of you was the righteous one, you or dad?"

Beverly turned the box over and handed it again to her son.

"Do you see the initials carved on the back of the box?"

"I see lots of initials."

"Look at the top one."

"It says BJD."

"That's me! Beverly Jean Davis."

Jeff was dumbfounded. "Wait a minute. You didn't put these initials on the box? They were already there when you found it?"

"That's right!"

"Did they explain how the box ended up being delivered here?"

"That they couldn't explain."

"So let me get this straight. A box gets delivered to this house with your initials on it because you are one of the thirty-six righteous people in the world."

"I know it sounds crazy, son, but that's exactly what happened."

"Mom, that was over twenty years ago. What have you been doing with this box since then?"

"Nothing really. I just keep it in the window sill above the sink."

"That's it?"

"Yep. And I let it do what it was meant to do."

"Soo when people go swimming in the lake they think the lake has magical powers but it's really this little box?"

"That's right, Jeffy. And then about fifteen years ago people started calling this Miracle Lake instead of Lake Milton."

"This is unbelievable!"

"I know it sounds crazy, honey, but every word is true."

Jeff pulled a chair up beside his mother and sat down. "Did you see the miracles, mom?"

"I did. I saw them with my own eyes."

"Like what, mom?"

"About two weeks after the box arrived I was at the market and I ran into Sylvia Turcotte. We used to play canasta together. "

"Yes, I remember Sylvia."

"Well, Sylvia was very upset because her husband was having serious heart problems. They said he had congestive heart failure."

"Yes, I'm familiar with that."

"She said he was at stage D and the only hope he had was for a heart transplant."

"Did the prayer box get the heart for him?"

"No, it worked even better. I brought the box to her house and within two weeks his symptoms were gone."

"Gone?"

"Gone completely, Jeffrey!"

"Holy"

"And that's not the only thing, Jeff. After that there was Edie Hinson's grandson. He had a terrible skin disease that turned his skin blotchy white. Here was a black kid that was turning white. Edie said all the kids at school made fun of him."

"And the prayer box again?"

"I had him sleep with the box for two nights and when he woke up the third morning his skin was perfectly normal. No blotches at all!"

"None?"

"Completely normal, Jeffrey. It was truly a miracle."

Jeff thought for a moment. "Mom, when dad got really sick why didn't the prayer box help him?"

"I asked that same question, but I was told that it can't be used for the immediate family, only to help others. Believe me, I tried everything, even slept with the prayer box in our bed. But it just didn't work for daddy."

"Mom" Jeff hesitated to speak.

"I know what you want to ask, honey. What should you do with the box when I die."

"I hate to ask."

"You must bury the box with me."

"What?"

"Jeffy, this is very important. You must place the box in my coffin and make sure that it is open."

"Okay, mom."

"I need you to promise me you will do that!"

"I promise, mom, but why?"

"I don't know why but that is what I was told. Maybe that is how it gets to the next person. I don't know. I just need you to promise."

"I promise mom. I promise"

"I'm tired now, Jeffy. I want to take a nap."

"Okay, I'll walk around the lake and fix lunch when I get back. The hospice nurse should be here any minute."

Jeff left his mother's bedside, gently placed the box back in the window, and headed out for his daily walk. As he watched the people swimming in the dirty lake water he now had new appreciation for what they were doing and why.

As he walked he thought about everything he had heard in the past twenty four hours. He was flattered that Pam wanted to try again but relieved that he had said no. And the story he heard from his mother was going to take a long time to digest.

About forty five minutes after he left for the walk he returned to the house. The hospice nurse was waiting for him at the door. Her head was down and she was shaking. She lifted her head and Jeff knew by the look on her face that his mother was dead.

She had lived just long enough to tell him about the prayer box.

CHAPTER 11

It took two weeks for Susan and Carla to renew their passports and make travel arrangements to Israel. Susan was careful not to talk to anyone else about the box or to use it in front of others.

At one point Susan asked Carla if she really wanted to go to Israel.

"I wouldn't miss this for the world," was her response to that question. "And wait till you see all the new clothes I bought for the trip."

When Susan told Dee Kalen next door that she was going to Israel, Mrs. Kalen handed her a five dollar bill.

"What's this for?" Susan asked.

"This is for *tzedaka*," the older woman explained. "That means charity."

"You mean like the singer, Neil Sedaka?"

"Oh I never thought about that," Dee said. "But I guess you're right."

"Carla told me he was Italian."

"No, honey I really think he's Jewish, but it really doesn't matter."

"You want me to give this to a charity in Israel?"

"Yes, honey. We believe that God will protect you on your journey if you are going to give to charity. So when you get to Israel please find some charity to give this money to."

"Thank you, Dee. That is so sweet," Susan replied, hugging her neighbor. "I promise I will do it."

The journey was scheduled from West Palm Beach to Newark and then on to Tel Aviv. It was a grueling pair of flights that would take over seventeen hours to complete.

The first stop in Newark proved very interesting for Susan. They had gone though the security check at Palm Beach International but were surprised to learn that they had to go through another security check in Newark before boarding the plane to Tel Aviv.

As they waited in line for the security checkpoint near the gate an attractive young woman in uniform came up to them and asked to see their passports.

"First trip to Israel?" she said as she examined their passports.

Both ladies nodded.

"You are traveling together?"

Another nod.

"And what is the purpose of your trip?"

Susan hesitated for a moment. She did not want to mention the prayer box so she said, "Just sight seeing."

Carla said, "Yes, we're sight seeing."

"And what sights are you going to see?" the young woman asked.

"The Western Wall is the main reason we are going." Susan replied "We have friends who are ill and we are going to put notes in the wall for them. We're hoping for miracles. My husband always wanted to take me there but he died before we could go so my friend Carla agreed to come with me."

The young woman looked carefully at both ladies. *This must be profiling*, Susan thought, I hope we pass the test.

"Are you Jewish?" came the next question.

"I am," Susan responded, "but she's not."

"My second husband was half Jewish," Carla added. The agent rolled her eyes up from the passport and looked closely at Carla.

"Did you have a Bat Mitzvah?" she asked Susan.

"Yes I did."

"And that's where she got her first kiss!" Carla added. Once again Susan was horrified by her dear friend's mouth. *Now we're cooked*, she thought.

But the security agent just laughed and said "me too!"

She handed back the passports and said "have a nice visit."

After having their carry on bags opened and checked thoroughly they walked into the waiting area at the gate.

Carla noticed that another security agent was positioned at the other end of the gate. Each time someone came up to go to the gate from this direction he stopped them and redirected them to the other end where the security checkpoint was. This happened several times.

A few minutes later a group of musicians carrying their instruments walked up and spoke to the security agent. Carla was surprised to see him allow them to enter the gate area without going through security.

"Did you see that?" Carla whispered to Susan.

"See what?"

"He let those guys come to the gate without going through security!"

"So?"

"So we're on this flight, too. What if these guys are terrorists and the guard is in cahoots with them?"

Susan laughed. "You watch too much TV, Carla. I'm sure there is a very logical explanation."

"Well, I sure as hell would like to hear it."

"Then why don't you go and ask the guard why he let them in?"

Carla took a few minutes to summon the courage to make her move but then she sauntered up to the security guard and said. "How are you?"

The guard nodded. "Just fine, ma'am."

"Can I ask you a question?"

"Sure you can."

"I'm concerned that you made everyone go around to the other side except the four musicians. How come they were let in without going through security?"

The security guard chuckled. "You really want to know?"

"Absolutely!"

The security guard pointed at the four men. "Those are the air marshals on your flight. Their job is to protect you."

It took only one second for his words to sink in. "Oh," Carla replied, "then I guess I shouldn't ask what's in those instrument cases."

"No, don't ask." said the guard with a grin.

Carla walked back to her seat and told Susan the whole story.

"Now you know why this airline has never been hijacked," Susan said.

Both women were able to sleep a little on the long flight. They arrived in Tel Aviv at four in the afternoon, local time. By the time they passed through immigration and gathered their luggage it was almost five.

The taxi ride from the airport to Jerusalem took about an hour. Their taxi driver was a nice man named Eli. He was a handsome man who looked to be about fifty. Carla called him "E-lye, like Eli Manning, the Giants quarterback," but he corrected her that his name is pronounced El-lee "like the girl," he laughed.

As Eli drove them through the crowded roads, he said, "Welcome to Israel."

"Thanks," Carla replied, "is it safe here?"

"Of course it's safe here," he replied. "Especially with me."

"Why are we so safe with you?" Susan asked.

"Because I am a retired captain in the Israeli Defense Force," Eli boasted, " I used to shoot terrorists and I have a gun in my taxi to protect you!"

"Oh, great," Carla whispered to Susan. "We have Barney Fife driving us."

As Eli fought his way through the heavy traffic, honking and yelling at the other drivers, he issued the following words of comfort to his passengers.

"The truth is you've got a better chance of getting killed by my driving than by a terrorist!" He let out a big belly laugh.

Those were the last words spoken in the taxi until it came to a stop in front of the King David Hotel.

It was a very impressive hotel to say the least. Two bellmen helped them with their luggage as they walked up to the front door. An armed guard checked their bags before they were allowed to enter.

"This is a fancy place," Carla whispered.

"It should be," Susan replied. "It's costing us five hundred a night."

"Whoa, I didn't know that."

"Well we get to split the cost, and the travel agent got us an upgrade to a deluxe room."

As they approached the front desk they were greeted by a smiling young man who welcomed them to the King David. He was short, dark, and had curly hair.

"Let's see," he said looking at their reservation. "I see you will be checking out on Sunday. Will you need a *Shabbos* key?"

"A what?" Carla replied.

"A *Shabbos* key. It's a special key that is used Friday night and Saturday by orthodox Jews. It doesn't require an electrical circuit like our standard key card. I assume you won't need one."

"That would be a correct assumption." Carla replied.

The two friends were exhausted. It was only 6 PM in Jerusalem, noon back in Florida, but neither had slept much on the overnight flight. As they entered their hotel room Susan began to hang up her clothes.

"Jenny told me the secret is not to go to sleep now or we'll never get adjusted to the time change."

Carla left her suitcase on the floor, removing only her makeup. "How about we get a nice dinner. I'm starving!"

They were directed by the front desk clerk to a nice Argentinian steak house just off Ben Yehuda, the main shopping area of the city. As they sat at the table Susan removed her cell phone from her hand bag and checked for wifi. Then she pointed the phone at Carla and began to send a Whatsapp video message to her daughter in New Hampshire.

"Hi Jenny. Here we are in Jerusalem and we're having dinner. Say hi, Carla."

Carla yelled. "Hi Jenny, I'm taking good care of your mom."

"Tomorrow is the big day for us," Susan said. "I'll let you know what happens. Love you and kiss the kids for me."

"That app is amazing," Carla said. "What is it?"

"It's called Whatsapp," Susan replied. "I think it's part of Facebook."

"It sends video messages?"

"Yes, it's amazing."

"So, how long does it take for them to get the message in the states?"

"They get it instantly. That's the beauty of it."

"Wow! But what happens if Jenny isn't there when you send her the message?"

"Then it's saved and she can listen to it whenever she has the time, just like a text message."

"Awesome! I have to get that app for my grandchildren."

"I bet they already have it."

"That's true. These kids are way ahead of me when it comes to this stuff."

After dinner they went straight back to the hotel. As they walked through the lobby Carla spotted several pairs of young men and women talking.

"Look," she said with a smile, "more shitters!"

CHAPTER 12

Jeff sat by himself for several hours reminiscing about his family. With Mom's death, he thought, I'm now the only one left. He took comfort in knowing that his mother would be buried between her beloved husband and son.

Jeff and Pam had purchased a cemetery plot together in Everett, Massachusetts. But it seemed highly unlikely that he would choose to be buried next to the woman who had hurt him so deeply.

He removed the prayer box from the window sill and placed it in a carrying case so that he could take it to the cemetery the next day. He hid the case in the master bedroom for now. He did not want anyone to see him placing the box in her casket, not even his son.

He was about to call Mickey to make arrangements for him to come when his doorbell rang. He opened the door to find Mr. & Mrs. Adams standing in his doorway.

"Hi there," he said.

"We hate to bother you, Doctor Morton," Mrs. Adams said, "especially at a time like this. But we really need your help."

"Oh, it's okay. How can I help you?"

Mr. Adams was staring at the floor. The two looked helpless.

"Oh, for goodness sakes please come in!" Jeff said as he ushered the couple into his living room.

Mrs. Adams began to speak. "Doc, do you remember when you offered to help us with our business problem?"

Jeff thought for a minute and recalled that they were facing the prospect of a large competitor moving in right next to them.

"It doesn't seem fair what they're doing to you," he said.

"It isn't fair," Mr. Adams responded. "And we have a meeting this afternoon with a lawyer who says he might be able to help us."

"Oh, that's good." Jeff replied. "When is the meeting?"

"Well, that's just it." Mr. Adams said sheepishly. "We're on our way to meet him now."

"And," Mrs. Adams interrupted, "we were hoping you would come with us. You're the most educated man we know. We're just simple people and we don't understand all this legal stuff."

"Now?" Jeff replied. "Gee, this isn't a good time for me. I'm trying to make arrangements for the funeral…"

"I know." Mr. Adams said. "My wife told me not to bother you but I thought it was worth a shot in the dark."

"We were hoping for a miracle," Mrs. Adams added. "And that's why we stopped here."

"But listen," said Mr. Adams. "We completely understand. I'm really sorry we bothered you."

Jeff thought for a moment as he looked at these two sad people. These are wonderful people, honest people, he thought. And they need my help.

"Just give me a minute." Jeff said as we walked towards the bedroom. He opened the drawer where the prayer box was hidden. He carefully removed the case and walked back into the living room.

Beverly had told Jeff all about the prayer box and the miracles it performed. The one thing she never said was whether or not it could work for situations like the one facing Mr. & Mrs. Adams. Was it only for illnesses? Here was one way to find out.

"Let's go!" He said as he walked out of the house with Mr. & Mrs. Adams. "I'll drive you in my car."

On the way to the law office Jeff reached into his case and made sure that they prayer box was open.

"What you got in the box, doc?" Mr. Adams asked.

"Oh, uh, just a few things I need for the funeral. I'm afraid if I leave them somewhere I might lose them. Old age you know?"

"I'm getting there," Mr. Adams replied.

In ten minutes they were at the law office of Vernon McGraw. Vernon was well known in the community as a lawyer who loved to take on the establishment.

As they walked in and sat down Vernon entered the room. He was a tiny man who looked to be about seventy years old. His small stature made it hard to imagine him as the feisty lawyer his reputation told of.

For fifteen minutes Mr. Adams spoke about the history of their station, how it had been built by his late father Albert in 1956 on a piece of land he had purchased from the Pennacook Indian tribe. Mr. Adams had started working in the station as a young boy in the seventies and took over permanently when his dad died in 1993. And now a large oil company was going to build a station right next door.

"These large companies can afford to sell gas at a loss for as long as it takes to put their competitors out of business. I've seen it happen to too many other family owned stations," he said.

Vernon McGraw listened intently for the entire time and, when Mr. Adams finished he spoke.

"I sympathize with you folks. I really do," he said softly. "And there is nothing I would rather do than stick it to the big boys. But I'm afraid in this case there isn't anything I can do. I researched the land title and it's clear. The city council is set to approve the site plan. It's a done deal."

Just as they were about to leave Mr. McGraw's office door opened and his secretary, Dorothy White walked in.

"This was just delivered by courier," she said. "I thought it might be important."

Vernon McGraw opened the envelope and read it for a moment.

"Dorothy." He yelled to his secretary.

"Yes, Mr. McGraw," she said reentering the office.

"Who gave you this?"

"It was just a courier. He didn't say where it came from."

Vernon nodded as Dorothy left the office. He turned to his visitors with a big smile on his face.

"We have to double check to see if this is real," he said. "But if it is there's no way that new gas station goes up next to you!"

"Why? What is it?" Mrs. Adams said excitedly.

Vernon McGraw stood up. "What I have in my hands is a contract signed by your father Albert Adams and the Chief of the Pennacook tribe."

"Contract?" Mr. Adams asked.

"It's a contract for the sale of the land in 1953. And in this contract it clearly states that no other gas station could be built on any other Pennacook property within five miles of your station."

"And the land next door? Is it?"

"It was purchased from the Penacooks. That I'm sure of."

"Oh lord. Thank you Jesus!" Mr. Adams shouted. He hugged his wife, hugged Vernon, and even hugged Jeff.

"Just leave everything to me," Vernon said. "This will be a lot of fun."

The three visitors left the office. As they reached the parking lot Mrs. Adam said, "Jeff, I'm so sorry we bothered you. If we knew about the contract we would never have asked you to come with us. We wasted your time."

Jeff looked at the case containing the prayer box. "It's okay," he said with a smile. "It was my pleasure."

CHAPTER 13

Susan was the first to awaken the next morning. She showered, got dressed, and woke up her friend. She went downstairs to the lobby and brought back coffee for each of them as Carla took her turn in the tiny bathroom.

By 10 AM they were in a taxi heading for the Western Wall. The driver took them to a parking area where they exited the cab and walked though a security checkpoint. More armed guards greeted them.

After passing through security the women walked to a large open area filled with people. Their attention was quickly moved to the wall that was in front of them. It was a large stone wall with hundreds of people standing in front of it praying. Men were on the left and women on the right, and a barrier separated them.

They made their way over to the women's side. As they approached the wall they could see several women placing little notes into the cracks in the wall. Most of them placed their notes in the wall, said a prayer, and then backed away from the wall without turning around until they were several steps back.

"Do we know what this lady looks like?" Carla asked.

"No but I know her name and she's very old and she's here every day sitting in a folding chair. That's all I know."

They saw one elderly woman standing near the barrier.

"Are you Dina?" Susan asked.

"Dina? No my name is Sarah."

"Do you come to the Wall often?" Susan asked.

"Every day." was the woman's reply.

"Every day?" Carla asked. "Why do you do that?"

"I come here every day to pray."

Susan moved closer to the woman. "And may I ask what it is that you pray for?"

"I pray for peace." The woman replied. "I pray that my children and grandchildren can live in a world where they are not surrounded by people who want to kill them."

"How is that working out?" Carla asked.

The woman chucked. "You know some days I feel like I'm just talking to a wall!"

Susan and Carla laughed as they watched the woman move closer to the Wall.

Carla spotted another elderly woman sitting about fifty feet back from the wall, all alone. "I think maybe that's her."

The two friends slowly walked up to the second elderly woman. She had wrinkled skin, a large scarf covering her hair, and she was dressed in a long skirt and a jacket even though the temperature was probably in the 80's. She was wearing glasses and appeared to be reading a prayer book.

"Dina?" Susan said hesitantly.

The old woman looked up from her prayer book. "Yes, I am Dina. Are you Susan Benjamin?" she said quietly.

Susan was startled to hear her maiden name. "Well, I am Susan Gold," she replied cautiously, "but my maiden name was Susan Benjamin."

The old woman smiled and nodded. "I know. I have been waiting for you."

"Waiting?" Carla asked, "how long have you been waiting?"

"Let's just say for a long time." The old woman replied.

"Then you know about the prayer box?" Susan asked as she reached into her handbag.

"No!" the old woman said sternly as she held up her hands. "Do not show me the box here."

Susan quickly forced the box down deep into her handbag. "Then when can you see it?"

The old woman whispered. "I want you to come to my house for dinner tonight. Then we can talk."

"Okay, where do you live?" Susan asked.

"I live in *Givat Mordechai*," the woman replied. "It's not too far. You can take a taxi. My address is 442 Shakal Street. Come at 6 PM."

"Okay," Susan replied as she wrote down the address.

"And please bring the box with you."

"Okay, I will." Susan said as the old woman stood up and walked away. Her chair remained.

"What just happened?" Susan asked.

"I think we just got a free dinner," Carla replied. "And now we have a whole day to kill."

Susan took out her cell phone and began to talk into it.

"Hi Jen," she said as she sent a Whatsapp message to her daughter. "I'm here at the wall and it's amazing! All of these people are placing notes in the wall hoping for a miracle. Love you."

In a few seconds Susan received a voice message back from her daughter. "Hi mom. We had a neighbor pass away today so I'll be going to the house after the funeral to pay my respects. The kids are in camp and I'm gonna pick them up in a few minutes. I'm glad you made it safely to Israel. Say hi to Carla for me."

"Are you gonna use that Whatsapp thing every day?" Carla asked.

"At least once a day, probably more," Susan replied. "This way Jenny can be right here in Israel with us."

"I can't believe I didn't know about this."

"We've got a few hours to kill," Susan said. "What would you like to do now?"

Carla pondered for a moment. "How about we get some lunch and then let's find a place to give away that five bucks Dee Kalen gave you."

"Oh yes, I almost forgot about that." She grabbed her cell phone and hit the Whatsapp button.

"Hi Jenny. What was then name of that soup kitchen you told me to visit?"

Within seconds Jenny's voice could be heard. "You mean the one from the Holocaust Survivor Cookbook? It's called *Carmei Ha'ir*. You should go there and make a donation."

The two friends walked away from the wall area to the parking lot where they boarded a taxi. Within a few minutes they were on Agripas Street in front of *Carmei Ha'ir*. Susan removed the five dollar bill that Dee Kalen had given her and together she and Carla walked into the soup kitchen.

They were surprised by what they saw. Tables were filled with families, soldiers, young and elderly people. Waiters took orders and brought food just like any other restaurant.

"This isn't a soup kitchen!" Carla whispered to her friend. "Are you sure we're in the right place?"

Susan checked the sign on the wall to see that it was indeed *Carmei Ha'ir*. She also noticed a Holocaust Survivor cookbook for sale on the counter.

"This is it," Susan replied. A tall young man with a beard walked over to their table. He was wearing black pants and a white shirt, just like all of the men they had met in Crown Heights.

"Welcome to *Carmei Ha'ir*," he said with a smile as he handed menus to the ladies. "What can I get you to drink?"

"Water will be fine." Carla replied and Susan nodded in agreement.

"Can I ask you something?" Susan asked the young man. "How can this be a soup kitchen? It looks like a regular diner to me."

The young man laughed. "A lot of people say that to us," he responded. "Our motto is 'all who are hungry shall eat.' We believe that everyone deserves to be treated with dignity, whether they have money or not."

"So none of these people have any money?" Carla asked as she motioned towards a group of elderly diners.

"Some do and some don't. Those who have money leave some on their way out the door. It's called a *tzedaka* box." He said, pointing towards a large wooden box hanging on the wall near the front door. "And those who have no money simply walk out the door. Everyone is treated with dignity and respect!"

"That's awesome," Carla said. "So how do you get enough money to do all of this?"

"Most of our money comes from donations," the young man replied. "One woman from the states has given us hundreds of thousands!"

"Is that the cookbook lady?" Susan asked. The young man nodded.

Susan and Carla ordered lunch and ate the meal. On the way out the door Susan placed the five dollar bill from Dee Kalen in the *tzedaka* box and added a twenty of her own. Carla added another twenty.

"I think we did our good deed for today." Susan said proudly.

"I think we're gonna be doing a lot of good deeds with that box of yours," Carla replied.

As they walked out of *Carmei Ha'ir* they turned left and strolled up Agripas Street to the open market. It was a huge market with people buying fruits, vegetables, bread, nuts, fish, and meats from vendors in the kiosks. People were pushing, reaching, and yelling.

"This is a madhouse," Carla said as she walked towards a flower kiosk. "Let's try to buy flowers to bring tonight."

Susan watched with amusement as her friend pushed and shoved her way to the front of the line. People were yelling at her in Hebrew and although Susan could not understand the language, it was easy to figure out what they were saying.

Carla eventually made her way to the man selling the flowers, grabbed a fresh bouquet and held out money for him. The man took Carla's twenty dollar bill and handed her back a handful of coins.

"So how much did he charge you?" Susan asked with a grin.

"Not a clue," her friend replied, looking bewildered as she examined the pile of coins in her hand.

"I think we should stop at an ATM and get some Israeli money, don't you?"

The two friends spent the rest of the afternoon in a taxi exploring the city of Jerusalem. At each historical sight they exited the cab and Susan sent a Whatsapp message to Jennifer, explaining the beauty and emotional impact of each place.

At six they arrived in front of Dina's home. It was an old building with three floors and Dina lived at the top. They walked up the cobbled stone steps carefully watching to make sure they did not trip. Susan counted a total of thirty two steps before they finally arrived at the front door.

"How does the old lady do this every day?" Carla whispered.

Susan gently knocked on the door, then harder and harder knocks until Dina opened the door for them. They entered into an apartment that looked like it belonged in the 1950's, linoleum floors, tiny old kitchen appliances, and rooms half the size of what we see in America today.

Dina invited the two women in, fixed them a cup of tea, and they sat around her small dining table. Slowly she reached into her bag and removed a box that looked very similar to the one Susan was carrying.

"I found this box in my apartment the day I arrived in Israel. It was called Palestine back in 1938. I was a young woman then and I came with my father. His plan was to establish a home in Palestine and then send for my mother and two brothers in Germany. But they never made it."

Susan noticed the look of despair that was etched on Dina's face. Dina stopped to sip her tea and placed a plate of cookies on the table.

"I started coming to the wall right after the war in 1967. After Jerusalem was liberated the wall became accessible to Jews. People started coming to the wall from all over the world placing notes in the cracks and hoping for miracles. Let's just say that my prayer box gave them a boost. Does the wall itself have healing powers? I really don't know. But I have come to the wall with my prayer box every single day except Saturday since 1967."

"About twenty years ago I received a visit from a woman who said she lived in Greece. She showed me her prayer box and told me that she knew she had very little time to live. She told me that there were a total of thirty-six prayer boxes in the world and she also told me who was in possession of each box. That's how I knew about you."

"You mean I had this box twenty years ago?" Susan cried. "I could have used it to save my husband?"

"I'm afraid the box can never be used for one's own family. It only works when you help others."

Tears welled up in Susan's eyes. "How could I be chosen to get this box and not been able to use it save the most important person in my life? That's cruel!"

Carla reached out and hugged her friend. "I'm so sorry sweetie."

Susan welcomed the hug and regained her composure. "But how did I have it twenty years ago and not know that I had it?"

"I doubt that you actually had possession of the box twenty years ago, but it was destined for you."

"Destined? How?" Susan asked.

Dina turned the box over and showed Susan the carvings on the back. "You see, these are the initials of everyone who has possessed this prayer box."

"We saw those letters," Carla said. "but they didn't make any sense to us."

"You see the initials on the bottom. These are yours, Susan."

"S.E.B." Susan read. "That's Susan Elizabeth Benjamin. That's me! I saw these before but I wasn't sure exactly what the letters were. And I never expected to see the initials of my maiden name on there! I never put two and two together. But how did these letters get on the box?"

"That is a mystery even I cannot solve."

"What about these other initials?" Carla asked as she examined the back of the box.

Dina looked carefully at Susan's box.

"Each set of initials denotes the person who possessed the box before you."

Susan examined the initials just below hers.

"MKL," she said as she carefully interpreted the writing.

"MKL?" Carla shouted. "Martin Luther King had this box before you?"

"That's MLK Carla. This is MKL!" Susan shouted.

"That stands for Marie Katrine Lafleur," Dina replied, sipping her tea.

"So who was the lady?" Carla asked. "Why did she have the prayer box?"

"Marie was known as Sister Katrine and she was the mother superior at a small orphanage just outside of Paris. Back then it was called *Village des Enfant*. Today it is a convent known as Convent Katrine. How she got the box and what she did with it is a mystery that you must solve for yourself. "

"Myself?"

"You must go to France to learn for yourself. It is a journey you will remember always and it will prepare you to use the box wisely."

"Hey Susie," Carla said as she walked away from the table to rinse her hands. "Didn't your dad come from France?"

"He did. He came to America in 1939 and thank God he did."

"So let's go there, I'm game."

"You know, Jenny spent a semester studying in Paris and she speaks fluent French."

CHAPTER 14

Carla called Air France to change their plane reservations so that they would stop in Paris for twenty hours before continuing on to the US.

"I wonder how much this change is going to cost us?" Susan asked.

"Cost us?" Carla responded defiantly, "It shouldn't cost us anything! You let me handle it."

Since their original reservation included a stop in Paris, Susan assumed it would be no big deal to stay over in Paris one night rather than the four hour layover that the original reservation included.

Carla called Air France and, after listening to three recorded messages and pressing several different numbers, was finally able to get through to a reservations agent who spoke English.

Carla calmly described the change she wanted to make and she was told that the new price would be three hundred dollars per person higher than the original tickets that they had purchased.

"Are you are out of your freaking mind?" she said to the reservations agent in classic Carla rant mode. "We're going to the same place we were going before and the only difference is we're stopping in Paris for a few extra hours. Why on earth would you make us pay so much extra money if we're not going anywhere different than we were going before?"

The Air France reservation agent calmly explained that this was their policy and there was nothing she could do about it.

"How about if we go into a lower class ticket?" Carla asked.

"I'm sorry, but you were already in coach and the only thing lower than that is baggage. We don't sell tickets to baggage." was the sarcastic response.

"How about if we offered to help serve dinner to the passengers?" Carla replied with an equal dose of sarcasm.

"Sorry, that's not allowed" was the quick response, "and besides, there's no dinner served on your flight anyway."

"Well for three hundred bucks we ought to get filet mignon!" Carla shouted. "You know my father was a US soldier during World War Two. He helped to liberate your country. If it wasn't for my father you'd be speaking German!"

"Ma'am, did you want to make this change or not?"

Carla could see she was defeated. She made the change, gave them Susan's credit card information for the extra six hundred dollars and got the new reservations.

"How'd you make out?" Susan asked with a smile.

"Damn, those French people are stubborn," Carla barked.

"I never knew your dad helped to liberate France?" Susan remarked as she hopped into bed.

"Neither did he! He told me he spent the whole war drunk in Chicago."

The two friends laughed.

*   *   *

They awoke early the next morning, took a taxi to Ben Gurion airport and eventually boarded a plane to Paris. They arrived in Paris early in the afternoon. Susan was bursting with anticipation as they walked out of Charles DeGaulle airport and into a taxi.

Their driver was a very friendly man who appeared to be in his forties. He was wearing a New York Yankees baseball cap, which pleased Carla to no end.

"You a Yankee fan?" She asked with a smile.

"No, *madame*," the driver answered in broken English. "I don't know anything about them. Last week a man from New York gave me this hat and I like it so I wear it."

"We need to go to Convent Katrine. Can you take us there?"

"Yes, madam. I don't know where it is but I will find out for you."

The driver then grabbed his cell phone and made a phone call, speaking quickly in French. After about two minutes he turned to the ladies and said "Yes, *madame*, I know where it is and I will take you there now."

"And how much is this going to cost?" Carla asked.

"You can go by the meter or you can pay me a flat rate of 40 euros. It's your choice."

"How much is that in dollars?"

"I think about 45 dollars."

"Okay, we'll take the flat rate. I don't want to be driving all over town. I want to go straight there!"

"You don't trust anyone do you, Carla?" Susan said.

"Not in this country that's for sure!"

"Thank you, sir," Carla said, "and by the way, what's your name? We never asked you your name."

The driver turned his head towards them, smiled and said "*je m'apelle* Henri. My name is Henri and it is nice to meet you both."

As they drove away from the airport Susan removed her cell phone from her handbag, opened the Whatsapp app and pushed the record button to send a message to her daughter.

"Hi Jen, we're here in Paris. Oh it's so exciting we're heading towards a convent and we're going to try to learn about who it was that had this box before me and how I ended up with it and whether or not she was able to use it to heal people."

She pointed the phone towards their driver.

"And this is Henri, our driver. Say hi, Henri!"

Henri turned around and smiled and waved, "Bonjour America!"

"I'm very excited about this journey, Jenny," Susan continued, "and I'm hoping that it will bring some much needed answers to me about this mystical box. I can't wait to tell you all about it after I speak with the people at the convent. Love to you and the kids. Mom."

"We should be there in about twenty minutes," Henri said as he navigated through the crowded streets, "as long as this traffic does not get worse than this and I will let you know when we get close."

About twenty minutes later they pulled down a tree lined street to a large house. The house looked to be well over a hundred years old, with a large front porch inviting people to use it. The house seemed to be in disrepair, definitely it needed a paint job, and the roof looked like it hadn't been cleaned in decades.

"This site doesn't look like a convent." Carla remarked as the taxi approached the front of the house.

"And just what exactly does a convent look like anyway?" Susan replied.

Carla pondered for a moment and then quickly blurted out, "Like the one in The Sound of Music."

"Of course it does," Susan replied with a giggle, "and there's Julie Andrews!" The two friends laughed at their own inside joke.

The driver stopped the car and asked for his money. Carla handed him a fifty dollar bill and said "keep the change".

Henri examined the bill carefully and sighed. "*Oui, madame*".

"I'm not sure how long we will stay at the convent." Susan remarked. "Would you like to come back later and take us to our hotel?"

Henri reached into his pocket and removed a business card. He held it over his shoulder and said, "It will be my honor to pick up you beautiful ladies. Please call me and I will come for you." He handed them a card with his name and phone number.

"And we will need a ride back to the airport tomorrow morning, can you do that too?" Carla asked.

"Why of course *madame*, it would be my pleasure."

CHAPTER 15

Jeff made arrangements for Beverly's funeral. He followed her instructions exactly. He invited exactly the people she wanted to a gravesite service at the Methodist Cemetery in Hooksett. Joe Rinds, the long time family pastor presided and he did a beautiful job. Jeff was careful to perform the two most important tasks his mother had requested. He placed the prayer box inside her coffin, with the top open as she had instructed. And he had her buried in the family plot right between his father and his brother.

"Mom will be happy now." Jeff said to Michael as the casket was lowered into the ground.

"She told me grandpa promised to be waiting for her in heaven with a big bouquet of roses," Mickey replied. "And I bet he will."

"He was always a man of his word," Jeff said with a smile, "but she said she told him to wait close to the entrance so he wouldn't get lost in there."

Michael laughed. "That doesn't surprise me at all."

"Grandma always said grandpa couldn't find his way back to the bed from the bathroom without a map!"

"But they really loved each other, didn't they dad?"

"Their's was a true love story, son."

After the service Jeff, Michael, his wife Deanna and their two children went back to the lake house to receive visitors. All of the neighbors came to give condolences. It was an outpouring of support that made Jeff feel very good. Everyone had kind and comforting words to say and many expressed their admiration for the devotion that Jeff had shown to his mother.

John and Mary Dawkins came. Mary was Beverly's closest friend at the Lake. They often went to Bingo together at the church and Mary was kind enough to take Beverly with her when she ran errands after Beverly could no longer drive herself.

"I loved your mother," Mary said as she wiped away tears from her eyes.

Jeff grasped both Mary's hands in his. "She knew that, Mary," he replied with a smile, "and she loved you too."

Michael moved close to his father and whispered, "Grandma had a lot of friends, didn't she, dad?"

"You know, Mick, grandma always told me that in order to have good friends first you have to be a good friend. And she was."

Jennifer Cohen stopped by with her children. Jennifer often chatted with Jeff during his daily walks around the lake and she was always asking about Beverly. Her children, nine year old Rachel and eleven year old Adam, were the same ages as Michael's kids so they often played together when Michael visited his grandmother.

Sylvia Genovese was there. She was a gruff woman about the same age as Beverly, although she would never admit to that. Jeff knew that Sylvia and Beverly were not on the best of terms but it was good to see her come by to pay her respects. Many more neighbors came, often bringing food. Jeff was so overwhelmed with food that he decided to give most of it to a local homeless shelter. Except of course for Hanna Jones' ribs. They were the best ribs he had ever eaten and he wasn't giving those up for anybody.

Mr. & Mrs. Adams stopped by. They had gone to the city council meeting when Vernon McGraw produced the old contact that Mr. Adams' father had signed with the Indian chief. Vernon had it verified and this caused the council to reject the site plan for the new station. Their nightmare was over.

"Did they ever find out who sent that contract to your lawyer?" Jeff asked.

"Nope," Mr. Adams replied. "But whoever it was saved our business for us."

And of course Janice Hanley made an appearance. As usual she was dressed inappropriately in a tight fitting dress that showed lots of cleavage. She made every effort to bend forward as often as possible in front of Jeff. He was most happy when she finally made her way out the front door.

Jeff was sitting and talking to his son when he heard the booming voice of his old friend Ernie Pantaloni.

"Jeffrey," Ernie said with his arms outstretched. Jeff stood to greet his old friend with a hug.

"Pants! I can't believe you made it!"

"Jeff, you know how much I loved your mom. She was more of a mother to me than my own mother was!"

"I remember," Jeff replied. "She would bring us food when we were studying for finals."

"And she was my best patient in dental school," Ernie replied.

"That's true," Jeff laughed, "she wouldn't let me get anywhere near her mouth, but you, you could do no wrong."

"I'm so sorry for your loss, my friend."

"Thanks, Ernie. Mom lived a long and happy life. Life didn't cheat her out of anything."

"I just wanted to stop by and pay my respects."

"Thanks Ernie, that means the world to me. Where are you heading now?"

"Actually I'm leaving tomorrow morning for Florida. I'm closing on a new house in Boca. You should stop by and see me some time."

"I'll do it Ernie, I promise."

Danielle Mauer, an attractive and well dressed lady who lived two streets away approached Jeff in the living room as he sat talking to Ernie Pants. Jeff had never seen her before. She introduced herself and asked if Jeff planned to stay in his mother's house.

"Probably not," Jeff replied. "I have another house in Massachusetts and now that I'm retired I really don't need the expense of two houses."

"So you will be selling this house?" Danielle asked.

"That's the plan." Jeff replied.

Danielle handed Jeff her business card. "I sell more homes in this community than all the other realtors combined!" she boasted. "Give me a call when you're ready. I'm a full service agent."

Jeff looked at the card and placed it on the table. By the time he looked up again Danielle was gone.

"I'm surprised she waited for mom to die." Michael said.

"She's trying to make a living, Mick." his father replied. "Can't fault her for that. And besides, if you wanted to sell your house who would you rather have, a polite real estate person or a pushy one like that?"

Both men smiled.

Shortly after everyone left, the door bell rang. Michael went to the door and let in the final visitor of the day. It was his mother Pam.

"Mom," he said as he hugged her. "We weren't expecting you."

"I won't stay long, Mick," she said. "I just wanted to give my condolences to your father.

Jeff walked towards Pam. "Hi!" he said. She looked beautiful in a long black skirt and V-neck top. She always dressed like a movie star, Jeff thought.

"You're looking mighty handsome today, Doctor Morton." Pam reached for Jeff. First she straightened his tie and then hugged him, pressing her body firmly against his. "I couldn't let this day pass without coming here, Jeff. You know how much I loved your mother."

"I know, Pam."

Pam took her ex husband's hand and walked him to the empty kitchen. "I really missed you the other night," she said. "I waited up all night."

"Oh really?" Jeff replied. "I decided it would be better if I didn't come."

"I get that, Jeffy," she said, taking his hand. "I'm not asking for you to trust me again. All I want is a chance to earn back your trust."

"This is difficult for me, Pam. I told you I've moved on with my life."

"I know Jeff, but you also told me there is nobody else in your life right now. That's true for me too." Tears trickled down her cheeks. "Jeff, we were meant to be together, not alone. We were meant be a family. A complete family with our son and his children. I am begging you, Jeff. Please give me another chance!"

Pam reached for her ex-husband again but this time he backed away. He was drawn to her beauty and charm but the pain of their separation and divorce was too much to overcome. He turned and walked up the stairs and into the bedroom. Pam was left alone to say her goodbyes to her son and his family.

CHAPTER 16

Jeff decided to remain in his mother's house until it was sold. Each day after his morning walk around the lake he spent many hours carefully going through all of his mother's belongings. He divided them into three groups- things he was going to keep, things he would sell, and things he would give away. Family photos he would keep, but his mother had a collection of thousands of photos so he had to decide which to keep and which to toss. Her clothes he would give away, first to her close friends and then to Goodwill. Her jewelry would be for Michael. There wasn't much but Jeff knew it was good quality. Everything else was give away stuff.

And then there was the house. For twenty years he had enjoyed visiting his parents in their cozy cottage on the lake, but it was clear now that the house was starting to show signs of age. He wasn't certain when it was originally built but he guessed it was close to fifty years old, and it was very dated. Beverly had wisely signed the deed over to her only son two years earlier.

As he was going through her things he saw the business card that had been given to him by Danielle Mauer the real estate agent. He dialed her number and she made plans to meet him at eleven thirty the next morning.

He spent the rest of the day going through his mother's things, watched TV and went to bed early.

The next morning he took his daily walk around the lake. As he approached the sandy beach and saw the people bathing in the murky lake water he couldn't help but think about the story his mother had told him about the prayer box. As a man of medicine every instinct in him told him to dismiss mom's crazy story. Of course whether or not the box had magical powers was irrelevant now since it had been buried twenty miles away in Hooksett. If only those people knew what he knew, he thought, they would probably go home. But then again, he thought, maybe not. Maybe the power of prayer is so strong that it can cause miracles to happen even without a prayer box. Never a religious man, Jeff was ready to move on, forget about the prayer box, and simply remember his mother for all of the wonderful qualities she had.

After his walk, Jeff showered and prepared for his meeting with Danielle Mauer. He had mixed emotions about selling the house and he was hoping that she could convince him to place it on the market.

At 11:30 sharp Danielle rang the front door bell. When he opened the door Jeff was surprised to see such a beautiful woman in front of him. He had seen Danielle after the funeral but he was so preoccupied that he didn't even remember her face. Danielle was tall with Sandy hair pulled up and back, showing her whole face. Not many women have the courage to do that, Jeff thought as he tried not to stare. Danielle was dressed in a red skirt and off-white silk top with a ruffle in the front. She appeared to be in her late forties or early fifties although, Jeff pondered, it really is impossible to tell these days. His ex-wife Pam looked at least ten years younger than she really was.

Danielle was carrying a brown brief case. She was professional yet still somehow very sexy. Just the opposite of Janice Hanley, he thought as he welcomed her into the house.

Within minutes Danielle had pulled out from her briefcase a series of aerial photos taken of the house.

"Wow!" Jeff said. "Where did those come from?" He studied the photos which were obviously taken from a plane or helicopter.

Danielle smiled. "I had them done after we met last week. It's done with a drone."

"A drone? Really?"

"Yes. I was anticipating your call and I wanted to be prepared. I have a service that I use whenever I list a house. It gives the potential buyer a great look at the house and how it fits into the neighborhood."

"That makes sense."

"In your case the areal view also accentuates the lakefront property you have." She reached back into her briefcase for some papers. "I know that I can sell this house for a good price Jeff and I am hoping you'll give me a chance to serve you."

Jeff was impressed. "So, it's been a long time since I sold a house. Exactly what is involved?"

"Just leave everything to me, Jeff," was Danielle's confident reply. "Here is the listing agreement."

She laid the papers out on the table.

"And what is your commission?" He asked.

"Standard sales commission in this area is six percent," she replied, "three percent for the listing agent and three for the selling agent."

Jeff began to look over the papers.

"But here's the good news," Danielle continued. "I am a full service agent. I plan to list your house and sell it too! I have a long list of people who are eager to move to the lake and they will be so excited when I show them your house. And when I am both the listing and selling agent you only pay four percent."

"So you think it will be easy to sell?"

"Easy? No not easy." She replied. "If it was easy anybody could do it. That's why you need me, because it takes a skilled professional to sell a house."

"So what needs to happen?"

"First, we need to get your house ready. It needs a lot of updating, the carpets need to be replaced, maybe the kitchen appliances. It needs a coat of paint. I'll know better after I bring in my staging team."

"Staging team?"

"Yes, these are the people who make a house look good for sale. The better your house looks, the more it will sell for. It's as simple as that."

"So how much will it sell for?"

Once again Danielle reached into her briefcase. She removed a series of papers and showed Jeff the recent sales and listings at the lake.

"Nothing is guaranteed of course, but I think you might have the highest sale price ever in this community."

With that Jeff signed all the papers and Danielle reached out to shake his hand.

"Now it's time for our first celebration," she said with a grin. "Let me buy you lunch."

"Sounds good to me," Jeff replied. He glanced at Danielle's left hand and noticed that she was not wearing a wedding ring.

Jeff and Danielle chatted over lunch for two hours. He was impressed by her beauty and her intelligence. He learned that Danielle was fifty-three, divorced, with two grown daughters. She began doing real estate after her divorce ten years ago because she had to earn a living. Soon she found that she not only enjoyed real estate but that she was very good at it. Now she was the top selling agent in her office. She also told him that she was so busy working that she never took the time for romance.

Jeff spoke briefly about his own divorce and how he had finally been able to put that behind him. He was ready to move on and selling the house an important step for him.

Danielle was doing most of the talking, but as she spoke he found himself staring at her and day dreaming about what it would be like to kiss her. He knew that was totally inappropriate so he suppressed the urge and continued to listen. There was something about her, though, that rekindled a spark that had been lost for a long time.

"I've been alone for four years," he said, "and I've never found a woman who could fill the gap in my life."

Danielle brushed back her hair with her left hand. "Well, that just means you haven't met the right woman yet," she said with a smile. "You are a very handsome man. I'm sure you have been told that many times." Now she was twirling her hair around her finger.

Those words were not new to Jeff. He had been told how handsome he was ever since he was young. He was even chosen prom king in high school over fifty years ago. He was tall and handsome and many women had told him he looked like Tom Selleck.

"No, I haven't," he lied. "But I really like hearing it from you."

Danielle pondered for a moment. "Do you like veal parmesan?" she asked.

"It's only my favorite," Jeff replied eagerly. "I have always said if I was on death row and they told me I could choose my last meal it would be veal parmesan."

"Well," Danielle said laughing, "I make a mean veal parmesan and I promise if you come for dinner tonight it won't be your last meal!"

"Let's do it then," Jeff said with a grin. He paused for a minute and reflected on what he had just said. "You know, I meant let's do dinner," he said. "I didn't mean let's do….it…you know"

Danielle giggled. "I knew what you meant," she replied. "So I'll see you at seven?" she asked, handing him another card with her home address on it.

"Wouldn't miss it for the world."

They both stood up, and Jeff moved towards Danielle. It was an awkward moment but it ended in a hug, which was his goal. As she walked away he thought, she looks as good from the back as she does from the front.

CHAPTER 17

Susan and Carla carried their suitcases up six steps to the front porch of the house. In front of them was a large double door with oval stained glass inserts. A small sign that said "Convent Katrine" was the only indication that they were in the right place. Susan gently knocked on the stained glass and within a few seconds the door was opened by a young woman who appeared to be in her early twenties. She was dressed in a nun's habit.

"Hello, I am sister Betrille," she said with a big smile.

Carla and Susan looked at each other and bit their lips to keep from laughing. Despite their best efforts their amusement was visible to the young lady in front of them.

"Yes, yes, I know," she said with a laugh. "I have seen the flying nun and you can laugh. It is OK."

"I'm sorry," Susan said suppressing her laughter. "I didn't mean to be rude. We came to see sister Katrine. Is she here?"

In a few minutes they were joined by a tall, stately woman who looked to be in her mid-70s. She had a very distinguished look that made it obvious to Susan and Carla that this was the woman in charge. She wore a gray and white habit with her hair completely covered. Her face showed signs of every one of the years that she had lived.

"Hello, my name is sister Maria." She held out both hands and grabbed each of her visitors hands between them. She had a soft and gentle but firm grip.

"It is so nice to meet you both. How can I help you?"

"We came looking for sister Katrine," Susan said quietly. "I was hoping she would be here."

"Sister Katrine passed away many years ago. I remember her well."

"Did you live here at the same time sister Katrine did?"

Sister Maria waved the women to follow her into the parlor, directed them to sit and gave them each a cup of tea.

She took a deep breath and began to speak.

"I was brought here in 1942 when I was just a very young girl. My parents were Jewish. They tell me that my name was Miriam. There were many Jewish children brought here to save us from the Nazis. Most of them were claimed by their parents after the war, but of course I was not. I learned later that my parents were both sent to Auschwitz where they were killed. I was raised here and I was baptized."

"You know, I am Jewish too!" Susan said.

"And you should always be proud of that. I took the vows and became a nun so this has been my whole life and even though I know that my roots are Jewish I take comfort in knowing that our Lord and Savior Jesus Christ had the same Jewish roots that I have."

"Please tell us about Sister Katrine," Carla asked. "What happened to her?"

"Sister Katrine ran this orphanage and she was like a mother to me. She raised me and taught me everything that I know until she passed away. Why are you so curious about her?"

Susan opened her handbag and showed the prayer box to sister Maria. The tall sister immediately stood up.

"Oh, my lord, I can't believe it!" she said as she examined the box carefully. "Where did you get this? How could you have this? This is impossible! This is absolutely impossible! Where did you get this box?"

"To be honest, sister, I don't know how I got this box." Susan replied. "It just appeared one day in my home in a box of things that I was moving from Massachusetts to Florida. Ever since then I have been on a mission to find out where this box came from and how I was able to get it."

"But what brought you here?"

"A lady in Jerusalem told us that Sister Katrine had a box like this so we came here to meet her."

Sister Maria stared at the box and held it in her hand. She stood perfectly still and then began to shake. Her upper lip began to tremble.

"But you see this is a box that I have known. It is a box that I have seen, a box that I have touched. I know for certain!"

"How can you be so sure that it's the same box that you have seen?"

Sister Maria turned the box over and showed one of the corners to the two ladies.

"You see this corner? You see that little crack? That happened when I dropped the box many years ago. I was so afraid when I dropped it. I was afraid that it would lose its powers because of what I had done. I was afraid to tell Sister Katrine what I had done. Of course she found out anyway and she forgave me and the box did not lose its mystical powers."

"How did Sister Katrine get the box?" Susan asked.

"She never told me how she got the box. It was here when I got here. People would bring children and sick elderly people from all over the area to visit Sister Katrine. She didn't want anybody to know about the box but people believed that if she laid her hands on them that they would get well. Of course it was not her hand, it was the prayer box. We were sure of that and so was Sister Katrine."

Carla finally spoke. "So the secret is to use the box for good deeds but not to let people know that you have it. "

"I guess that's right," Sister Maria replied, "because that is certainly what Sister Katrine did. And she told us that it can only be used to help others, not to help yourself."

"I guess that's why she died. The box couldn't save her."

"Yes. We begged her to use the box for herself but she refused."

"So what did you do with the box after Sister Katrine died?"

"That's what has me so confused. Sister Katrine insisted when she got sick that we place this box in her coffin and of course we fulfilled her wishes. I personally put the box in the coffin with Sister Katrine just before it was lowered into the ground in our cemetery. We made sure to leave it open because that was our instruction."

"That's impossible," Susan said. "This can't be the same box. How would it have gotten out of her coffin and into a box in my garage? It makes no sense."

Sister Maria smiled and said, "Many people have tried to make sense of works of the Lord and they have failed. That is why we call it faith. We believe in the power of our Lord without questioning how he does it. "

"Where is Sister Katrine buried?"

"Actually, we have a graveyard on our property. Would you like to see her grave stone?"

Both women nodded in agreement and they headed out the back door about 100 yards to a small area of the yard where there were about a dozen gravestones. Sister Maria walked them over to the largest one.

Susan looked at the gravestone of Sister Katrine and she froze. Her mouth was wide open. Her eyes wide open. She couldn't believe what she was looking at.

The gravestone marking was clear

Sister Marie Katrine Le Claire

September 1, 1877 - June 3, 1956.

"Holy shit!" Carla whispered. "June third is your birthday!"

"I know," Susan replied, "and 1956 is the year that I was born. That means Sister Katrine died the very day that I was born and this box was placed in her coffin the very day that I was born. It's unbelievable. I'm just blown away. I don't know what to say."

Sister Maria walked over to Susan and hugged her for what seemed like several minutes before either one of them could speak.

"Just as I said, Susan, the Lord works in mysterious ways and I hope that you will do as much good with this box as Sister Katrine did."

As the two women hugged Sister Betrille spoke up. "Sister, do you think we could use this prayer box one last time before it goes back to America?"

Sister Maria released her grip on Susan and said "You're right, sister. Let's bring the box to Sister Jeanne. "

"Who is Sister Jeanne?" Carla asked, "and do you think the box can really help her?"

"Sister Jeanne is the oldest member of our convent. She is almost 88 years old and she has been suffering from arthritis for the past 10 years Now she's confined to a wheelchair and her hands are so crippled that she can't even read her bible. Maybe the prayer box can give her comfort and less pain as she lives out the final years of her life."

In a few moments the women were back inside the convent and Sister Maria knocked on the door of Sister Jeanne's room.

"Entree," Sister Jeanne said. She was sitting in a wheel chair. The Holy Bible was sitting on the table next to her

As the women entered, Sister Jeanne immediately recognized the prayer box. "*Oh mon dieux!*" she said.

"This kind woman brought it from America," Sister Maria replied. "Do you remember this prayer box?"

"*Mai oui.*"

"Well, this is exactly the same box. We don't really understand how this woman in America was able to get it but she has brought it back here and now we want to open the box for you, Sister Jeanne."

Gently, Sister Maria opened the box and set it down on the table next to the Holy Bible.

"I'm not sure we can stay long enough to really help her." Susan said.

"I remember," Sister Maria replied, "that it really only took a few minutes of the box being open for it to begin working. There weren't necessarily immediate results but only a few minutes is all it took for the prayer box to work it's mystical wonders."

Sister Jeanne stared at the box for several minutes, saying nothing, and then she closed her eyes and began to pray. A few minutes later she slowly reached her hand onto the table and took the Holy Bible and opened it. She began to read it. Tears streamed down her face and Sister Maria's face, too.

"This is the first time she's been able to hold the Bible in many, many years." Sister Maria said. "I'm so grateful that you came and I'm sure that her final years here will be filled with so much more spiritual fulfillment because of you. God bless you both!"

Susan wiped the tears from her eyes, walked over to Sister Jeanne and hugged her.

Sister Jeanne said, "*Merci beaucoup, merci beaucoup, je t'aime.*"

"Maybe it's time to call Henri," Carla said, breaking the emotional stream in the room.

"You're right." Susan said. She reached into her handbag, removed Henri's card and dialed his number. Within 20 minutes, Henri was outside waiting for them.

"Bonjour, beautiful ladies!" Henri said as he opened the door to let them in and he placed their suitcases back into his trunk.

On the ride to the hotel in Paris, Susan gleefully sent a Whatsapp message to her daughter, Jennifer.

"Jenny, you won't believe what happened here. We found out where the box came from. It was from a wonderful nun in an orphanage that saved Jews from the Nazis. And you won't believe it but she died exactly the day I was born! They buried the box in her coffin. I can't wait to come home and tell you all about it."

While Susan sent her Whatsapp message, Henri was on his cell phone talking to someone in French. Neither Susan nor Carla paid attention to what he was saying and neither of them could understand or speak French anyway.

As they approached the front entrance to the Renaissance hotel Henri asked, "So what time would you like me to pick you up for the airport trip in the morning? It's only about a fifteen minute trip to the airport from here."

Carla checked her new itinerary and said, "Our flight leaves at 11:00 and I like to get there early so perhaps you should pick us up at 7:30, okay?"

"I will be here, Madame. You can count on me."

CHAPTER 18

Jeff walked around the lake again early that evening. He was excited to be having dinner at Danielle's house and he wondered where it might lead. He was intrigued by Danielle's beauty and intelligence, but wondered if she was interested in him as client or a potential lover. He certainly didn't want to make a fool of himself by coming on too strong, too soon.

As he walked towards the lake, he spotted Jennifer Cohen. She was outside of her house on her cell phone and she appeared to be in distress. He walked towards her and waited for her to finish her call.

"Is everything alright, Jenny?"

Jennifer was disheveled and appeared to be in panic mode. She had always been calm and friendly but now she was frantic.

"My mom's in trouble, Jeff, and I can't reach her to warn her!"

"Trouble? What kind of trouble?"

Jennifer pondered for a few seconds. "I can't tell you the details, but she's in France and her life is in grave danger!"

"Grave danger? Oh my God." Jeff replied. "Is there anything I can do to help?"

"No," Jennifer yelled. "I just need to reach her to warn her. I've been sending her Whatsapp messages but she's probably sound asleep right now. I came outside because my wifi is down and I get better service outside the house than inside."

"Do you think she'll see the message when she wakes up?"

"She should, but that might be too late."

"Oh my, I see. So you need to talk to her now."

"Yes, but I have no idea how to do that." Jennifer was crying and shaking.

"Where in France is she?"

"That's the problem. I know she's in a hotel but I have no idea which one. She made a last minute change in her plans and she didn't tell me what hotel she was going to. I need to call her but I have no idea what hotel to call."

Jeff took a deep breath. "Okay," he said. "Let me help you."

"How?"

"Let's start with the city. Is she in Paris?"

"Yes, I'm pretty sure."

"Okay, so that narrows it down. Has she been to Paris before?"

"I think so but that was before I was born."

"Do you have any idea what hotel chain she usually stays at when she travels?"

Jennifer thought for a minute. "Usually Hilton or Marriott."

Jeff reached in his pocket for his cell phone. He began working with it. "I have the Marriott app on my phone." He punched in a few things and the looked up at Jennifer. "There are nineteen Marriott properties in Paris. You and I are gonna call every one of them until we find her! What is her name?"

"Susan Gold." Jennifer replied. "And thank you so much!"

"If this doesn't work we'll try Hilton."

With that, Jeff gave Jennifer a list of phone numbers. The two of them called Marriotts and each time asked to speak with Susan Gold.

Finally, after about seven calls, Jennifer was ecstatic. "I found her!"

"Great! Where is she?"

"She's at the Renaissance near the airport. They're putting me though to her now."

Jeff watched as Jennifer warned her mother of the danger that she faced. As she talked she walked away from Jeff, making it clear that she did not want him to hear the details.

CHAPTER 19

The two friends were exhausted from their day and the emotion of learning about the prayer box. They ate a late dinner at the hotel and then went back up to the room to get a good night's sleep.

Susan was sound asleep when the hotel phone rang at midnight. It was the front desk.

"Ms. Gold, we have an emergency phone call for you from a woman who says she's your daughter, Jennifer. Would you like me to put the call through?"

"Oh my God, yes, yes, yes, please put her through, put it through!"

"Mom?"

"Oh my God!" Susan yelled, waking up Carla.

"Oh my God, oh my God, Jennifer! Jennifer, what's wrong Jenny? Is it one of the kids? What is it?"

Susan was hysterical. Her whole body was twitching. "Tell me, tell me please!"

"Mom, I've been trying to reach you for hours! I didn't know what hotel you were in so I called every hotel in Paris until I found you."

"But what is it? What is it, Jenny? What's the problem? Is it the kids? Is it you? Is it David? Tell me, please tell me. You gotta tell me what the problem is!"

"No, mom, everything is fine here. But I'm calling to warn you."

"Warn me? Warn me about what?"

"Mom, remember when you were sending me a Whatsapp from the taxi cab today?"

"Of course, honey, I was excited. I just wanted you to know what we learned today."

"Well, you not only let me know what you came to France to do, but you also let your taxi driver know too. You must have talked about it in the taxi."

"I guess we did, but so what? What are you talking about, honey?"

"While you were sending your Whatsapp message to me, your driver was speaking French to someone. I don't know who but I understood every word he was saying and I played it over and over and over again to make sure I got it right. Mom, he's trying to get that box from you. He said he's picking you up tomorrow morning to take you to the airport but he has no intention of actually taking you to the airport."

Susan began to shake again. "What do you mean, Jenny? What do you mean?"

Jenny's voice was trembling. "He's bringing another guy named Claude with him and they're not going to take you and Carla to the airport but they're going to take you somewhere where they'll take the box and kill you, mom! That's their plan, mom. Please promise me, mom, do not get in the taxi with that man. Do whatever you have to do to get out of there safely away from him and don't tell anyone about that box. Please mom. Promise me, mom. Get yourself to the airport and call me when you get there to let me know you're safe. Okay?"

By this time Carla was wide awake and listening to everything.

"This is what the rabbi meant in New York when he told us we had to be careful, that people would do anything to get this box from us," she said. "He knew what he was talking about and we've got to get out of here now. We've got to get to the airport."

Susan pondered a moment. "I don't know if that's a good idea, Carla. What are we going to do at the airport? It's probably closed. It's what, it's like one o'clock in the morning."

Susan walked towards the hotel room phone. "Let's find out what time the airport opens and let's get a taxi to take us to the airport first thing so that we're long gone by the time Henri comes back to pick us up."

Their flight to Miami was scheduled for 11 AM. Susan called the front desk and asked if they knew what time the airport opened. After a short wait they received a call back and they were told that the airport counters open at 5 AM. But they were also told that they could not check in until four hours before their flight which would be 7 AM.

"If we can get there by six-thirty and we can get through security then we'll be safe." Susan said as she began to pack her suitcase. "There is no way they can get us once we're through security so let's have a taxi pick us up at six and take us to the airport. Better yet, let's not even rely on a taxi. Let's see if we can get some kind of a special limo service to pick us up, somebody who's more trustworthy than just a taxi driver."

Once again, Susan called downstairs and the front desk arranged for a limousine to pick them up at six AM to take them to the airport. For the next several hours neither woman slept for one minute. They packed and showered and they worried. They talked, they cried. At 5:45 they were in the elevator heading to the lobby for their limo to pick them up.

As the elevator reached the lobby level it opened and Carla immediately pushed the button to close the doors.

"What are you doing?" Susan asked. "Why did you shut the doors, Carla?"

"Look." Carla froze. "That's Henri sitting in the lobby with another guy. It must be that guy that he's bringing who's supposed to kill us. They're sitting in the lobby waiting for us. We can't go down there!"

By now both women were in full panic mode. Carla was shaking and Susan was crying.

"My God," Susan shrieked in a loud whisper. "What are we gonna do?"

Carla regained her composure. "We're going back up to the first floor," she said calmly, "and we're going to find an exit with some stairs to take us down to the outside of the building."

Within minutes the ladies walked down the first floor hallway until they reached an exit sign. They carried their bags down the steps and through the exit door. Carefully, Carla opened the door to see where it had led them.

"Aw shit," she whispered. "We're back in the lobby! We've got to go back upstairs."

Susan began to cry again. "Oh my God, I can't handle this any more. The suitcases are too heavy!"

Carla said, "Open the prayer box, Susan. Right now!"

"What are you talking about?" Susan said. "What do you want me to do that for?"

"Because we need that prayer box more than anybody ever has! Our lives depend upon opening that prayer box."

"But it can't work for us!"

"What do you mean 'us'?" Carla growled. "Maybe it won't work for you but it should work for me!"

Susan nodded. She reached into her handbag, opened up the prayer box and set it gently back into her handbag still open. The two friends then carried their bags back up the stairs to the first floor. They wandered through the narrow hallways of the first floor until they eventually came to another exit sign and another set of stairs. They walked down the stairs carrying their bags and when they came to the bottom, Carla once again peeked through the door. This time they were outside the hotel.

Quickly, they walked around the side of the building until they arrived at the front of the building. A black limousine was waiting with an elderly driver smiling at them.

"It worked!" Carla whispered.

Susan walked up to the limo driver and said, "Are you here for us? We're going to the airport." Carla looked back at the front door to see if Henri and his accomplice were there. They were not.

"*Oui madame,*" the driver said. "Are you ready?"

The driver quickly put their bags in the trunk of the limo. They jumped in and Carla said "Please take us quickly. We are going to be late for our flight unless you hurry!"

"*Oui madame*," he said and off the limo sped.

As they were driving away Susan looked back in panic.

"Oh my God, it's them! They saw us into getting in the limo and now they're following us! Oh my God, what are we going to do Carla?"

Carla slowed and lowered her voice in a soothing manner. She grabbed her friends hand.

"Driver, please take us directly to the airport and I will tell you exactly where we want you to stop."

"Make sure the box stays open until we get on the plane," she whispered to Susan.

For the entire length of the fifteen minute drive both ladies peeked out the back window. They could see Henri and his taxi following them. As they approached the airport the driver said "What airline, *madame*?"

Carla looked over and saw a police car sitting in front of one of the terminal entrances.

"Take us right over there," she said calmly. "Park right behind the police car."

"But what airline are you on?" the driver asked.

"It doesn't matter," Carla said firmly. "I want you to park right behind that police car."

As soon as their limo stopped, Carla jumped out of the car and walked right over to the police officer. Henri and his accomplice pulled up right behind them.

"Please help us," she said. "The men in that taxi behind us are trying to kill us!"

The police officer looked at her and said "I not speak English, *madame*."

Carla walked closer to the officer and pointed at the taxi until the officer looked back. As soon as he was seen Henri drove away quickly.

Susan breathed a sigh of relief. "But he didn't understand a word you said!" she remarked to her friend.

"Yes, that's true," Carla replied. "But our friend Henri didn't know that!"

For the first time in hours they both laughed. It was a nervous laugh for both of them.

Carla and Susan grabbed their bags, paid the limo driver, and walked inside the terminal. They were nowhere near where they were supposed to be so they just kept asking for directions until they finally reached the Air France terminal. It took about fifteen minutes before they were able to check their bags.

Once they checked their bags and walked through security, Susan said, "I think we're safe now, Carla. I think we're finally safe."

Carla said, "Let's not be so cocky about this, honey. They could still be coming after us. You know, maybe they went to get passports. Maybe they're going to buy tickets for our flight."

"But they don't know what flight we're on. And they don't even know where we're going."

"You're right about that but we should still be cautious. Let's make sure we stay together the whole time. And make sure that prayer box stays open."

Susan peeked into her purse and saw the prayer box. She checked frequently to make certain that it remained open.

"You know, they can't get through security with a gun or a knife or anything that could hurt us," she said calmly. "I think we're going to be okay."

For the next three hours, the two friends sat together at the gate with their heads spinning around looking at every man who walked in and around their gate. They were suspicious of everyone and still wondering if they were going to be safe. It wasn't until they finally boarded the plane and the door was closed that they felt they finally had escaped.

As soon as she sat down, Susan sent a Whatsapp message to her daughter back in the States.

"Jenny, we're on the plane and we're going to be home safe. I love you."

This was a day they would never forget.

The nine hour plane ride should have given the ladies ample opportunity to finally rest after the sleepless night before, but both were so keyed up, so excited, and so nervous that neither one could sleep. Even on the plane they kept looking around behind them to see anybody who might have resembled Henri or his notorious friend. Each time a man walked by their seats they stared at him carefully to make sure it wasn't Henri.

When they arrived in Miami, they finally had an opportunity to relax. As they came off the plane through customs and immigration back home to the United States they felt completely safe the first time in over twenty hours.

Danny picked them up with Carla's Jeep for the two hour ride home back to Stuart. Finally in the car, both ladies fell sound asleep.

CHAPTER 20

Jeff called Jennifer later that day and was relieved to learn that her mother had made it home safely. He was more than curious about the reason for her danger but, he thought, maybe some day Jennifer or Susan herself would fill him in.

More importantly it was time to get ready for his date with Danielle. He showered and shaved. It took him awhile to decide what to wear. He knew that he was several years older than Danielle but he didn't want his clothes to make it so obvious, so he ruled out the flowered shirt and fedora that he had purchased in Jamaica. But on the other hand, he didn't want to look like a man who was trying to look much younger than he really was, so he tossed aside the blue jeans and Patriots jersey.

After several false starts he finally settled on a pair of black slacks and a red Tommy Bahama sweater. Under the sweater he wore a silk black tee shirt. He topped off his ensemble with three shots of Light Blue cologne aimed at his neck. The sales clerk at Macy's had told him that this cologne always drove women wild, and he was hoping it would work on Danielle.

As he walked towards the front door, he stopped to take one more look in the mirror. Perfect, he thought.

He chose to walk the three blocks to Danielle's house. Better not to have his car sitting outside, he thought, no need to give the neighborhood gossips something to talk about.

In five minutes he was at Danielle's front door. She lived in a new upscale townhouse development that was built on the lakefront. The building of these homes had caused quite a stir a few years ago because the developer had purchased ten lakefront homes and then immediately tore them down to build townhouses. Some of the neighbors, including Jeff's mother, were not happy about the project, but the developer prevailed and most people accepted the fact that the new townhouses were a big improvement over what was there before.

When Danielle opened the front door, Jeff was stunned. She looked absolutely beautiful. She was wearing tight blue leggings with flowers and a creamy colored silk top with ruffles. She looked to Jeff like a model. She greeted Jeff with a big hug and said, "Oh, wow, you smell delicious."

Light Blue did it again, Jeff thought, as he hugged her back. The hug lingered for a lot longer than normal "friendly" hugs do. Jeff could smell Danielle's hair and it smelled really good. Everything about her was perfect and he found himself not wanting to let go.

"Come in," she said as she finally broke the hug. "You look really handsome tonight."

"And you look beautiful," he replied. The physical attraction between them was palpable. Jeff wondered if they were going to have dinner first or skip right to the bedroom.

After what seemed like a long pause she finally said, "Come in, please! I fixed you a drink, Hendricks and tonic with cucumber, right.?"

"Uh, right, but how did you know?"

Danielle smiled, "I always do a little research on my clients. I hope you don't mind?"

Jeff was a little surprised by this but he wasn't going to say or do anything that would screw up this night. "Of course not! I'm flattered."

Jeff sipped his drink, paused for a minute, and sat triumphantly "I think I figured it out."

"Figured what out?" Danielle replied as she poured herself a glass of Cabernet Sauvignon.

"It was that drone, wasn't it?"

"Huh?"

"The drone," Jeff said with a smile. "When you shot the aerial photos of my house you zeroed in on my liquor cabinet. That's where you saw the Hendricks."

Danielle laughed. "Guilty as charged," she replied. "No. I'm good but I'm not that good." She chuckled and sat down on the sofa next to Jeff, making sure that their thighs touched. It sent an electric charge up Jeff's thigh.

"Actually," she said, with a grin, "you were drinking Hendricks and tonic with a cucumber when I first met you at your mothers house."

"Of course," Jeff said. "I was, wasn't I?"

Danielle nodded, put her wine on the coffee table, took the glass from Jeff's hand and gently placed it on the table. Then she leaned close to his face and said, "I know you want to kiss me tonight, so let's get that out of the way now, shall we?"

Their kiss was soft and gentle at first, and then more intense as it lingered. Jeff could never remember a kiss like this, even from Pam. They both stood up and he held her tightly in his arms as the kiss continued for what seemed like ten minutes. They only paused to breath once in a while and then their lips locked again.

Danielle broke away from Jeff for a moment and, without hesitation, she took his hand in hers and led him to her bedroom.

Dinner came later, followed by another drink and then another visit to the bedroom. This time they stayed in the bedroom all night. Jeff was glad that he had chosen to walk to Danielle's house.

CHAPTER 21

When they arrived back in Stuart two hours later and pulled into Susan's neighborhood, there was a line of cars parked in the street near Susan's house.

"Oh shit!" Danny said, loud enough to wake up both his mother and her best friend.

When Susan awoke she saw the cars and said, "What the hell is all this? What are all these cars here for? I don't understand. What are they doing here?"

"I think that might be my fault," Danny said sheepishly.

"What did you do, Daniel?" Carla barked. "What could you possibly have done to bring all these people here in front of Susan's house? What?"

"Well, you see a couple days ago I was at The Ale House and I was sitting next to this attractive young woman. We began to talk and I bought her a drink and I was telling her about my motorcycle. She was very fascinated by motorcycles and wanted to go for a ride with me so we went for a ride back to my apartment and one thing led to another and, you know."

"Get to the point!" his mother shouted. She was annoyed that her son had created this mess. "How did these cars end up in front of Susan's house?"

"Well," Danny said, "I might've told her about my accident, and I might've told her about the prayer box, and I might've told her that it saved my life."

"You MIGHT have told her?" Carla said angrily. "Is that why all these cars are here? How did they all find out about it?"

"Oh, wow, ah, two days ago," Danny continued "I got a call from a reporter from the Palm Beach Post. She said her friend told her that I had an accident on my motorcycle and then a prayer box miracle saved my life and she wanted to ask me about it. So I talked to her and the next thing you know..." Danny reached underneath the front seat of the car and pulled out a newspaper. "The next thing you know this came out."

Carla grabbed the newspaper and looked at the headline. In big bold letters it said "MIRACLE PRAYER BOX SAVES LOCAL MAN." It was pretty clear from the article that the prayer box was here in Stuart and that the box belonged to a local woman.

"But you didn't give them my name and address, did you?" Susan asked angrily.

"Well not exactly," Danny replied.

"What do you mean 'not exactly'?" his mother barked.

"Well," he said , "I did give them your name but I didn't give them your address. But I guess they were able to find your address just by looking it up in the directory, and so I guess people read about it and I guess people want to be here and here they are. I guess they're hoping for some kind of miracle for them, too."

As the Jeep pulled closer to Susan's house they stopped behind a lineup of parked cars. Carla told Susan to lie down in the back seat.

Susan said, "What are you trying to do?"

"Just trust me, honey! Lie down in the backseat and don't move. I'm going to handle this."

Carla walked out of the car and up to the front of Susan's house. There was a line of people standing in front of her house. Women carrying young children and babies, elderly people with crutches and walkers and wheelchairs. It was unbelievable, Susan thought, that all these people needed a miracle from my prayer box.

As Carla began to walk past the crowd several people yelled at her.

"Hey, you can't cut in! Go to the end of the line!" It was a mob mentality and getting dangerous. There were several hundred people waiting for a miracle.

Carla stood on the front porch of Susan's house and yelled to the crowd.

"I'm not cutting in front of anybody. My name is Carla. It was my son who was in the motor cycle accident. I'm Susan's best friend and you're wasting your time here, folks. Susan went to Israel with the box and she's not gonna be back for quite some time. You're all gonna be standing out here in front of this house for God knows how long. So if you're smart you'll just go home, take care of your own business, and don't expect a miracle from this house today."

"When will she be back?" someone shouted from the crowd.

"I have no idea," Carla lied. "I can only tell you it's gonna be a long time before she comes back here, so go home."

Carla then walked back to the Jeep. From behind she could see people start to mumble and then slowly they began to disassemble, get back in their cars and drive away. It wasn't until the last car drove away that she was able to tell Susan it was all right to sit up in her car.

They waited for twenty minutes to make sure nobody would see them and then quickly Susan jumped out of the car wearing one of Carla's biggest hats and ran into her house. She was relieved to be home but apprehensive as well.

"I don't know what to do," Susan said to her friend. "I want to help people if I can but I don't want these people coming to my house. This could be dangerous. Some people might try to take the box away from me. I'm not gonna let strangers in my house. What should I do when they come back. Should I call the police?"

"I don't think that's the right thing, Sue," Carla responded. "Maybe you need to just take a little vacation right now. This has been very stressful. Why don't you go up and see your daughter in New Hampshire for a while. Maybe this whole thing will blow over in a couple weeks if they realize that you're not coming back with the prayer box."

Susan grabbed her cell phone and called Jennifer immediately.

"Hi mom," Jennifer respond. "I'm so glad you're home safe and sound. I was worried sick about you this whole time. Did you have any other problems?"

"Well, not till I got home, honey, and then it seemed like all hell broke loose around here."

"But were they still trying to get that box away from you? Are there still bad people coming after you?"

"No, honey, not bad people, actually good people."

"What do you mean, mom? I don't understand."

"Well, it's a long story but let's just say that the whole world knows I have this prayer box now and they were all lined up outside my house looking for a miracle."

"Mom," Jennifer yelled, "this whole prayer box thing is ridiculous! We have to get you out of there now! I want you to come up here to Miracle Lake. I miss you and the kids miss you, too. You know, maybe if you stay here for a while people will forget about the prayer box and then you can go back home safely."

"Okay, honey. I'll fly to Manchester tomorrow. Can you pick me up at the airport?"

"Of course, mom, just let me know when you're gonna be there and I'll pick you up. I'm really looking forward to seeing you and I'm so glad you're safe. I love you."

"I love you too, babe."

CHAPTER 22

Susan spent the night at Carla's house and returned home before sunrise. She sneaked into her house, packed, and Carla drove her to the airport in West Palm Beach. She checked several times to make sure that the prayer box was still in her handbag.

Six hours later, after a layover in Baltimore, Susan's plane landed at the Manchester airport. When she arrived at baggage claim she was surprised to see her daughter waiting for her. She was so overcome with emotion from all that happened that she rushed up to Jennifer, hugged her, and began to sob. For two minutes mother and daughter hugged. Not a word was said, nor was a word needed.

When the bags arrived on the carousel Susan and Jennifer grabbed them and headed for the parking lot where Jenny's Lexus SUV was parked. "This is a great car!" Susan said as she entered the front seat.

"I know," her daughter replied as she started the engine. "I really didn't want it but David insisted that a doctor's wife had to drive a luxury car."

Together, mother and daughter drove the thirty miles to Miracle Lake. They talked about the kids for the first few minutes but then Jennifer broke the ice and began talking about her mother's experience.

"So how many people were waiting in front of your house?" Jennifer asked.

"Well, I couldn't tell exactly because I was hiding in the back seat but Carla said there was about a thousand people there."

"A thousand? You mean there were a thousand lunatics waiting for you?"

"Honey, I don't think of them that way. They might just be people who are searching for a miracle."

"You know, mom," Jennifer replied, "I really think this whole prayer box story is nonsense. I mean, do you really believe that little box has magical powers to save people's lives?"

"I didn't at first, honey, but after I saw what it did for Carla's son and so many others I just had to do what I did."

"Yeah and it almost got you killed!"

"Something funny about that, honey."

"Funny?" Her daughter said. "What could possibly be funny?"

"I don't mean funny like haha funny. I mean strange. They told me the prayer box can't work on me or my family, but I used it to save Carla from the bad guys and that saved me, too!"

"You know, David and I talked about it," Jenny replied. "He thinks it's crazy too."

"I would expect that from him. He's a doctor."

"Yeah but he's a pretty open minded guy. But he still thinks there's no such thing as a prayer box. He says it's just as crazy as the people who jump in our lake and think they're gonna be cured of anything."

"I agree about the lake. I think that's just an old wive's tale. But who knows?"

"You know," Jennifer said, "Rachel has been having headaches so I was thinking about taking her for a swim in the lake. I guess it can't hurt."

"Headaches? How bad are they?"

"Not too bad. David checked her out and he said we should wait a week to see if they go away. If not he'll do an MRI to see what's going on."

They stopped at summer camp to pick up the grandchildren, Rachel and Adam. Both greeted their grandmother with hugs and kisses. A few minutes later they were home at Miracle Lake.

The Miracle Lake house was a summer getaway for Jennifer and the kids. They had purchased the house for a rock bottom price just after the real estate market crashed in 2008. Rachel was newborn and Adam was two. David was busy with his medical office in Lexington so he only came up to the lake on weekends. Many of the other women had the same situation as Jennifer, alone with their kids Monday through Friday all summer waiting for their husbands to arrive Friday night and then leave again Monday morning. The women often referred to route 93 as 'hubby highway'.

"This is a great place you have here, Jenny." Susan said as she grabbed her suitcase from the back of the SUV.

"The kids and I will be here for another seven weeks and we want you to stay with us."

"I don't know, Jenny. That's a long time. What do you do up here?"

"Every week day I take the kids to camp at 8:30. The kids are in camp all day. At 9:00 I take my walk around the lake and then I have tennis from 10:30 to noon."

"Do you have room for me on the tennis court?"

"Of course we do, and if not we'll make room. The girls all love you and you're as good as they are."

"Not bad for an old lady, huh?"

"Not old either, mom!" Jenny replied as they both giggled.

"So what happens after tennis?"

"We usually go out to lunch. We drink Prosecco and talk about stuff."

"Hmm. I like the Prosecco part. What do you girls talk about?"

"When I first got here we all talked about babies because we all had them. Then we talked about schools and camps."

"And now?"

"Now we mostly talk about whoever isn't there!"

"Oh, I'm so proud!" Susan said sarcastically. "I can't wait to see you on Real Housewives of Miracle Lake!"

Mother and daughter laughed together. It was the first time either had laughed since Susan was in Paris.

As they entered the house. Jenny said, "Seriously, mom, you're welcome to stay here as long as you want. You can even stay after we go back to Lexington if that's what you need to do."

"Thanks, honey," Susan replied, "but I really want to get back to Florida."

"Okay but don't be in too big of a hurry. It must be sweltering heat there now."

"That's what everyone says," her mother replied. "At least everyone up north says that. But we really never get too much above ninety degrees. And we have a pool and air conditioners so it's never a problem for me."

"I know, mom. You always hated the cold. But you have to stay here until that prayer box story dies down. Any idea how long that will take?"

"I have no idea. Carla says she'll stop by my house every day and tell people they're wasting their time waiting for me. And then she'll let me know when the coast is clear."

Mother and daughter sat at the kitchen table sipping tea.

"Mom, what are you gonna do with that box?"

"I'm definitely gonna keep it, honey. I believe that it really works and I wanna help people like all of the others are doing."

"The others? What others?"

"Yes, Jen, there are other people who have boxes like mine. I was told that there are thirty-six of these boxes in the world."

"Only thirty-six? And you have one of them? That's like hitting the lottery! No wonder people are after you to get that box!"

"That's what scares me, Jenny. But up here nobody knows anything about the box."

"So let's keep it that way, mom, okay? I don't want to put you or me or especially the kids in any danger."

"Oh my," Susan replied with a grimace, "I never thought about that. Maybe I should go somewhere else."

"No, mom. You're staying right here. We will figure this thing out together."

"Thanks, hon. I want to join you for your walk around the lake tomorrow morning. That always clears my head."

"Sure. I ordered pizza for dinner. I hope you don't mind. The kids love it and it's been a busy day for me."

"Lots of Prosecco?" Susan asked with a grin.

She spent the evening playing board games with the kids. At one point she asked Rachel about her headaches.

"They're not too bad, grandma," Rachel replied.

"That's good, honey," Susan said. "But make sure you let mommy and daddy know if they don't go away."

"I will, grandma."

CHAPTER 23

Jeff was awakened at 8 AM by a gentle stroke from Danielle. Her touch made it clear that she was ready to go again. Jeff was glad that he had a good night's rest in between sessions. At his age things didn't always work as well as he wanted. With Danielle's assistance they worked just fine all three times.

Jeff dozed off again and was awakened a short time later by a love tap on his butt. Danielle was dressed in a business suit and heading towards the bedroom door. "I have to go to work, sweetie," she said. "You can stay as long as you like and let yourself out whenever. There's coffee on the counter." And with that she was gone.

What just happened, Jeff thought. Was this a new relationship or just a one night stand with a horny real estate agent? He figured he would find out sooner or later, and either way it was a lot of fun!

He moved towards Danielle's front door and carefully opened it to see who was outside. At first, Mr. and Mrs. Adams walked past the house so he stayed inside until the coast was clear. Then he quickly walked the three blocks back to his house. He changed into his shorts and walking shoes and headed for the path around the lake.

* * *

Susan woke early the next morning, fixed pancakes for breakfast for everyone, and drove to camp with Jennifer and the kids. On the way back they stopped at Starbucks for coffee and then headed home. Susan called

Carla and learned that there was still a large crowd of people waiting by her house.

"I'll bet Carla is giving them hell!" Jennifer laughed.

As they were about to leave the house for their morning walk, Jennifer handed Susan a tube of lipstick.

"What's this for?" Susan asked as she reluctantly took the tube and applied it to her lips.

"I don't know," Jennifer replied. "It's the first time I'll have you with me and sometimes we meet people and I think we should both look our best."

Within minutes they were on the lake front walking path.

No sooner had they begun their walk than Jennifer spotted Jeff. He was about one hundred yards ahead of them and, since he usually walked at a faster pace than Susan, there was no way the two ladies were going to catch him.

"Let's walk in the other direction, mom," Jennifer said firmly as she pivoted and began to walk the other way around the lake.

Susan was surprised by this move but followed her daughter's lead.

"Why this way, honey?" Susan asked.

"Oh, uh, it's the sun. Sometimes it's blinding when we walk the other way."

Jennifer didn't mind telling a little white lie to her mother. Ever since she had first run into Jeff on the path a few weeks ago she had been planning to find a way for her mother to meet him. Jeff was tall, handsome, and charming, a perfect match for Susan. It had been well over a year since her dad's death and perhaps now was the right time for her mom to meet someone.

* * *

Jeff continued his walk around the lake. He stopped for a moment to chat with Mr. & Mrs. Abrams. They expressed their condolences about his mother and moved on. Then Jeff spotted Janice Hanley. Once again she was dressed in a fancy outfit, tight pants and top that accentuated her large breasts. It was, as it usually was, totally inappropriate for walking around the lake. But that was Janice. She was the last person he wanted to see today.

"Why, Jeffery, we must stop meeting like this!" Janice said in what appeared to be an imitation of Mae West. Next he expected her to say, "Why don't you come up and see me sometime?"

Don't quit your day job, he thought, as he smiled at Janice.

"Morning, Janice," Jeff said curtly. "Sorry I can't stop to talk today. I've got real estate people meeting me in a few minutes."

He didn't mind lying to Janice Hanley. He had no interest in her and there was no way he was going to say anything that might lead her to think otherwise.

As he quickly walked past Janice, Jeff's thoughts once again turned to Danielle. He was turned on by Danielle and he certainly enjoyed the sex he had with her last night, but he wasn't sure if she was serious about him or just using him for sex. In sixty eight years, he thought, I have never been used for sex. So why fret about it now ? Why not just enjoy it? The truth was that he was not built that way. All his life he had been a "one woman guy" who gave his heart and soul to every relationship. Even when he first suspected that Pam was cheating on him he never used that as an excuse to do the same thing to her. It wasn't until after they separated that he took any interest in other women.

He remembered the first night after Pam walked out on him with her fitness coach. There he was, a sixty four year old man who was a free agent for the first time after thirty four years of marriage. He remembered walking into a night club that catered to the "senior crowd." He arrived at 7 PM to find the place totally empty. He sat at the bar and ordered a Hendricks and tonic. Fifteen minutes later one woman, who appeared to be in her sixties, walked in and, even though the bar was completely empty, she plunked herself down in the seat right next to him. He remembers that she was wearing way too much makeup and he didn't like the smell of her perfume, which apparently she had bathed in.

For almost an hour the two of them talked. He bought her a glass of wine and they talked and talked. Her name was Diane. They talked about their exes, their children, and grandchildren. He didn't find Diane attractive at all. As they talked the bar began to fill up. Lots and lots of attractive women came in and sat down. One in particular kept looking at him and smiling. She was hot and he really was interested in meeting her, but he was too polite to dump Diane. As if by divine intervention, at one point Diane must have noticed Jeff's wandering eye.

"You know, you don't have to sit and talk to me all night," she said.

Jeff did not hesitate. He shook Diane's hand and said, "It was very nice meeting you." Then he walked directly to the other woman, sat down next to her, and ordered another drink. Three drinks later he was on his way to the woman's apartment. He remembered waking up in her bed the next morning knowing that he would never see this woman again. He vowed never to do that again. But was that how it was going to be with Danielle? She was his real estate agent but was she really interested in him for any other reason. Time will tell, he thought, and I am wasting way too much time obsessing about Danielle.

* * *

Susan and Jennifer continued their walk, stopping for a moment at the sandy beach to watch people bathing in the lake. Mothers were dipping young children into the murky water and then saying prayers as they looked up to the sky.

"So what do you think, mom?" Jennifer asked. "Is this as good as your payer box?"

"I have no idea, Jenny," Susan replied, "but I wouldn't be surprised if it was. There must be a reason people keep coming back here to the lake."

"Maybe one of the other thirty-six is a fish in the lake!" Jennifer joked. "I hope he doesn't get caught!"

Shortly after they passed the beach area, Jennifer spotted Jeff walking towards them.

"Mom," she whispered. "That's Jeff Morton. He's the one whose mother just passed away."

"Uh huh."

"He's really handsome!" she whispered again

"Uh huh. I guess so."

"You met him two years ago."

"Oh really? I don't remember."

Jeff walked up to the two ladies.

"Good morning, Jenny!" Jeff said with a big smile. He reached his hand out to Susan.

"And you must be Jenny's mom, Susan. It's been awhile but I remember you."

Susan placed her right hand in Jeff's right hand. He grasped the top of her hand with his left hand so that it was engulfed between his two hands. She wondered how this stranger remembered her name.

"Mom is here visiting from Florida, Jeff. She'll be here for a while."

"Only a short visit I'm afraid," Susan added.

Jeff released Susan's hand. He smiled and said, "Well, I hope you enjoy this slice of heaven for as long as you stay."

"Thanks."

"I'm sorry to learn about your husband."

"Oh, thank you. I miss him a lot. And Jenny told me that your mom passed away recently."

"Yes," Jeff replied. "She was a wonderful lady."

"Mom," Jennifer said. "Remember the night I called you in Paris?"

Susan was surprised to hear her daughter mention this. "Ahh, yes, of course I do."

"It was Jeff who helped me find you. We called all over Paris until we finally got to you."

"Oh well aah okay…aah then I guess I owe you a big thanks, Jeff!"

"It was my pleasure to help," Jeff replied. "And maybe someday you'll tell me what it was all about."

Susan was about to speak when her daughter interrupted. "Maybe someday, Jeff, but now is not the time I'm afraid. Too painful and too fresh."

"That's okay," Jeff replied. "I don't mean to pry into something that's none of my business. It was nice talking with you, Jenny, and it was nice to see you again, Susan."

Jeff began to walk away when Jennifer said, "Jeff?"

"Yes?" Jeff responded.

"Mom and I would like to thank you for helping me find her in Paris. Are you free for dinner tonight?"

Jeff was surprised by the invitation and he quickly pondered whether or not he would be seeing Danielle again this evening. Was Jenny trying to set me up with her mother he thought. For the past few years he had been invited to dinner by several young women only to find their mothers waiting to meet him.

He looked at Susan and saw someone special. She was the total opposite of Danielle, and Pam too for that matter. She was short, dark, and understated. But she was also very pretty with amazing blue eyes and a beautiful smile. He certainly wouldn't mind getting to know her better if that was what this was all about.

"Sure!" He said happily. "What time, and what can I bring?"

"We eat early, so, six o'clock, and just bring yourself, okay?"

"Done!" Jeff said as he walked away.

Susan was the first to speak. "I can't believe you did that, Jenny!"

"What did I do that was so wrong, mom? He's a great guy!"

"I'm sure he is, Jenny, but you made me look like a desperate woman! I'm not interested in him or any other man for that matter!"

"Relax, mom, it's not a date. I just felt like we both owed him something. He probably saved your life!"

"I hope he understands what it is because I am not interested. No way, no how, no ma'am!"

Jenny laughed, "I think you doth protest too much, mom! Just have dinner and don't worry about anything."

Susan shook her head. "Okay, if you say so. But what are we gonna fix for dinner?"

"Let's stop at the market and pick up something up after lunch."

* * *

Jeff had decided to do a second lap around the lake but, after spying Janice Hanley coming his way, he quickly turned around and returned to the safety of his house. He immediately moved to the bedroom where his cell phone was charging. On his phone were three missed calls from Danielle. One contained a voice message.

He hit the speaker and play buttons and heard the sound of Danielle's voice.

"Hi, handsome. I've been trying to reach you all morning. Hope you got a good rest at my place. Hey listen, I wanna stop by with my staging crew this afternoon. We should be there around two. I have a key if you're not home. But I hope you'll be there 'cause I wanna see you."

CHAPTER 24

Susan and her daughter returned to the house and quickly changed into tennis clothes. Susan hadn't thought to bring a tennis outfit but she and Jennifer were the same size so she easily fit into Jenny's clothes. Jennifer also had an extra racquet for her mother to use.

Just as they were about to leave for the courts Susan opened the top drawer in the chest in the guest bedroom. Hidden under all of her underthings was the prayer box. It had been a couple of days since she last looked at the box and she felt good knowing that it was hidden and secure.

The two women drove five minutes and parked in the lot next to the tennis courts. During the drive Susan called Carla for an update. The crowd was smaller, Carla said, but still a lot of people.

"These are really nice courts for a community your size." Susan remarked as they exited the car with their racquets slung over their shoulders.

"I know," Jennifer replied. "They just resurfaced them. We're lucky to have tennis players on the board of the homeowners association."

Waiting for them at their court were two women, Abby Main and Diane Markstone. Abby was the younger of the two, in her late thirties Susan guessed. She was tall and very athletic looking. A formidable opponent, Susan figured.

Diane was quite a bit older and appeared to be out of shape. But it didn't take long during their warm-ups for Susan to realize that Diane would be the tougher opponent. While Abby was tall and quick it was Diane who was clever and crafty with her shots.

Susan was no slouch at tennis. She had played for years in USTA events and was rated a 4.0 on the skill level scale. This rating placed her in the top 10% of all amateur women in her age bracket and she was very proud of it. Her daughter was a strong 3.5 level player and together they were a tough team to face.

The first set was a real struggle, as Susan tried to find her stroke. It had been a long time since she had last played and the rustiness was apparent. The mother daughter team lost the first set seven games to five. The set took almost an hour to play.

After the set the ladies moved into the covered gazebo for a cold drink and a few minutes rest. As they sat and chatted, Abby's cell phone rang. It didn't take long for Susan to notice the panic on Abby's face as she listened to the call.

"When? How? No!" Abby shouted into the phone. "Where are they taking him?"

The other three women stared at each other in disbelief. Abby ended the call and she began to shake. Her whole body was convulsing.

"What happened, Ab?" Jennifer shouted.

"It's, it's Michael," she shouted. "He drowned!"

"All three women shouted "NO!"

"They found him at the bottom of the pool and they tried to revive him. They're taking him to the hospital now."

"Is he still alive?" Susan asked.

"I don't know. They don't know. Nobody knows!. I have to go there." Abby began searching frantically for her keys. "I gotta go right now!"

Jennifer noticed that Abby's keys were on the ground. She picked them up and said, "I'm gonna drive you, Ab. What hospital is it?"

"Concord." Abby replied.

Jennifer took her friend's hand and guided Abby to her car. She handed her own car keys to Susan.

"Mom, please take my car back to the house."

"Okay, honey," Susan replied. "Let me know if there's anything I can do."

Susan watched her daughter and friend drive away. As she got into Jennifer's car she thought there is something she could do. I need to get the prayer box, she thought.

Susan quickly drove home, wondering how she would find Concord hospital. She had never been there before, thank God, and she had no idea where it was. As she drove towards Jennifer's house she saw a familiar face. It was Jeff.

She stopped the car and rolled down the passenger side window.

"Jeff?" she said loudly. "Hi, I'm Susan, Jennifer's mom."

Jeff smiled and walked over to the car. He placed his head inside the open window. "Of course, I remember. Hi, Susan, nice to see you again."

"I need a favor, Jeff."

"Sure, anything."

"Can you give me directions to the Concord Hospital?"

"Sure thing," Jeff said. "I took my mother there quite a few times. Is everything okay?"

"Well, no, actually. One of Jenny's friends has a son who drowned."

"My God!"

"I need to get to the hospital right away. Can you tell me how to get there?"

Jeff responded quickly. "I'm gonna do more than that. I'll drive you there. I insist."

Susan thought about protesting but quickly realized that this was her best option to get to the hospital fast. "Okay, thank you so much." She replied. "I just need to stop by the house to pick something up."

"Okay let me get my keys and I'll pick you up in one minute." Jeff ran into his house as Susan drove away.

Susan parked the car in front of her daughter's house, ran into the bedroom, opened the drawer and removed the prayer box. Then she grabbed her largest handbag and gently placed the box inside. It's important, she thought, not to let anyone know I have this prayer box. She didn't want a repeat of her Florida fiasco.

In a few seconds, she was outside the house and Jeff was waiting for her with his silver Mercedes.

The drive to Concord hospital took fifteen minutes. Along the way they talked about the situation.

"Is the boy still alive?" Jeff asked.

"I don't know," Susan replied. "That's the same question I asked."

"Well, the fact that they took him to Concord is a good sign. Perhaps there is hope. They have a great trauma unit there."

Susan took a deep breath. If only she could get there with the prayer box before it was too late. "How much longer?"

"Only two more minutes. It's just around the corner. I'll let you off at the emergency room entrance and then park the car."

Susan was surprised by this. "Thanks. I really appreciate this, but you don't have to stay."

Jeff did not respond. He pulled his car up to the large sign that said "Emergency Entrance." Susan jumped out of the car and ran into the hospital with her handbag.

Jeff began to drive away but then decided to park the car.

When Susan arrived at the emergency waiting room, Jennifer was sitting in a chair using her cell phone. "Mom!" she said. "I was trying to reach you."

"Oh, my cell phone is back at the house. But I came anyway."

"I was trying to get you to bring the...". She then stopped talking and mouthed the words "Prayer Box."

"That's exactly why I came here, honey." Susan whispered. "It's in my handbag."

Mother and daughter waited in silence and both were surprised when Jeff walked in. He was stoic.

"I'm here just in case you need me for anything." He said as he sat down beside Susan.

The three sat in silence for fifteen more minutes until finally Abby came out. Her face was ashen. All three stood up to greet her.

"How is he?" Jennifer asked.

Abby took a deep breath. "They asked me to step out for a few minutes, I'm not sure why. He's breathing on his own."

"That's a good sign," Susan said.

"I know it is," Abby replied. "But the problem is he was under water for so long without oxygen going to his brain that they think he might be brain dead." Abby broke down and began to sob. She fell into Jennifer's arms.

"Can I get you anything?" Jeff asked, hoping to make himself useful.

"How about a cup of coffee, Ab?"

Abby nodded.

"I'll get coffee for all of us," Jeff said. He immediately headed for the hospital cafeteria.

Jennifer helped Abby into a chair and held her friend's hand. "We're all here for you, honey."

Abby took a deep breath and began to talk quietly.

"You know, when I was pregnant with Michael they knew in the first trimester that he had Downs Syndrome." She wiped tears from her eyes.

Susan walked over to the emergency room desk and brought back a box of tissues.

"They told me I could abort the baby if I wanted to but I said absolutely not! He was my baby and I was gonna love him no matter what!" She paused to take a tissue out of the box. "John didn't want me to keep the baby and it almost caused a divorce, but when he held that baby for the first time he loved Michael as much as I did."

"Does John know what happened?"

"I called him. He's on a business trip in Chicago and he's taking a plane here as soon as he can get one."

"I'll stay with you until John arrives." Jenny reassured her friend.

"Thanks, sweetie. I need you. Michael is all I have," she continued. "We never had another child after him. Maybe we were afraid. I don't know. We just didn't try."

Just then Jeff appeared with coffee. He handed each of them a cup with creamers and sugar packets.

Abby sipped her coffee. "Michael is the sweetest boy I have ever known," she said with a smile. "He has only goodness in his heart. He's the best thing that ever happened to me!!"

She broke down sobbing again. "He begged me to let him go to camp with the other kids. I didn't want to do it but he was so sad I couldn't deny him. My God, please help him. He's only eight years old!"

"What's happening right now?" Susan asked.

Abby gathered herself to answer. "Right now he's in a coma. They'll wait to see if he wakes up and they'll keep monitoring his brain activity."

Susan caught her daughter's eye. She glanced at her purse as if to say 'let's get the prayer box in that room'. She reached into the handbag and made sure that the prayer box was open.

"Abby, I'd like to be with you when you go back in if that's alright with you." Jennifer said

"Okay," Abby replied. "I think only immediate family can go in but I'll tell them you're my sister."

Both women stood up and walked out of the waiting room. As she stood up Jennifer grabbed her mother's handbag. Jeff and Susan were left alone together in the waiting room. Jeff immediately noticed the short tennis skirt and sleeveless top Susan was wearing. It was obvious that she was freezing.

"Cold?" He asked.

"It's like a refrigerator in here."

"I'll be right back."

With that Jeff dashed out of the waiting room. He returned five minutes later with a blanket. He gently placed the blanket on Susan's lap.

"I had this blanket in back of my car because mom was always cold," he said.

"Thank you," came the reply from Susan. What a kind and considerate man this is, she thought to herself.

They sat for several minutes without talking until Jeff once again broke the ice. "This boy needs a miracle."

Susan pondered those words and thought about all of the miracles her prayer box had produced. She was hoping for one more. This situation was very similar to Carla's son, Danny. He had been declared brain dead after his motorcycle accident and the prayer box had brought him back to life. Could it work again?

"I had a brother named Michael," Jeff said quietly. "He died very young. I named my son Michael to honor my brother. My mom couldn't bear to call my son Michael so we've always called him Mickey."

"I'm so sorry for your loss." Susan replied.

"My brother fell off a roof and died. It was devastating for the entire family."

"I'm so sorry to hear that, Jeff."

Jeff sat quietly for a moment. He thought about how much he had missed having Michael in his life. "I wish my mom was here right now." Jeff said, "She might have been able to save this boy."

"Oh? Was she a doctor?" Susan responded quickly.

Jeff realized what he had said. He had let the emotion of his brother's death get to him. His mother had always kept her prayer box secret. Maybe he should not be talking about it. But then again, now that she was gone and the box was buried with her what difference did it make? And maybe knowing that miracles can happen would be comforting right now.

"It's a crazy story," he replied.

"Crazy? In what way?"

Jeff was now at a fork in the road. If he continued the conversation he was all in for telling Susan about the prayer box. He thought for a few seconds and then let it all out.

"You're not gonna believe this," he said.

"Try me," Susan replied. She wrapped the blanket tightly around her body.

Jeff cleared his throat. "My mom had this box."

Susan could not believe the words she was hearing. "Box?" she said. "What kind of box?"

"It was a little wooden box," he responded. "She called it a prayer box."

Susan's heart began to race. She couldn't believe what she was hearing. She tried to remain calm and resist the urge to shout out about her prayer box. "Where did it come from?" she asked

."That's the strange thing," Jeff replied. "She never knew where it came from." He sipped his coffee and continued. "It just showed up one day many years ago."

"Did she use it to help people?"

"Yes, she did. But she never told anyone about it, not even me until the day she died."

"So where is this prayer box now?"

"Funny thing. She insisted that I bury it with her, and I had to open it before I placed it in her coffin!"

This was incredible, Susan thought. What are the odds that she would meet the son of one of the only other thirty-five people in the world who had a prayer box?

A moment later Jennifer came into the waiting area with a big smile on her face. She was carrying her mother's handbag. "He woke up!"

"And?"

"And he said, 'Hi mom, where am I?'"

"So, he's okay?"

"Yes!! The doctors said only one in a thousand survive what he went through."

"I'm so happy," Susan replied, hugging Jennifer.

"Listen, mom, I promised Abby I would stay with her until her husband gets here. Jeff, would you mind taking my mom home?" She handed the handbag to Susan.

"Of course not," Jeff replied as he headed for the door. "Do you need me to come back and get you?"

Jennifer thought for a moment. "Oh, that's right, I drove Abby's car. The kids need to get picked up at camp at four."

"Don't worry about a thing, honey. Jeff will take me home and I'll pick up the kids from camp. If you need a ride home just let me know."

"Thanks, mom." They hugged again as Susan walked outside with Jeff.

As they pulled out of the hospital parking lot, Jeff said, "That was a true miracle!"

"Amazing!" Susan replied as she checked for the prayer box inside her handbag. She reached in and closed the lid.

"Can I ask you something personal?" Jeff asked sheepishly.

Oh my, Susan thought, is he going to ask me about my prayer box? But how could he know about it?

"Well, you can ask," she said. "But I might not answer!"

"Fair enough," Jeff laughed. "When I helped Jenny find you in Paris she said your life was in grave danger."

"Yes, it was."

"So, can I ask why anyone would want to harm a wonderful person like you? I hope everything is okay now."

Susan sat silent for several seconds. What should I tell him? I wish Jenny hadn't said anything, but then again I might be dead if she hadn't asked for his help.

"Everything is fine now, Jeff!" she replied.

CHAPTER 25

In a few minutes Jeff and Susan arrived back at Jennifer's house. Jeff dropped Susan off and, as she stepped out of his car he said, "Are we still on for dinner?"

"Oh," Susan replied. "I forgot all about that."

"Look." Jeff responded quickly. " It's been a long day and you both must be exhausted. Let's reschedule for another day."

At first Susan wanted to insist that he still come that evening but then she realized that she had no food in the house, she had to pick up the kids, and Jenny might not be back until very late.

"I think that might be better," she replied. "I'll check with Jenny when she gets home and I'm sure she'll call you to set it up."

"No problem. Have a nice day."

With that, Jeff drove to his house. As he approached the house he came upon five people carrying boxes from the house into an awaiting cargo van. As he walked through the front door he saw more people wandering through the house and moving things around.

"What the hell is going on?" he shouted.

"Oh hi, handsome!" came Danielle's voice as she walked down the staircase. "This is my staging team." She pointed to each one and spoke their names.

"Okay, nice to meet you all. So what the hell is your staging team doing to my house?"

Danielle walked towards Jeff and smiled. To Jeff it seemed like a condescending smile. "Look, sweetie," she said, "this is a wonderful house that was lived in by a sweet little old lady for twenty years. Your mom was ninety years old when she lived here and this is a perfect house for a ninety year old."

Jeff was beginning to grasp the concept. "Okay."

"So we all know that the people who buy this house will not be ninety years old. And we want to make the house attractive to the buyer. We want the potential buyer to easily see their family living here. That's what a staging team does."

"But what are you doing with all my stuff?

Danielle laughed, again condescending in Jeff's eyes. "Don't worry, handsome," she said as she showed him a document from her briefcase. "I rented you a storage garage so all your stuff will be safe and secure until the house is sold."

"But I have to live here!" Jeff protested.

Danielle took his hand and walked him to the kitchen. She opened one of the cabinets. "Look inside." She said.

"Okay," Jeff said as he peeked into the cabinet. It was filled with serving trays that his mother used to entertain guests. "What's wrong with this?"

"It's full, Jeff! That's what's wrong with it. It's filled to the gills."

"So?"

"So when a potential buyer looks in the cabinets and sees them full it makes the kitchen look too small for their own things. We want them to see cabinets that are less than half filled so they can envision their own things fitting easily into the cabinets."

"So you want to fool them."

"We're not fooling them, silly boy! We're just giving them a chance to see themselves living here. We do the same thing with your closets because we don't want the buyer to think the closets are too small."

"Okay, so what else?"

"Well, we will remove all of your artwork from the walls and we'll replace them with, shall I say, more neutral things. I already mounted the aerial view of your house so potential buyers can see it when they walk through the house."

Jeff was beginning to grasp the concept. "Okay then, do your thing."

"Oh, and we'll also have a crew come in to shampoo all of your carpets and wax the tile floors."

"Okay, is that it?"

"And my photographer will be here soon."

"Anything else?"

"Just one final thing," Danielle said with a smile. "We have a *Feng Shui* expert coming in this evening to rearrange all of your furniture."

Jeff sighed and shook his head. He always thought that his mother's house was decorated and arranged beautifully. He was disappointed to learn about the changes and he was thankful that mom wasn't here to see what they were doing to her house. But if this would help sell the house for a good price then he was all for it.

"Okay," he said sheepishly. "But tell me, how much is all of this costing me?"

Danielle laughed. "Oh, don't you worry about that, sweetie." She said. "I'll give you the bill when we're all finished. But you'll get it all back when you sell the house because we're gonna get the highest price ever for a house on Miracle Lake."

"From your lips to God's ears." Jeff said.

"I always do what I say, Jeff!" she replied. "Now be a good boy and take a little ride. You can come back after four. We should be finished by then."

"Okay," Jeff said as he walked towards the front door.

"Wait," Danielle called to him. He stopped and turned in her direction.

"Can we do dinner tonight?"

Jeff remembered that he had postponed his dinner with Jennifer and Susan so he instinctively said, "Sure."

"Great," Danielle replied. "Pick me up at seven."

* * *

Susan returned to Jenny's house and surveyed the refrigerator to see if there was something she could fix for dinner. Since she found nothing easy and she didn't know when Jenny would be home she decided that pizza was the best option. Besides, she thought, that's the kids' favorite meal. She texted Jenny to make sure that she had permission to pick the children up from camp and then made the short drive to get them.

As she drove past Jeff's house she noticed Danielle going out of the front door. It doesn't matter who she is, Susan thought. But for some strange reason it did matter to her. Could that be a girlfriend? Who cares? She tried to tell herself, but she found herself feeling jealous, which she kept telling herself was ridiculous. What claim did she have to Jeff? None, of course.

A few minutes later she was in front of the camp and she watched as Adam and Rachel were escorted to her car. Adam was eleven. A very handsome boy indeed but also very short. Jenny had told Susan that Adam hated being the shortest kid in his class, and he especially hated that his nine year old sister was a half inch taller than he was. It appeared that Adam inherited the Gold genes from his mother when it came to height while Rachel took after her father who was over six feet.

"Hi, grandma!" both kids shouted as they entered the back seat of the car. Both buckled their seat belts.

"How was camp today?" Susan asked.

"Good," was the answer in unison.

Good? Susan thought. Is that all I get? I guess that's typical of kids today. You spend thousands on camps and other programs for them and all they can say is 'good.'

"How is your headache today, Rachie?"

"Good." Rachel replied.

"Good?" Susan inquired. "You mean good like 'I have a headache' or good like 'I don't have a headache?'"

"Don't," was the curt response from Rachel.

It was obvious that the Cohen kids were not big conversationalists. At least not with their grandmother. Within seconds, each had their iPhones on and were very busy doing something that was totally foreign to Susan.

"Would you guys like pizza for dinner tonight?"

"Yeah, we love pizza!" At last there was a touch of enthusiasm.

"How do you like your pizza?"

"Pineapple," Adam responded.

"Yeah, pineapple!" His sister shouted.

Pineapple on pizza? Susan thought. Can there possibly be a worse tasting pizza than that? Oh well, we have always given the kids what they want so why stop now.

In a few minutes they were back at the house and Susan took a shower. By the time she finished Jenny was home.

"Everything okay?" Susan asked.

"Michael is doing great, mom," Jennifer replied. "He was sitting up and eating dinner when I left. He was talking to his mom and he seemed like his old self. I honestly believe that prayer box made a difference."

"You think so?" Susan said with a grin.

"Yes, I do. I really do."

"Not a skeptic any more?"

Jennifer paused. "Well, not completely."

"Sit down, Jenny." Susan said as she poured two glasses of wine. "Have I got a story to tell you!"

Susan told her daughter about her conversation with Jeff. She related how Jeff's mother had one of the prayer boxes and that she had never told anyone. She told her daughter how Miracle Lake got it powers not from within the lake but from that prayer box, how Jeff had buried the prayer box in his mother's coffin, and how Susan was the only person he had told about it. Jennifer sat mesmerized as she listened.

At one point Jennifer said, "I need another glass of Prosecco. One just isn't enough for this story!"

"Jenny," Susan continued, "what an amazing coincidence that I would meet a man whose mother was one of the thirty-six righteous people who have a prayer box."

"Mom," Jennifer said calmly. "I don't believe this is a coincidence."

"What do you mean, honey?"

"Mom, I believe that you and Jeff both came here to this lake for a reason. It's no accident that you arrived here around the same time as Jeff did, that his mother died just before you got here, and she told him about the prayer box, and that you were the only person he told about the prayer box. Does all that sound like a coincidence to you, mom?"

Susan pondered for a moment. "No, I guess not. It really doesn't sound like just a coincidence."

"I think it's possible that you and Jeff were meant to meet and maybe even that you were destined to be together."

"Whoa, slow down!" Susan barked. "I think you're taking this way too far!"

"No, I'm not, mom. You've seen the miracles from your prayer box. Why couldn't your meeting Jeff be another one of the miracles?"

Susan took a deep breath. "First of all, I'm not ready for another man in my life. And second of all, I think he has a girlfriend."

"No, I don't think so," Jennifer replied. "I see him walking every day and I've never seen a woman with him. And we often stop to talk and he's never mentioned a woman in his life. He's been divorced for a few years."

Susan then described the woman she had seen leaving Jeff's house.

"Oh!" Jennifer laughed. "That's not his girlfriend. That's Danielle Mauer. She's his real estate agent."

Although she would not admit it, Susan was relieved to hear those words.

"That's interesting," she said in a matter of fact tone.

"Speaking of Jeff, we did invite him to dinner tonight, didn't we?"

"Yes, we did, honey, but he and I both decided this was not a good night so we need to reschedule."

"I'll invite him for tomorrow night. I want to hear more about his mother and her prayer box."

"I'm afraid you can't, mom."

"Why not?"

"Jeff told me about the prayer box in confidence and I don't want him to know that I discussed it with you."

"Oh, well, did you mention anything about your prayer box?"

"No, honey. I'm afraid to tell anybody. I don't want to create any problems for you and the kids."

"Okay, that makes sense, mom." She paused for a moment. "If I can't ask him about his mother's prayer box then I guess that means we'll have to arrange for some alone time for you and Jeff."

"Uh huh."

"I'll ask him to join us tomorrow tonight. Let's do salad and lasagna."

Susan called Carla for another update. Each day fewer and fewer people were showing up at Susan's house, hoping for a miracle. The latest count was about twenty cars.

"They're still out there!" Susan said as she hung up from Carla. "Oh, by the way, I asked Rachel about her headaches and she said they were gone today."

"Oh, that's good." Jennifer replied. "It seems like they come and go every other day. David says that he'll check her out when he comes up to the lake this weekend. If she still has a headaches he'll take her to Concord for an MRI."

"MRI? That sounds serious."

"No, mom, it's just a precaution. I'm sure she's fine."

"It sure is nice knowing that you have a pediatrician in the family."

"I know, mom, it's very convenient."

"We could have used one when you were growing up."

"Oh please, mom, don't get me started. Every time I sneezed or coughed you panicked and wanted to drag me to the Emergency Room! Thank God for daddy!"

Susan smiled as she remembered her late husband. "Yes," she said, "daddy was always the calm one in our family, wasn't he." She paused for a moment. "I miss him so much, honey!"

"Me too, mom." Jennifer replied as mother and daughter hugged. "Me too."

CHAPTER 26

Jeff returned to his house at about five and was relieved to see that the staging team was gone. Also gone was half of everything his mother owned, and this was after he had personally gone through the house and removed a lot of things. It's amazing, he thought, how much stuff can be accumulated over twenty years.

He had mixed emotions about seeing Danielle this evening. Yes, she was beautiful, sexy, vivacious, and smart. But she was also overbearing, condescending, and in some cases, rude.

As he showered and dressed he decided that this would be his last date with Danielle. He would join her for dinner, take her home, and say good bye. After tonight, Danielle Mauer would be his real estate agent, nothing more and nothing less.

He also decided that he would like to get to know Susan Gold much better. After revealing his mother's secret to her he felt that he must have a connection with Susan. Why else would he have done that? And he found it interesting that she never challenged him on what he was saying about the prayer box. She just accepted it. But it also seemed like she too had a secret to tell. Why would her life have been in danger in France?

Jeff finished preparing and left his house just before seven. He drove three blocks to Danielle's house and she was waiting for him when he rang the bell.

"Hi, handsome," she said with a smile, "I've got a great restaurant for us tonight. I made a reservation for seven thirty at Casa Bella. It's a little bit of a ride but it's definitely worth the trip."

Danielle's aggressiveness with him at his house today was continuing now, Jeff thought. Maybe he was being too sensitive. After thirty years with Pam he was used to a strong woman, but he was having a hard time warming up to Danielle's aggressive personality. Maybe she reminded him too much of his ex.

"Okay," he said quietly. "Let's go."

They made the drive down route 93 to Manchester and eventually pulled into the parking lot of Casa Bella. As they walked in the maitre d' greeted them. He was an elderly man who looked to be as wide as he was tall.

"*Bongiorno*, Danielle," he said with a big smile.

"*Ciao*, Antonio," came Danielle's reply.

"Your usual table is ready," the fat man said. "Right this way *signora*."

Jeff found it interesting that Antonio had never even acknowledged his presence. As they sat down at their table he said, "How often do you come here?"

"Oh, at least once a week," Danielle replied. "I try to bring every new client here."

Jeff was happy to hear those words from Danielle. Even though they had been together for only two days he had decided that Danielle was not a long term interest for him. The fact that she considered him nothing more than a "client" would make what he planned to tell her later much easier.

Their dinner lasted for two hours, with special wines served for each course. He had to admit it was one of the best meals he had ever had. As Danielle talked during the meal she continued to reinforce Jeff's belief that she was not for him. She was an expert and very opinionated about every subject, especially politics. And even though her political views were similar to his he was turned off by the vitriol she expressed for those on the other side.

As Danielle continued to drink wine and talk she became more and more animated, more and more outrageous. During the course of one meal Jeff learned that the World Trade Center was taken down not by terrorists, but by the US government. JFK was killed by the CIA, diet soft drinks will kill you, global warming and recycling are communist plots, the moon walk was faked, the Russians are poisoning our water supply, and cartoons have subliminal messages that are influencing the minds of young children.

Every time Daniel opened her mouth he was turned off, but she was sexy, very sexy. She wore a tight fitting top that was cut low. Jeff had to force himself not to stare at her breasts during the meal. The more dumb things Danielle said, the more Jeff stared at her breasts. Several times it occurred to Jeff that she was doing all the talking. She apparently had no interest in getting to know him.

During his years as a dentist, Jeff had become very good at one sided conversations. With the patient unable to talk it was up to him to make the conversation. He was a real pro at innocuous discussions about the weather and sports, but he always stayed away from anything controversial, especially politics and religion. Why lose a patient because you offended them? It just wasn't worth it.

Jeff was proud of the fact that he had a good filter for his opinions. But Danielle did not. Apparently, whatever thoughts came into her head soon came out of her mouth.

At nine thirty they finished dinner and returned to Jeff's car for the ride back to Miracle Lake. Danielle continued to talk about everything that was wrong in the world. As they got close to his neighborhood, Danielle said, "Let's stop at your place. I want to see the finished product from the staging team."

Within minutes, they were inside Jeff's house. Danielle walked around, moving furniture and straightening wall hangings. As she explored each room she mumbled things like "okay" or "no."

When they reached the master bedroom, she excused herself and walked into the master bathroom. She closed the door as Jeff waited for her. Within a couple of minutes, Danielle walked out of the bathroom wearing nothing but her high heels.

She walked up to Jeff and began to unbutton his shirt. "I guess you didn't get the memo about the dress code for tonight!"

Jeff was turned on. What straight man wouldn't be, he thought. This was a woman he had absolutely no romantic interest in but, what the heck?

Danielle removed all of Jeff's clothes, exploring his body with her hands and mouth as she did. They spent the next thirty minutes in his bed. It was even better than the previous night, he thought.

When the sex ended, Jeff lay in bed with eyes wide open. Danielle snuggled up next to him and rested her head on his shoulder. As they lay together, Jeff practiced what he would say to Danielle. He would tell her that he liked her a lot, that he still wanted her to be his realtor, but that he didn't want to continue their relationship. But as she rubbed her hands on his body the words became much more difficult to find.

Jeff glanced at the clock radio next to his bed. It was eleven fifteen. "Would you like to stay?" he asked softly. Danielle responded with a passionate kiss. Another round of sex followed and then Jeff fell asleep without telling Danielle what he had planned to say.

He was awakened in the morning by an alarm from Danielle's cell phone. She too was awakened and she jumped up out of bed and headed for the shower. It was eight AM.

"I've got a meeting with a potential client this morning," she said loudly from the bathroom. "He wants to meet me at his office before he opens at nine."

Jeff lay in bed and watched as Danielle emerged from the bathroom. She was as naked as she had been the night before. This was a stunning woman. There was no doubt about that. But definitely not for him.

"I don't want to do this any more."

"Do what honey?"

"This," Jeff replied, motioning to himself in bed. "You can be my realtor but this has to stop."

"Aren't you having fun?"

"There's someone else, Danielle."

"Someone else?" Danielle replied. "So what difference does that make? We can still have fun."

"No Danielle, I'm not built that way. You can still be my realtor but not my lover."

"Okay," Danielle replied. "No problem. I'll call you after my meeting."

Danielle finished dressing, touched up her makeup, and left the house at eight-thirty. Jeff was stunned by her emotionless reaction to what he had said. I made the right decision, he thought.

CHAPTER 27

Susan and her daughter had spent the evening reminiscing about Steven Gold. He had been such a wonderful husband, father, and grandfather, a role model for every man. They both agreed on that. Susan missed her husband and best friend and Jennifer missed her dad.

"Mom," Jennifer said quietly. "I think daddy would want you to meet someone who could make you happy."

Susan thought carefully for a moment. "I know, honey. He loved me so much he would want me to be happy. But I just can't help but feel like I would betray him if I found another man."

Jennifer hugged her mother. "I know, mom, and that's what makes you so special. But when the right man comes along hopefully you'll remember what I said about daddy."

Susan had a hard time falling asleep that night as she pondered the words she had heard from her daughter. Mother and daughter both woke the next morning in time to drive the kids to camp. As they sipped their morning coffee Jennifer said "I'll call Jeff and invite him for dinner tonight."

"Do you think we can walk around the lake with him this morning?" Susan asked. It was then that she realized that she was beginning to have feelings for Jeff.

"Of course, mom," Jennifer replied with a grin. "Jeff's out there every morning between nine and nine fifteen. If we time it right we should run into him.

"Why are you grinning?" Susan asked defiantly.

"Grinning?" Jennifer replied. "I wasn't grinning!"

"Yes, you were. You were grinning. I know a grin when I see one, Jenny!"

Jenny was enjoying the back and forth with her mother. This was the first time her mother had ever expressed any interest in a man since Steven had died.

"Mom, it's okay if you like Jeff."

"If I 'like' Jeff?" Susan said sarcastically, using her fingers to make air quotation marks as she uttered the word 'like'. "What, are we in junior high school? I think he is a very nice man."

"And handsome, too!" her daughter interrupted.

"Okay, and handsome, too."

"And that prayer box. We can't forget that!"

"Of course not, honey. I have a lot more questions to ask him about that."

Adam and Rachel came down stairs dressed and ready for camp. They each grabbed a pop tart from the toaster as Rachel said, "Let's go, mom. We've got a field trip today and we can't be late."

Jennifer, Susan, and the kids left the house at 8:30. In two minutes they were driving past Jeff's house. Susan was just about to make her daily call to Carla when she spotted Danielle leaving the house.

"That's the same woman I saw there yesterday!" she whispered.

"Yes, that's Danielle Mauer, the real estate agent." her daughter replied.

"Still think she's just his real estate agent?"

"I dunno, mom. To be honest, I don't know of any real estate people who make house calls that early!"

Now Susan was jealous. How could Jeff fall for a woman like that, she thought. I bet Danielle slept with every male client she had! Susan mentally slapped herself across the face. What am I doing, she thought. And besides, there might be a logical explanation for what she saw. Probably not, she thought.

The kids were dropped off at camp and Jennifer made her call to Carla. The crowd was down to ten cars as more and more people had given up on finding the prayer box. Perhaps Susan could return home in a few days. But did she want to leave Miracle Lake right now?

They made the short drive back to the lake. Before she left the car, Susan checked the mirror on the sun visor of the car to see if her hair and makeup were okay. Mother and daughter quickly headed towards the walking path and, as expected, there was Jeff. He had seen them coming and waited for them before he began his walk.

"Hi ladies!" He said with a big smile. "Will you join me?"

"Sure, "Jenny said as she walked towards Jeff. Her mother followed behind.

For the first ten minutes the conversation was superficial. They talked about the weather. As they approached the beach area, Jennifer said, "So are you gonna sell the house Jeff?"

"Yes." Jeff replied. "I always loved coming here to visit mom but I can't afford to keep up two houses now that I'm retired."

"Do you have a real estate agent?" Susan asked matter of factly.

"Yes, I'm using Danielle Mauer. I heard she's the top agent for this community."

"I've heard a lot of things about Danielle!" Jennifer laughed.

Susan winced upon hearing those words come from her daughter's lips. Don't go there, Jenny, she thought. Please don't go there! She tapped Jenny's leg to get her attention and shook her head.

"You have?" Jeff replied. "Like what? What have you heard?"

"Oh, ah." Jennifer stammered. "I've heard she's very aggressive and she gets houses sold fast."

"I'm really not sure I want the house to be sold fast." Jeff replied. "I'm enjoying living here at the lake and I'd like to spend the rest of the summer here before I leave the country."

"Leave the country?" Susan asked.

"I volunteered for World Health Teams and I'm scheduled to leave on October first."

"What is World Health Teams?" Jennifer asked.

"It's a charitable organization that started about thirty years ago. It sends doctors, dentists, and other health care professionals to countries where they're badly needed. There are some places where kids have never seen a doctor or a dentist in their lives."

"My mom was a dental hygienist for a long time, Jeff!" Jennifer said.

"Oh really," Jeff replied. "That's great!"

"Well, yes. I worked for Doctor Adler in Lexington for many years, but I retired about ten years ago." Susan added. "So where will you be going?"

"Not sure yet," Jeff replied. "I haven't got my assignment. I think it will be in South or Central America, but it could possibly be in Africa. Wherever they send me, I'll go."

Susan was now even more impressed with Jeff. He is a kind and selfless man, she thought. But learning that he was leaving the country was disappointing.

"How long will you be gone, Jeff?" she asked.

"The normal assignment is one month."

Susan was happy to learn that it was only a one month assignment.

"It sounds quite challenging." Jennifer said.

"Yes, it's very challenging." Jeff replied. "I understand the conditions are atrocious, sometimes they don't even have electricity. But you know, life has been very good to me and I feel like this is my way of giving back."

The walk ended and they headed back towards their houses.

"We'll see you at six, okay?" Jennifer said.

"Wouldn't miss it for the world." came Jeff's reply.

As they walked back into the house, Jennifer turned to her mother and said, "There's a special place in heaven for people like Jeff. He's a good man, mom!"

Susan was daydreaming. "Yes he is, honey. Yes he is!"

* * *

Susan and Jennifer changed into their tennis clothes and headed for the courts. They were happy to see Abby there with her partner Diane.

"How is Michael doing today?" Jennifer asked.

Abby flashed a big smile. "He's doing great!" she said. "He ate like a horse at the hospital last night and all he wanted was to come home and go back to camp."

"That's fantastic!" Susan said.

"Yes, it is. John spent the night with him at the hospital. I stayed until eleven but when I saw father and son curled up together in the hospital bed sound asleep I kissed them both and came home."

"This is such a miracle!" Jennifer said.

"One thousand to one, they told me," Abby replied. "I called this morning and they'll be sending him home as soon as the doctor releases him."

The four women then played a rousing game. Susan was surprised by how well she played. Perhaps my stroke is coming back, she thought. Mother and daughter won both sets.

After tennis they decided to stop for lunch at the Bread Factory. They had just ordered soup and salads when Jennifer's cell phone rang. Susan listened intently to what she was hearing from the call.

"Oh, hi Brenda!" Jennifer said. Then she paused and said "Okay, I'll be there in ten minutes. Get Adam ready too, please. I'll take him home too."

"What's up, Jenny?"

"That was Rachel's camp counselor." Jennifer said. "Rachel has a bad headache. She threw up and she wants to come home."

Susan shook her head. "This is serious, Jenny."

"I don't know, Mom. David is coming up to the lake tonight and we'll see what he says."

They picked up their order to go and headed directly for the camp. Rachel and her brother were waiting with the counselor. Jennifer got out of the car and spoke to the counselor as the kids buckled up in the back seat of the Lexus.

"Is it really bad, Rachie?" Susan asked.

Rachel was crying. "It really hurts, grandma!"

Jennifer returned to the car. "Daddy will be here tonight honey and he'll make you feel better," she said lovingly. "Let's get you home and you can rest until he gets here."

When they arrived home Jennifer gave her daughter children's Tylenol and put her to bed. Adam immediately marched to the TV set and began playing a video game. It looked like a violent game. Adam was working a controller and he was killing bad guys left and right.

Susan sat down on the sofa next to her grandson and said, "Can I play with you, Adam?"

Adam looked puzzled. "Grandma, you don't know how to play this game, do you?"

"Well no, but maybe you can teach me."

Adam rolled his eyes. "It's very complicated, grandma. Took me a long time to learn. Maybe you can just watch me for a while."

In a few minutes Jennifer came downstairs. "She's sleeping," she said.

"I hope this is nothing serious," Susan said as she watched more bad guy killing on the TV screen.

"Me too, mom, me too." Jennifer paused for a moment. "You know, mom, I hate to do this again, but I don't think it's a good idea for Jeff to come over for dinner tonight. You know, David will be here and he'll be tending to Rachel. And she doesn't feel good."

"Of course, Jenny. He'll understand."

"I hate to cancel Jeff two nights in a row."

"Yeah, me too."

"Hey! Why don't you and Jeff go out for a bite to eat? You said you had a lot of questions to ask him and this will give you the time and the privacy to ask."

Susan was excited at the prospect of a private dinner with Jeff. "Okay, I'll give him call!"

Jeff was at the florist picking out a bouquet to bring to Jenny's house. He was excited to see Susan again and, while he was bringing the flowers to Jennifer, he really wanted them to be for her mother. His cell phone rang, and he was pleasantly surprised to hear Susan's voice. He was disappointed, however, when she explained that her granddaughter was sick and they had to cancel the dinner tonight. He quickly gathered his thoughts and said, "Do you think we could go out for dinner, just you and me?"

Susan laughed on the other end. "I guess great minds think alike, because I was gonna ask you the same thing!

"Pick you up at six?"

"Sounds great!"

CHAPTER 28

Jennifer's husband, David arrived at the house shortly after five PM. He kissed his wife, hugged Susan, and immediately went upstairs to check on his daughter. He returned about twenty minutes later.

"The headache is back and she's nauseous." He said. "I checked a few other symptoms and I don't like what I'm seeing. I'm gonna take her to Concord tomorrow for an MRI."

"What does that mean, David?" Susan asked. "Is this a serious problem?"

David lowered his voice. It was obvious that he did not want his son to hear what he was about to say. Adam was totally immersed in his video game so that was highly unlikely.

"We won't know until we look at the scan," he said in a calm voice. "But headaches like this usually don't occur in young children unless something's going on."

"Something?" Jennifer shouted. "Something, like what?" She was beginning to lose it.

David grabbed his wife and hugged her. "Honey," he said, "this could be nothing, so let's not panic. But if it is something I promise you our daughter will have the finest doctors in the world to take care of her!"

"Do you want me to stay home and help with anything?" Susan asked.

"No, mom. There's nothing any of us can do right now. Go get ready for your date."

"Date?" David asked. "You have a date, Sue?"

Susan nodded. "Jenny will tell you all about it."

Susan went upstairs to the guest room, showered and dressed for her dinner date with Jeff. She studied her clothes for quite some time and was disappointed that she hadn't brought more things from Florida. She had a lot of pretty dresses at home but she never anticipated staying more than a few days in New Hampshire. And who expected someone like Jeff to come along, she thought. She was about to settle for something less than desired when her daughter entered the bedroom holding a black dress.

"Mom," she said, "you taught me that the little black dress is often the best choice, so here you go!"

Susan showered and dressed and, by the time she arrived downstairs, Jeff was waiting for her. He was as tall and handsome as ever, wearing black slacks and a silky gray shirt. He looked at Susan and said, "Wow! You look sensational!"

"Oh, this old thing?" She laughed, and so did Jeff. One more thing I like about him, Susan thought. Check off the boxes!

Jeff held the door as Susan entered the passenger seat of his car. When he assumed the driver's seat he said, "Do you have a favorite type of food?"

"Anything you choose is fine," she replied. "I'm not picky."

"How about sushi?"

"That's one of my favorites!"

In a little over ten minutes, Susan and Jeff found themselves sitting on opposite sides of a table at Sushi King. As they perused, the menu Jeff said, "I've been here a few times and it was always great."

The waiter took their drink orders, sake for Jeff and plum wine for Susan. Each took one sip before Susan said, "Jeff, I'm so glad I met you."

"I feel the same, Susan."

"I have so many things I want to know about you," she said.

"All you have to do is ask." Jeff replied. "I have no secrets."

"Except the prayer box!"

"Yes, of course. How could I forget that!"

"We'll get to that." she replied. "But first I want to know about Doctor Jeffrey Morton. Tell me about your life."

Jeff thought about that question and realized how different Susan was from Danielle. She was truly interested in him as a person, and that made him like her even more.

For the next fifteen minutes Jeff told Susan his life story. He started as a kid growing up in Malden, Massachusetts, losing his older brother, admiring his dad and eventually becoming a dentist to work in his dad's dental practice. He told her about his marriage to Pam, their son Michael and his family, the betrayal and divorce, and of course his mother and how much she meant to him. The only interruptions came when the waiter asked if they were ready to order. The first two times they both said no but eventually they ordered miso soup and a variety of sushi rolls.

"I heard they call you Doctor J," Susan said with a smile. "How'd you get that name?"

Jeff chuckled and then replied. "When I was at UMass I played on the basketball team with Julius Irving."

"You mean THE doctor J?"

"Yes, but at first the guys on the team always called me Doctor J because I was in pre-med. Julius liked it and when I graduated he sort of adopted the name for himself."

"Were you a good player?"

"Well, let's put it this way," Jeff answered. "You know when there's a timeout and the players on the court come over to the bench?"

"Uh huh,"

"Well, I was one of the guys who stood up to let them sit down!"

Susan laughed. "You're a funny guy!"

"I've been talking too much, haven't I?" Jeff said.

"No, not at all. You are a very interesting man and I thank you for sharing your story with me."

"Okay, now it's your turn." he said as he sat back and allowed the waiter to place his soup bowl in front of him.

"Wait." Susan said. "Before we start with me there's one more thing I'd like to ask."

"Sure."

"I hope you won't get upset."

"Try me. I'm a pretty easy going guy."

Susan took a deep breath. "Is there anyone else in your life right now?"

Jeff smiled. "You mean like a woman?"

"Of course I mean a woman, silly!" Susan loved that she felt comfortable enough to say those words to him.

"Actually," Jeff began, and then paused to collect his thoughts.

As he paused Susan's heart skipped a beat.

"Just recently I was dating my real estate agent," he continued.

"You mean Danielle?"

"Yes, that's right."

"So what happened?"

"I broke it off with her."

"Oh," Susan said. She was happy to hear those words from his lips. "Is it okay if I ask why?"

"Actually, there were two reasons I won't be seeing Danielle. For one, our personalities clashed and we really didn't get along very well."

"Is that one reason or two?"

Jeff laughed, "No, that's all reason number one."

"So, what was reason number two?"

Jeff hesitated. "I met you!"

"Oh my!" Susan said instinctively. She was thrilled to hear it. "Now, can I tell you something?"

"Absolutely. It has to be your turn to talk now."

"My husband died a little over a year ago. fifteen months to be exact. He was the love of my life."

"I know, and I'm so sorry."

"Thanks, Jeff. When Steven died I told myself that no other man could ever measure up to him so I was never going to let myself get close enough to any man because I didn't want to be disappointed."

Jeff sipped his sake. "And yet, here you are!" he smiled.

"Here I am!" Susan said softly as she lifted her wine glass to toast with Jeff's sake.

The rest of the dinner went perfectly. The two of them talked and talked and they laughed and laughed. Susan told Jeff about her life growing up in Newton, about her parents and her two older brothers. She told him about her career as a dental hygienist, she spoke lovingly about Steven and her life with him, about Jennifer and how hard they had tried to have a second child. Jeff listened with compassion and understanding.

As they talked they learned that they had so much in common that it was "almost creepy," Jeff said. They even shared a background in dentistry.

Jeff looked at Susan throughout the meal. This is a beautiful woman on so many levels, he thought. She is attractive, but not in a showy way. She is smart, but anything but a know-it-all. And she is even a Red Sox fan! What more could a man ask for?

On the ride home Susan thought about asking more questions about the prayer box, but the evening had gone so perfectly that she didn't want to say anything to spoil it. They arrived at Jennifer's house at eleven PM and it appeared that all of the lights were out. Jeff opened the car door for Susan, took her hand, and walked her up the stairs to the front door.

"I had a wonderful evening!" Susan said.

"Me too." Jeff replied "I hope we can do it again."

"I'll be heartbroken if we don't!"

Jeff placed his hand around Susan and gently pulled her towards him. Their lips met in a tender kiss that lasted for several seconds. It was a perfect kiss.

"Good night!" They both said in unison.

CHAPTER 29

Jeff walked into his house and immediately headed for the shower. As he exited the shower and entered his bedroom he was surprised to see Danielle sitting on his bed. She was wearing a bright red outfit that was tight and sexy.

Wrapped only in a towel, Jeff was caught off guard.

"Hi, handsome!" Danielle said with a smile. "I'd ask if that's a gun under your towel or are you just happy to see me but I don't see a gun!"

With that she playfully reached for the towel. Jeff backed away, grabbing the towel, and keeping it safely covering his lower body.

"What are you doing here?"

"I came over to show you the ad we're gonna run in the two local real estate magazines. I'll be submitting them tomorrow morning and they should come out in next week's editions."

"Oh, okay," Jeff replied. "Give me a minute to get dressed and I'll meet you in the living room."

"Sure, sweetie. I'll make us a cup of coffee."

Jeff dressed quickly and walked into the kitchen. He took a sip of coffee and asked Danielle to join him in the living room. She walked in and sat down on the sofa. Jeff deliberately chose to sit in a chair facing her rather than sit beside her.

"You look serious, handsome," Danielle said. "Is everything okay?"

Jeff paused to make sure he chose the right words. "Danielle, I thought I made it clear that I didn't want this deal."

183

Danielle laughed. "Deal? What deal? I don't know what you're talking about, sweetie!"

Jeff took a deep breath. "Look," he began. "This has been a difficult time for me. I retired from my job and buried my mother a short time later. Now, I'm trying to sell her house and move on."

"I get that."

"I had a great time with you the past few days," Jeff said as he searched frantically for the best words to use. "But the truth is I am not interested in a relationship with you right now. That's what I was trying to tell you the last time we were together."

He wondered how Danielle would take this. Would she be disappointed? Angry? He quickly found out.

"Relationship?" Danielle said with as grin. "So that's what you think this is, a relationship?"

"Well…"

"Well, it's not, sweetie. It never was and never will be a relationship!"

"Then what would you call it?" Jeff asked.

"Sweetie, have you ever heard of the term 'friends with benefits'?"

Jeff understood exactly where she was going with this. "Of course I have," he replied. "and I'm not interested in that, with you or anyone else for that matter. I met someone else that I'm really interested in and this has to be over!"

Danielle laughed again. It was one of her condescending laughs that Jeff detested so much. "Honey, you must have been reading way too much into this. It's not 'over' because it never 'was.'"

"Okay that's fine with me."

"Sweetie, do you remember when I first met you after your mother's funeral?"

"Yes."

"Well, I told you then that I was a full service agent."

Jeff was quick to respond. "And now I understand what you meant by that."

Danielle laughed again. Jeff was not surprised that she could take this so lightly, and he was happy that he was learning about Danielle now, and not later. He also knew now that his feelings for Susan were real.

"So, I guess you do this with all your clients, huh?" Jeff said sarcastically.

"Only the good looking ones!" Danielle replied.

"You're a piece of work!" he mumbled.

"And it looks like you've got yourself a new piece of ass!" she barked.

Jeff stood up from his chair. He stared straight at Danielle. "You know what?" he said. "I think I'm gonna stay at the lake for the entire summer. I won't be selling the house now. These ads won't be necessary. Cancel them and cancel the listing too."

"So, what? Are you firing me as your agent?"

"That's exactly what I'm doing!"

"Oh come on, Jeffy boy. Did I bruise your ego?" Danielle said sarcastically as she stood up and approached Jeff. He backed away.

"I think you should leave now," he said sternly.

Danielle stared at him for what seemed like minutes. He stared back and was determined not to back down. Finally, she gathered her papers and walked towards the front door.

"Good luck, Jeff," she said, and walked out the door.

Jeff took a deep breath and poured himself a Hendricks and tonic.

* * *

Susan was excited. Her mind was racing as her thoughts kept turning to Jeff. She and Jennifer talked for a few minutes before Susan decided

185

to walk to his house and surprise him, hopeful that their date would continue.

"Not a good idea, mom." Jennifer offered.

"You're right, honey," her mother replied."But I'm going anyway."

Susan walked to Jeff's house, hoping to spend more time with the man she was fast falling in love with. As she walked she practiced what she was going to say to Jeff, but then settled on nothing more than big kiss. That should do the trick, she thought.

As she approached Jeff's house she saw Danielle walking out the front door and down the steps. She was buttoning her blouse. What could she be doing here this late, Susan thought. He told me that he was through with her, so what is doing she at his house?

Danielle walked down the steps and came right over to Susan. She had a big grin on her face. "Are you Jeff's new girlfriend?"

"Just a friend." Susan replied stoically.

"He's a real player, honey," Danielle said, licking her lips in an obvious fashion. "A real player." She walked towards her car and drove away.

Susan was stunned. She was speechless. She turned and walked back to Jennifer's house, fighting tears every step of the way.

It was difficult falling asleep, and only a sleeping pill finally allowed her to stop hearing Danielle's words over and over. When she awoke the next morning she was eager to tell her daughter about her what she saw at Jeff's house.

Her personal pain was tempered by the sight of her son-in-law walking out the door with his daughter. They were on their way to Concord Hospital for an MRI that would determine if Rachel had a serious problem. Jennifer was crying at the kitchen table.

"We should be back in a couple of hours." David said.

"When will you get the results?" his wife asked.

"I'm gonna stick around and read the films myself."

"Bye, mommy. Bye, grandma," Rachel said. "Don't worry, daddy says this won't hurt at all!" It was obvious that the little girl had no concept of the gravity of her situation. And perhaps that is for the best, Susan thought.

Susan sat down and rubbed her daughter's shoulders. This had always kept Jenny calm, even when she was little.

"How about we go for a walk around the lake this morning?" Susan asked.

"Good idea, mom. I could use some fresh air and I need to do something to get my mind off this."

Mother and daughter quickly put on walking clothes and shoes and headed out the front door. Standing in front of the house was Jeff.

"Hi!" he said with a smile. "I was just stopping by to see if you wanted to walk with me this morning?"

"Not today!" Susan replied curtly as she abruptly closed the front door, leaving Jeff stunned on the other side.

It occurred to Susan that she hadn't yet told Jenny anything about her experience with Danielle at Jeff's house.

"Mom," Jennifer said, "what the hell was that about?"

"He had that woman at his house, Jenny."

"Danielle?"

Susan nodded.

"So, she's his realtor. No big deal."

"What realtor shows up at 10 PM, Jenny? None that I've ever seen."

"It could be innocent, mom," Jennifer replied. "You should at least give him a chance to explain."

"You know what Danielle told me?" Susan said. "She said he was a real player. A real player."

"At least give him a chance, mom."

"I'm not ready for that. Not right now anyway." Susan replied.

The two women did chores around the house to keep their minds occupied until David returned with Rachel. Later, Susan called Carla for the latest update from Florida. Carla told her something had developed and she would call back this evening.

"What's up with Carla?" Jennifer asked.

"I don't know, honey," Susan replied, "but it sounds like something big."

"Maybe someone tried to break into your house."

"I don't think so, Jen, she would've told me that."

A moment later, the front door opened and David walked in. Susan knew right away that something was wrong. David was never good hiding his emotions. Susan hugged her daughter and sent Rachel off to play video games with her brother. When she was out of earshot David began.

"I was with the radiologist when he looked at the scan," he said quietly. "She has a tumor. There is no doubt about that."

"Oh my God!" Jennifer cried. "My baby!"

"What type of tumor is it, David?" Susan asked.

"That I can't tell you." David said. He was visibly shaken.

"How can you find that out?" Susan asked calmly.

"I'm gonna take her to Mass General next week."

"Next week? Why wait until next week? Why not this week?"

"I want her to be seen by Stan Carpenter." Jeff replied. "He's the world's most renowned specialist in pediatric neurology. He's on vacation and he'll be back next week."

"Can't she see someone else? I hate to wait that long."

"I spoke to Stan and he wants to see her himself. He says that the extra week won't make a difference in her treatment. This tumor has most likely been growing for years."

Jennifer broke down completely, "Is she gonna die, David? Is our baby gonna die?"

David held his wife tightly until she took a deep breath. "Honey, remember what I told you. Rachel is gonna get the best doctors and the best treatment the world knows."

Susan went into the bathroom and brought back a box of tissues for her daughter.

"We need to stay strong for Rachel." Susan said.

"You're right, Sue," David replied. "Let's try to keep calm until we know for certain what's going on."

CHAPTER 30

One week had passed since Susan had last spoken with Jeff. Several times each day her cell phone rang and she saw Jeff's name appear on the screen. Each time she chose not to accept the call.

"Why won't you at least talk to him, mom?" Jennifer asked on several occasions.

Susan was adamant. "I lived with your father for over 35 years and he never once gave me a reason not to trust him. Never once, Jenny."

She paused to catch her breath and compose her thoughts. "Then I meet this guy, a stranger, and within two weeks I can't trust him."

"So he owes you an explanation, mom."

"No, honey. He doesn't owe me anything. He can live his life anyway he wants. I just don't want to be part of it."

"But mom, there might be an innocent explanation. For God sakes at least tell him why you're upset."

"I'll think about it, honey."

Susan decided to walk around the lake by herself, but made sure that her timing would not let her cross paths with Jeff. She was not going to have a relationship without trust, and there was nothing he could say to her at this point that would change her mind. So why take it any further with him, she thought.

She stopped several times to chat with people she had gotten to know. One of the great things about this community, she taught, was the warmth of the people. It was like one big family. As she walked she could not help but look for Jeff. On the one hand she wanted to avoid him, but on the other hand, perhaps in a small way, she was hoping to see him.

She had completed three quarters of her walk when her cell phone rang again. This time it was Carla.

"Hey, Susi Q!" came Carla's booming voice.

"Carla, what's happening there?"

"First of all, everything is okay."

"Thank God for that! I was afraid there was some trouble at my house."

"Nah." Carla replied. "We keep having the same few people show up every day looking for you and I keep telling them the same thing. But they must have nothing better to do cause they keep coming back!"

"So what's the big news then?"

"Oh yeah, you won't believe this, Susie."

"I won't even know it till you tell me for God sakes! What the hell is it?" Susan yelled. She knew that Carla was sometimes absent minded but this was ridiculous.

"Yesterday, there were two men in business suits who showed up at the house. They were sitting in a car in front of your house when I got there."

"Who were these men?"

"Well, at first I was afraid they might be bad guys like the kind we ran into in France, so I tried to ignore them. But after a while one of the men got out of the car and asked me if I knew where you were."

"Oh! You didn't tell them, did you?"

"Of course not! I told them I didn't know where you were. Maybe you were somewhere in Europe."

"And what did they say?"

"They asked if I had any way to get in touch with you. I said sometimes you called me from wherever you were but I didn't know how to contact you."

"That was smart of you, Carla."

"Hey, this broad wasn't born yesterday you know?"

"Then what?"

"Then the guy handed me his business card and asked if you would contact him. Turns out he's a New York lawyer."

"No way I'm gonna do that, Carla,."

"Wait, Susie, there's more."

"I'm listening."

"This morning the guy showed up at my house."

"Did you let him in?"

"Not at first, but after we talked outside I did."

"And what did he want from you?"

"This is the part you won't believe, Susie. He handed me a check for a million dollars."

"A million?"

"Uh huh, a million bucks."

"And what did he want for his million dollars?"

Susan could hear Carla clear her throat on the other end of the phone.

"Here's the deal, Susie. If you give him the box I get to cash the million dollar check and you get two million!"

"Two million?"

"That's what he says."

"So who is this guy that is willing to pay three million bucks for the prayer box?"

"His name is Benson. He just said that he's a lawyer who represents a client in New York."

"Well, I hope you told him I'm not interested in his money!"

"No, Susie, I just told him I would talk to you whenever you called."

"Did he say what they wanted the prayer box for?"

"I asked him that and he said he didn't know. He was a lawyer representing his client who wants to buy the box and that's all he knew."

"Well, I'm not interested in selling the prayer box, Carla!"

"I thought you would say that Susie, but please just listen to me."

"Go ahead."

"You know, things have been tight for me since my last divorce. I've got a deadbeat ex who never comes through with my alimony checks. I'm living day to day, week to week trying to make ends meet."

"Can't Danny help you?"

"Danny got fired from his job at the Hilton and now he's trying to pick up odd jobs to help out. He can barely take care of himself, Sue!"

Susan thought for several minutes before she responded to Carla.

"Look, Carla, I know things are tough for you but I can't imagine giving up this prayer box for money."

"I know how you feel, honey. All I'm asking you to do is think about it. Think about all of the good you can do with two million dollars. And yes, I'm asking you to think about me, your best friend, and how this would help me."

Susan was breathing heavily.

"Will you at least think about it, Susie? That's all I'm asking"

"Okay, Carla," Susan said reluctantly. "I'll call you in a couple of days."

As she ended the call she looked up to see Jeff standing in front of her. She began to walk away but stopped when he said "Sue, please talk to me."

"Jeff, I…."

"I don't understand, Sue, what did I do?"

"Please leave me alone, Jeff."

With that Jeff walked away. This would be his last attempt to talk to Susan. What might have been, he thought.

*　*　*

Susan returned to the house and went into her bedroom to get dressed for dinner. Two minutes later her son-in-law knocked on her bedroom door.

"Sue, can I talk to you for a minute?" David asked.

"Sure," Susan responded and opened the door. David came inside the room and sat on the bed.

"I need your advice, Sue," he said stoically.

"Sure, David, anything."

"It's Rachel," he said, his voice quivering, "It's really bad!"

"Oh no, David!"

"I'm not a neurologist but what I have shown the MRI to several other doctors this week and they all say the same thing. It looks like something called pontine glioma."

"What's that?"

"It's a tumor on the brain stem."

"Brain stem?"

"The brain stem is the part of the brain connected to the spinal cord. It is in the lowest part of the brain, just above the back of the neck. It's the part of the brain that controls breathing, heart rate, and the nerves and muscles used in seeing, hearing, walking, talking, and eating."

"Oh my God, David, what does this mean?"

"Susan, I hope I'm wrong. But if my diagnosis is correct there may be no hope for my Rachel." With that he began to cry. "And I can't bear to tell Jenny about this. It will break her heart! I've been holding back all week, trying to avoid telling Jenny, but I feel like somehow I am betraying her."

David cried for two minutes. Susan said nothing until he regained his composure. "What happens next, David?"

"On Monday we'll take her to Mass General to see Stan Carpenter. They'll probably do another MRI there for better delineation." David was sniffing between sentences. "Then Stan will tell us what he finds and what the next steps are."

"So what are you going to tell Jenny in the meantime?"

"That's why I'm talking to you, Sue." David took a deep breath. "Should I tell her what I think now or wait until we see Stan Carpenter? Keeping this from her has been eating me up inside."

Susan thought for a moment. "David, there's nothing Jenny can do right now except worry. She's already falling apart over this. I think you should wait to see what the other doctor says."

"Okay, thanks. That's what I was thinking, but I appreciate your advice. And please, don't tell Jenny that I talked to you about this."

"Of course, David, of course I won't."

David hugged his mother-in-law and walked out the door. As he reached the door he turned and asked "Can we use your prayer box for our little girl!?"

Susan was hesitant to answer this question. "I was told, in no uncertain terms, that the prayer box won't work on me or my family, only strangers."

"That doesn't seem fair, does it?"

"No, David, it sure doesn't."

As David walked away Susan thought about the prayer box that Jeff's mother had. He had buried it with her. Could it still work? Could it help Rachel?

She was very hurt by what she saw at Jeff's house the and especially by what Danielle had said about him. But this was about Rachel, not about her feelings toward Jeff. She needed Jeff and she needed the prayer box right away.

She grabbed her cellphone and called Jeff.

Jeff was shocked when he the call come through from Susan. Had she changed her mind?

"I'd like to talk if it's okay with you Jeff."

Jeff took a few seconds to respond. "Of course, Sue. I was hoping that I would hear from you. It's been over a week and I don't know what's going on with us."

"Can you pick me up at six?"

"I'll be there."

* * *

Jeff picked Susan up at six for the start of a very somber drive. Susan was quiet for the first few minutes as they drove out of the neighborhood.

After what seemed like several minutes of silence Jeff broke the ice. "I know you're upset about your granddaughter," he said. "but I need to ask you why you won't answer my calls. Obviously I did something wrong, but I don't know what it was. If you tell me then maybe I can fix it."

Susan pondered for a moment, finally summoning the strength to confront Jeff about Danielle. "I walked back to your house after you dropped me off last Saturday night."

"Oh?"

"I was hoping to see you and continue our date."

"I sense a big 'but' coming."

Susan took a deep breath. "I ran into Danielle as she was leaving your house."

"I see."

"Jeff, I will not be made a fool of!"

"I would never do that, Sue. That's not who I am."

"That's the problem, Jeff. I don't know who you are. We've only known each other a short time and I fell head over heels for you, only to find that you were still seeing Danielle."

"That's not how it was, Sue. You have to believe me."

"You told me you broke up with her, Jeff. I believed you but that was a lie."

"No Sue, you've got it all wrong."

"I don't think so. I know what I saw."

Susan was beginning to cry. Jeff reached across the seat to touch her but she pushed his hand away.

"Please let me explain."

"I'm not ready for that yet, Jeff. Right now I can only focus on my granddaughter. I need your help."

As Susan explained what she had learned about Rachel's condition Jeff was aware of the emotional burden this placed on Susan.

"You said you need my help," Jeff said. "I'll do anything, just tell me what I can do."

Susan was quick to respond. Her thoughts quickly turned from her anger with Jeff to her very sick granddaughter. "You said you buried the prayer box with your mother, right?"

"That's right, and I would dig it up in a minute if it meant helping Rachel, but I think it takes a court order to do that."

"It might not be necessary to dig up the box, Jeff." Susan said.

"Why not?"

Susan hemmed for a moment. She was not ready to reveal the truth about her prayer box, but she would if it meant saving her granddaughter. She knew that her prayer box would be of no help to Rachel, but Beverly Morton's box certainly could.

"Well," Susan said, choosing her words carefully. "Do you remember telling me that your mother asked you to keep the prayer box open when you placed it in her casket?"

"Yes! Yes she did." Jeff replied. "Those were her explicit instructions. And I did open it before we closed the casket. Why? Does that make any difference?"

Susan spoke softly. "Jeff, I've heard a little about these prayer boxes, and I think there's a possibility that it can work from inside your mother's grave."

"Really?" Jeff asked. "Where did you hear this?"

"That's not important right now, Jeff, but I'd like to bring Rachel to your mother's grave site tomorrow to see if it helps."

"Of course," Jeff replied. "anything to help Rachel. And I will do whatever it takes to try to save her. I only hope that you will eventually give me a chance to prove to you that I am not a liar and a cheater."

Susan did not respond. Instead she asked "Can you pick me and the kids up at one o'clock tomorrow?"

"Absolutely." Jeff replied. He started to ask again for a chance to explain but chose not to.

Their drive ended at Jennifer's doorstep. Susan popped out of the car without a kiss, without a goodbye.

CHAPTER 31

Sunday was always a quiet day in the Cohen lake house. No camp for the kids, no tennis for Jennifer, and usually David was there for the weekend. This Sunday was particularly difficult as Jennifer searched for things to keep Rachel's mind, and her own, preoccupied, so as not to keep thinking about the brain tumor. Her own mind was preoccupied with thoughts about Rachel and, in addition, she could not get Jeff out of her mind either.

Was I too hard on him, she thought. Here he knows how angry I am and yet still he is willing to help save my granddaughter. That speaks volumes about the man, she thought.

Shortly after lunch Susan launched her plan.

"Jenny, Jeff is picking me up to go for ice cream in a few minutes. Can we take the kids with us?"

"I don't know, mom. I think Rachel needs to rest at home."

David walked into the kitchen and heard the conversation. "I think that's a good idea, honey," he said. "She'll enjoy the ice cream and there's no risk in taking her."

Jennifer sighed. "Okay, it sounds like doctor's orders!"

As Susan headed for the front door her daughter said, "Did you patch things up with Jeff last night?"

Susan shook her head, no.

Within minutes, Susan, Adam, and Rachel were in Jeff's car, headed towards Dairy Queen. Susan noticed that Jeff had brought two bouquets of flowers.

"Are those for your mother's grave?" she asked.

"One of them is for her." He replied ."And the other is for you—- if you will let me give them to you."

Jeff reached out the flowers toward Susan. She thought for a minute and took them from his grasp. "Thank you," she said.

"Sue, I didn't sleep at all last night. All I could think about was you. And the thought that I hurt you just kills me."

Susan looked at Jeff and whispered, "Please, not here, not now."

After a silent few minutes of driving they arrived at the ice cream shop.

"Can I get a blizzard, grandma?" Adam asked. "That's what mom always gets for us."

"Sure you can," Susan replied. "What is it?"

"You don't know what a blizzard is, grandma?" Rachel asked, "We get them all the time!"

"I love blizzards too, kids!" Jeff added, as he turned towards Susan. "It's like an ice cream smoothie."

"I want Peanut butter cup!" Adam said.

"And what's your choice, Rachel?" Jeff asked. He tried too maintain a happy face even though he was burning inside.

"Chocolate chip cookie dough."

The kids piled back into the car with their blizzards as the adults each ordered a small cone. Susan began to pay for the order when Jeff stopped her.

"Please," he said as he opened his wallet. "Let me get this."

Susan smiled. Up until last she was finding more things about Jeff that she really liked. But can he be trusted, she asked herself. Was she ready to let him explain himself? She hoped to know the answer when the timing was right, but right now they needed to get to the cemetery.

"Kids," Susan said carefully. "Jeff would like to make a stop on the way home."

Rachel and Adam were so immersed in their blizzards that neither heard nor responded to their grandmother. Jeff drove twenty miles to Hooksett and, as they passed the gates of the cemetery Adam finally realized that they weren't at his house. "Where are we?" he asked.

"It's a cemetery, honey," Susan replied. "Jeff just wants to drop off some flowers at his mother's grave."

By this time both children had finished their Blizzards and were totally involved with their iPhones. Jeff drove into the parking lot and found a space as close as possible to his family grave site. It would only be a short walk to the grave.

"Hey, kids," Susan said as she turned towards them. "The rules say that we can't leave you alone in the car so we need you both to come with us."

"Oh, do we have to?" Rachel whined.

"That's the rules," Jeff said.

"What rules?" Adam said defiantly. "I don't see any rules!"

"Look," Susan responded quickly. "Jeff was nice enough to buy you ice cream. The least you can do is walk with us to pay your respects to his mother."

Adam groaned, but both he and Rachel reluctantly got out of the car and followed Jeff about a hundred yards to his family grave site.

The site was marked by a large stone that said MORTON. Under the family name the stone was divided into three sections. The far left section had the name

MICHAEL

April 12, 1947

October 1, 1967

On the far right the stone had the name

DONALD

June 14, 1923

May 5, 2014

The middle section of the stone was blank, and the ground in front of it was still fresh with dirt from the hole having been dug recently. His father and brother's sections were covered with grass.

Jeff stood solemnly in front of the grave and said, "Hi, mom, the engraving for you will be done next week."

Susan walked beside Jeff. He smiled at her as if to say thank you. He reached out his hand but Susan did not take it. He then turned towards Rachel and handed her the bouquet of flowers.

"Rachel," he said. "would you do me the honor of placing these flowers down on top of my mother's grave?"

Rachel looked stunned to be asked to do this. She hesitated until her brother said, "Go ahead, Rach."

Rachel accepted the bouquet from Jeff and slowly walked towards the gravestone. At one point she hesitated as if to again ask permission to walk on the grave. Jeff nodded as Rachel bent down and gently placed the flowers on Beverly Morton's grave.

She began to walk back when Susan said, "Wait, Rachie, stay there for a second. I want to get a picture of this."

"Grandma!" Rachel protested, but Susan was not taking no for an answer. She reached into her handbag and removed her cell phone.

"Okay, now let me get a shot of this," she said as she snapped the photo. "Now Adam, you get in the photo with your sister."

For five minutes Susan kept finding reasons to take more and more photos while Rachel was standing directly above the buried prayer box. She wasn't sure how long it would take for the box to work, or if would it even work at all, but she was determined to give it ample opportunity to perform one more miracle for her granddaughter.

As they walked back to the car, Rachel turned to her brother and said, "That was so weird!"

"Old people!" Adam replied

Twenty minutes later, Jeff's car pulled up in front of Jennifer's house. Both Jennifer and David were waiting outside for them.

"Where have you been?" Jennifer yelled to her mother as she exited the car. "We were worried sick, It doesn't take that long to get ice cream!"

"Oh I'm so sorry, Jenny," Susan replied. "Jeff had some flowers for his mother's grave and we just went to drop them off."

Jennifer turned to her daughter. "Are you okay, Rachel?"

"Yeah, mom. It was kinda fun!"

As he was leaving Jeff turned to Susan and asked "Can I call you later?"

Susan nodded her approval.

After Jeff left the house Jennifer turned to her mother and asked, "Is everything okay with you two?"

"Not yet, honey, not yet."

A few minutes later Susan's cell phone rang and she noticed that the call was from Jeff. For the first time in a week she answered his call.

"Sue, I'd like to take you to dinner tonight. I hope you will say yes. If your answer is no I will be heartbroken but I promise I will never bother you again."

Susan hesitated for a moment. She held her hand over the speaker and whispered to Jennifer. "He wants to see me tonight."

"Go, mom!" was her daughter's fast reply.

Susan returned to the call. "Okay, can you pick me up at six?"

"I'll be there."

"Remember, mom," Jennifer said after Susan finished her call. "He's a good man. And the fact you both had prayer boxes means that you were brought together for a reason."

"I'm hoping to see the goodness in him tonight, honey."

CHAPTER 32

Jeff picked Susan up on time. She had two admit that she was happy to see him and she hoped that he would have a good explanation for the Danielle late night visit. This was it. Either she trusted him or their relationship was over.

Jeff drove away from Jennifer's house and, as soon as he exited the community he found a secluded spot to stop the car. He immediately turned to Susan.

"Sue," he said quietly, "I fully understand why you are upset with me. But I hope after you hear this you will see that I am not a dishonest man."

"Okay, Jeff," she replied sternly, "you helped Jenny find me in Paris and you did a wonderful thing for my granddaughter today. I will always be grateful to you, and for that I certainly owe you a chance to explain. But I'm just telling you, it better be good."

Jeff took a deep breath. "I did have a relationship with Danielle. It was very short, and, as soon as I realized my feelings for you I broke it off with her. I told you that and it was the God's honest truth."

"Okay then, what was she doing at your house late at night?"

"As my realtor she had a key to my house, and when I came home from our date she was sitting in the house waiting me. I never invited her to come over."

"She was waiting for you? Waiting for what?"

"Honestly, she wanted sex. That's all it was to her. There was no feeling behind it, just sex."

"So, did she get what she wanted?"

"Absolutely not!" Jeff turned and looked Susan straight in the eye. "I was furious that she was in my house so I fired her as my realtor on the spot and told her to leave. That must be when you came walking up to the house."

"Yes it was," Susan said. "But when I saw her she was buttoning up her blouse."

"That could only have been her putting on a show to get back at me. I told her there was someone else and I guess she figured you were that someone."

"She asked if I was your girlfriend."

"And what did you say?"

"I said I was a friend. And then she told me that you were a player."

"A player? Me? That's laughable, Sue. For my entire life I have aways been a one woman man. I have never been anything even close to a player."

"I didn't know, Jeff. We've only known each other for a short time."

"Yes we have, Susan, but the truth is that I am falling in love with you. And I would never, ever, do anything to hurt you."

Susan looked in Jeff's eyes and saw that he was crying.

"You know," Jeff continued, "throughout my life I have done plenty of dumb stupid things that I regret. But I have never deliberately been mean or dishonest to anyone."

Susan's guard came down. She was ready to believe Jeff and she was angry at herself for shutting him out this past week. This is a good man, she thought, a decent man, and I almost let him go.

"Go back to the falling in love part again," she said with a grin.

"It's true, Sue. I am falling in love with you. Please believe me!"

"I'm starting to believe you, Jeff," Susan replied. "and I'm starving. So let's go to the diner, okay?"

"Thank you for believing me and giving me a chance to explain. I feel horrible that this almost caused me to lose you."

"Well, I'm still here."

"So, can we please put this whole thing behind us and pick up where we left off?" He reached out his hand and this time she took it.

"I'm willing to try."

They arrived at the diner and sat down to eat. Jeff loved the diner because they served breakfast all day long, including dinner time.

"This place amazes me," Jeff said as they sat down at a booth. You can order any kind of food here, Chinese, Greek, Italian, Mexican, it doesn't matter. And it's all good!"

Susan ordered a Greek salad and Jeff ordered the big breakfast which consisted of two eggs over easy, two pancakes, two link sausages, and a pile of home fried potatoes. Susan looked at Jeff's dish when it arrived and she joked, "Is there another person coming to help you eat all that?"

Jeff laughed, which made Susan very happy. She appreciated that Jeff had such a positive outlook on life and that he was able to find humor in so many things. He was even able to laugh at himself.

"So you are not a liar, or a cheater, so is there anything wrong with you, Jeff?" Susan asked with a smile. "Anything at all?"

"Wrong?" Jeff quickly replied. "You mean like, am I an axe murderer or something like that?"

"No, I'm sure you're not an axe murderer." Susan paused for a second. "Are you?"

They both laughed as the absurdity of the conversation became evident.

"No," Susan continued. "You said you did a lot of dumb things so I was wondering what is it about you that's not so perfect."

"Hmm," Jeff replied. "Let me think." He placed his index finger under his chin and feigned deep thought. "Well, I must tell you that I snore."

Susan took a brief moment to soak in Jeff's comment. Does this mean that he expects us to be sleeping together? I'm certainly not ready for that, she thought.

"Well, that's not a problem at all for me," she said. "My Steven snored so loud that he would often wake himself up!"

"Oh geez, I'm not that loud. At least I don't think so."

"I used to listen to music on my iPod every night and that drowned out the snoring."

"I see that the lady is as smart and resourceful as she is beautiful!"

Susan spoke in her best Scarlett O'Hara southern accent. "Why Doctor Morton, are you trying to seduce me?"

"Well, this is our third date," Jeff laughed. "and you know what they say about third dates."

"No, what do they say about third dates?" Susan was enjoying the back and forth. She had missed that when they were apart.

Jeff took a bite of food from his plate. "Well, actually, I don't remember. But it must be really good!"

The two laughed. Their conversation had gone back to the cute banter that she loved so much. She was completely ready to put the Danielle incident behind them.

But then the conversation once again turned serious when Jeff asked, " So what happens next with Rachel?"

"I'm not sure," Susan replied. "Jenny and David are taking her to Mass General tomorrow and I guess then we'll know for certain."

"I hope the prayer box works for her, Sue."

"Me too," she replied. "Me too."

Jeff took a bite of food and said, "Let me ask you something."

"Sure."

"You told me you know something about prayer boxes, and you said my mother's prayer box might still work if it was open in her coffin. How did you know that, Sue?"

Susan gathered her thoughts and responded slowly in a whisper. This was the moment she had been waiting for. She took a deep breath and said, "Because I have a box, too."

"You have a prayer box?" Jeff started shouting, but quickly realized the need for privacy. The words "prayer box" were mouthed, not spoken.

"I do, Jeff. And, just like your mother, I don't know how it got to me."

For the next hour, Susan told Jeff the whole story about her prayer box. She told him about her trips to New York, Israel and France, about meeting Dina Eliezer at the Wailing Wall, about visiting the grave of Sister Katrine in Paris, and how some men tried to kill her and take the prayer box.

"Now it all makes sense to me," Jeff said. "So that's why your life was in danger."

Susan nodded. "Yes, and what are the odds that you would run into my daughter just as she was trying to reach me to warn me?"

"It's amazing," Jeff replied.

Susan completed her story, telling Jeff about the mob scene in front of her Florida house and how that was what had brought her to Miracle Lake this summer.

Jeff was fascinated. "And then you met me," he said, "and I went and told you that my mother had a box just like yours!"

"Yes, and you can imagine how I felt about that."

"But, why didn't you tell me your story then?" he asked

"I really didn't know you at first, Jeff, and I was afraid to tell anybody." She reached across the table and took Jeff's hands in hers. "But things are different now. At least for me they are. I shouldn't speak for you."

"I'll speak for myself, Susan," Jeff replied. "What I told you in the car is the absolute truth. I am falling head over heals in love with you, Susan Gold."

"Oh, me too!" Susan blurted out immediately. "And I'm so sorry that I doubted you."

"It's okay. I fully understand. I know it's only been a short time, Sue, but that's all it took for me. I think you are an amazing woman!"

"And that's exactly what I told Jenny about you!" Susan replied with a grin. "You know, she's been trying to fix us up since the day I got here."

"That means a lot to me, Sue. I wouldn't want Jenny to feel that it was too soon."

"I really don't know what the so called rules are. How long is a widow supposed to wait?"

"I don't know the answer to that question, Sue," Jeff said. "But if Jenny's okay with us being together that means that maybe she feels that her dad is also okay with it."

"My Jenny is a very wise young woman. She always has been."

Jeff lifted his coffee cup. "Well then, here's to Jenny!"

"And here's to us."

They each stood halfway up and reached across the table until their lips met.

They sat back down and Susan said, "Jeff, do you think it's a coincidence that we met?"

Jeff thought for a minute. "You know, I'm a big believer in fate," he said. "And I honestly believe that God brought us together with our two prayer boxes."

Susan smiled. "And I'm so glad he did!"

"Hey, let me ask you something." Jeff offered. "If you have a prayer box then why did we have to take Rachel to my mother's grave?"

"I don't know if your mother told you this but I was given specific instructions that the prayer box would not work on me or my family. I received it to do good deeds for others, not for myself."

"You know, now that you mention it, she did tell me that. I asked her why she didn't use it when my dad got sick and that's what she told me."

"But I learned something in France." Susan said quietly.

"What was that?"

"You see, I found the grave site of the lady who had the prayer box before me. She died the exact day I was born!"

"Wow!"

"And the nuns told me that when she died they buried the box open in her casket and it still performed miracles even after she died."

"Oh God! Please let my mother's prayer box save Rachel!"

Susan chose not to bring up the subject of Carla and the three million dollars, but she would definitely do it soon. She valued Jeff's advice on how to handle it.

They left the diner in Jeff's car and he invited Susan to come back to his place for a nightcap.

"It's been a long day," Susan said. "And tomorrow I'll be in charge of Adam when Jenny and Dave take Rachel to Boston. Is it okay if I take a rain-check?"

The minute those words left her mouth Susan began to worry. *Did I make a mistake? This man and I just expressed our love to each other and I brushed him off. What will he think of me?*

Jeff reached across the seat and took Susan's hand in his.

"It's okay, sweetheart, I understand completely," he said lovingly. "I hope that we can be together for a long time and we'll have plenty of time for nightcaps."

As Jeff kissed Susan goodnight all she could think about was how lucky she was to have this wonderful man in her life, and how she had almost let him go.

"Please pray for Rachel," she said as she walked into the house. She was so happy to have Jeff back.

CHAPTER 33

The next day, Susan watched as her daughter left the house with her son-in-law and granddaughter.

"Call as soon as you know something," she whispered to Jennifer as they walked out the door.

She made breakfast for Adam and drove him to camp. On her way back she stopped at Jeff's house, rang the doorbell and waited two minutes for Jeff to open the door. He was still in his pajamas, short pants and a tee shirt. Even though he was disheveled he still looked fabulous to Susan.

"Hi!" he said with a wide grin. "Come in, please!"

As she walked in she realized that this was the first time she had ever been in Jeff's house. She looked around at the sparse decorations. Jeff noticed what she was doing and said, "Welcome to my staged house!"

"Oh, it's nice!"

"Yeah, real nice." Jeff laughed, "and sterile!"

As she explored the surroundings Susan noticed a framed aerial view of Jeff's house. "This is great!" she said. "How did you get a picture like this?"

"Oh," Jeff replied, choosing his words carefully. "That's something realtors do when they sell houses. I guess it's done by a drone."

"Did you put the house on the market?"

Jeff moved close to Susan and kissed her gently on the lips. "No I thought I would but I'm having second thoughts. I haven't listed it yet and, like I said, I fired Danielle. I might never sell this sell house."

"Really, why not?"

"I love Miracle Lake, Sue," he said quietly. "I love my walks around the lake, the beauty and serenity of the place. But once mom passed I really had nobody to give me a reason to stay here. Until now!"

Susan thought about what Jeff was telling her. Was he planning to stay at Miracle Lake because of me? Is he expecting me to move in with him and stay here? It's way too early to make a decision like that, she thought.

"Let's walk," she said as she grasped Jeff's hand.

"Okay, let me get my sneakers on."

* * *

The ninety minute ride to Boston was very somber. Hardly a word was spoken. Rachel sat in the back seat playing games on her iPhone as her parents sat silently in the front seats. On the back seat next to Rachel was a manila envelope containing the films of the MRI that was done at Concord Hospital.

They arrived at Mass General Hospital and found their way to the neurology department. Stan Carpenter was waiting for them in the lobby. He shook David's hand, hugged Jennifer, and reached out his hand to Rachel.

"Hi, Rachel," he said with a smile. "My name is Doctor Carpenter. How are you feeling today?"

"Good." Rachel replied.

At that moment a young woman in a white lab coat came into the lobby. She had a stethoscope around her neck. She smiled as she approached.

"Rachel, this is Doctor Lewis," Stan said. "She's going to examine you and give you another MRI like the one you had on Saturday. This one will give us a little more information."

Rachel nodded.

Stan Carpenter turned to Jennifer. "Mom, will you go with Rachel for the exam please?" Stan said. "Dad and I will look at the last MRI and then we can all get back together shortly."

With that, Jennifer and Rachel exited the lobby with Doctor Lewis. David and Stan walked into Stan's office. David opened the manila envelope he was carrying. In an instant the films were placed on a light box and the two doctors were looking at the images of Rachel's brain.

Stan Carpenter stood with hand on chin and stared at the images for several minutes. David watched and waited for his friend to speak.

"It's not good, Dave," Stan said firmly.

David took a deep breath. "That's what I thought," he replied.

Stan pointed at the screen. "You see this?"

David nodded.

"Pontine glioma," Stan said.

"That"s what I thought," David replied. He then opposed for a moment to gain his composure. "What can you do for her, Stan?"

Stan sighed. "Well, I'm afraid operating would be impossible. About the only treatment we have is radiation."

David gulped. His worst nightmare was about to be confirmed.

"But that won't save her."

Stan placed his hand gently on his friend's shoulder. "I'm so sorry, Dave. I wish there was something else I could say."

Two minutes later there was a knock at the door, and in walked a lab technician with Rachel's MRI films. "We didn't wait for a radiologist, Doctor Carpenter. We knew you wanted these, stat!"

"Thank you, Sarah," Stan said, as he removed the films from their envelope. He quickly placed the new films on the light box to compare them to the ones David had given him.

"Wait a minute!" he yelled. "Sarah, I need you!"

Sarah hurried back into the room.

"These are the wrong films," Stan said sternly. "Please go back and get me the right ones. And quickly!"

"Yes, sir," Sarah replied and she ran out of the office.

"I can't believe this can happen in the best hospital in the world," Stan said. "I'm sorry, Dave, but it should just be a few more minutes."

The two doctors waited five minutes until Sarah returned with another set of films. Once again Stan placed them on the light box and yelled, "What the hell is going on here?"

"I'm sorry, sir." Sarah said.

Stan picked up the phone and called Paula Resnick, the head of the Radiology Department. "Paula," he said sternly, "We've got a problem."

*   *   *

In minutes Susan and Jeff were on the lake path walking and talking. As usual the conversation was easy. When they passed by the sandy beach they saw people bathing in the water.

"I wonder if Miracle Lake is still performing miracles now that my mother's prayer box is gone?" Stan asked.

Susan pondered a moment and replied. "Well, maybe my prayer box is doing the job now."

"Oh, I never thought about that," Jeff said. Then he paused, smiled, and added, "I guess you'll just have to stay here then. Miracle Lake needs you, Sue!"

They walked in silence for a few minutes until Susan decided that the time was right to tell Jeff about the money offer.

"I spoke to my friend Carla yesterday."

"She's the one who went with you to Paris, right?"

Susan nodded. "Carla's been my closest friend for years, Jeff. She was there for me when Steven died, she was there when I found the prayer box, and she went with me to Israel and France to learn about the box. Now she's checking my house every day while I'm gone."

"She sounds like a dear friend, Sue." Jeff replied. "I hope I can meet her some day."

"So, yesterday Carla called me and told me that a man offered her one million dollars, and me two million, if we would give him the prayer box."

"Really? And why does this man want the prayer box so badly?"

"He wouldn't say. He just said he was a lawyer representing a client who wanted the box."

"So what was your answer?"

"My answer was absolutely not, but then Carla told me how badly she needed the money and I started to have second thoughts."

* * *

In a few minutes Doctor Paula Resnick was in the office with Stan and David. They exchanged pleasantries as Stan walked over to the light box.

"Here's the MRI that was done on David's daughter ten days ago at Concord," he said.

Paula stared at the MRI on the screen. She immediately looked at David and said "I'm so sorry!"

Stan then placed the two sets of MRI films that he had received from Sarah.

"And these are what are supposed to be the MRI films for the same girl that were taken at our hospital today!"

"That's impossible!" Paula said as she looked closely at the film.

"Is there something wrong with our equipment?" Stan asked.

"Absolutely not," Paula replied firmly.

"Then maybe you can explain to me how a nine year old girl can have a Pontine Glioma on Saturday and it completely disappears on Monday!"

Paula paused for a moment. "The only thing I can think of, Stan, is that the problem was at Concord. Maybe they gave Dave the wrong films."

"No, that didn't happen," David responded quickly. "I was there for the test and I looked at the films the second they were ready."

"Okay," Stan said, "none of that matters right now. Paula, can you repeat the MRI one more time right now?"

"Of course, and I'll be right there to read it myself."

David and Stan sat quietly in the office as they waited to hear from Paula. In a few minutes the phone rang. Stan answered, listened for a moment, and said, "Okay, thanks."

He then turned to David and said "Dave, your little girl has no tumor. She's as healthy as any nine year old can possibly be!"

David began to cry. This time they were tears of joy. He hugged his friend and said, "Thank you! It makes no sense, but thank you so much!"

"I'd like to take credit for this, Dave," Stan said. "But this was something far bigger than me! Let's keep checking her every six months just to be sure."

One minute later Jennifer and Rachel walked into the office with Doctor Lewis. David hugged his wife and daughter and said, "She's fine honey, she's fine!"

Jennifer broke down. She hugged her husband, her daughter, and Stan Carpenter too.

"But" she began to say.

"We don't know what happened," her husband replied. "All we know is that somehow between a week ago Saturday and today that tumor just disappeared!"

"Her examination bears that out," Doctor Lewis interjected. "She has no symptoms."

"So, how do you feel right now, Rachel?" Stan asked with a smile.

"Good." Rachel responded. "Can I get a blizzard on the way home?"

"Honey, you can have anything you want!" her mother replied.

CHAPTER 34

After their walk Susan and Jeff drove to the diner for brunch. As they sat down in the same booth they had been seated in before, Jeff said, "One more time and we can call this our place!"

Susan laughed. "Wouldn't it be fun to have a place where everybody knows your name?"

"Like Cheers!" Jeff said, remembering the old TV show.

"NORM!" they both shouted in unison. People at three other tables turned to see what they were yelling about. Susan and Jeff giggled like two school kids.

They ordered ice tea and then the conversation reverted to Carla and the prayer box.

"You said you were having second thoughts," Jeff said. "What thoughts were you having?"

"Well, on the one hand, I have seen the miracles that the prayer box can do and I want to continue helping people."

"And, on the other hand?" Jeff asked.

Susan thought for a few seconds. "But on the other hand, Carla is my best friend and I can't bear the thought of letting her down."

"I see."

"What do you think I should do, Jeff?"

Jeff thought carefully before he spoke. "Let me ask you this, Sue. Why do you think you were chosen to have the prayer box?"

"I really don't know, Jeff. I've been asking myself that same question since the day I found it!"

"My mother said something about thirty-six righteous people."

"That's right, and for some reason I am one of the thirty-six."

"Yes, you are," Jeff said. He reached across the table and took Susan's hands in his. "And do you think that one of the thirty-six righteous people should sell the prayer box to someone who is not?"

"You're right, Jeff, of course not," she said. "But would a truly righteous person turn her back on her best friend?"

"I don't think so," Jeff answered. "But I think she would try to find another way to help her friend."

"Another way? I wish I could think of another way."

"Well, I believe it'll come to you, Sue. You're a true friend and I am certain that you'll come up with a way to help Carla without having to give up the box."

"I wish I had a good idea."

"Maybe the prayer box itself will provide the answer for Carla."

"You think it can, Jeff?"

"Let's take it one step at a time Sue. First let's find out what happened with Rachel."

"Oh my God, Rachel!" Susan shouted. "I completely forgot! I didn't bring my cell phone. I bet Jenny is trying to call me. Can we go home now?"

With that, Jeff reached in his wallet and left a five dollar bill on the table. They jumped into his Mercedes and raced back to Jennifer's house.

Susan ran to the bedroom to retrieve her cell phone. Sure enough there was a missed call from Jennifer. Quickly she hit the buttons and dialed Jenny.

"Mom, I've been trying to reach you!"

"Where are you, honey?"

"We're at the Dairy Queen, mom. Rachel's eating a blizzard."

"What did the doctor say?"

"Mom, it's a miracle! Rachel has no tumor!"

"No tumor!" Susan shouted.

Jeff heard those words and began dancing around the room. He was ecstatic.

Susan ended the call and gently placed her phone in her handbag. "She said it was a miracle, Jeff. It was a miracle!"

The two danced and hugged and kissed. They hugged and kissed their way to Susan's bedroom. Within seconds they were in the shower together and shortly after that they were in bed. Soon after that they were lying in each other's arms.

This felt different for Jeff. He had always believed that love and sex belonged together. His romps with Danielle were nothing like that. But now he had found a woman to truly love.

They both dozed off, but were awakened by the sound of Jennifer's voice. "Mom, we're home!"

Jeff jumped out of bed naked. He ran to the bathroom where his clothes lay on the floor and quickly dressed.

A quick knock on the door and Jennifer opened it to enter in the room. Susan was still in bed, still naked under the sheets.

"Are you okay, mom?" Jennifer asked.

"Oh sure, Jenny," Susan replied, trying desperately to act casual.

Her attempt was foiled, however, when a loud noise came from the bathroom.

Jennifer smiled at her mother. "Mom, is someone here with you?"

Jeff opened the door sheepishly and walked out of the bathroom.

"It's me," he said with the look of a little boy caught with his hand in the cookie jar. "I'm sorry, I dropped a cup in there."

Jennifer's smile widened. "Well, I guess you guys made up," she said as she walked out of the room. "I've got so much to tell you, mom."

As soon and the door closed Susan lifted herself out of bed, wrapped in the sheet. She walked over to Jeff and hugged him. They kissed and she ducked into the bathroom to get dressed. Jeff waited for her to come out before they both walked downstairs to the kitchen.

Jennifer smiled when she saw the two lovers. "So, how was your day?" she asked with a wry grin.

"Oh, we had a great day, Jenny," Susan replied. "And we're so happy about Rachel!"

"Yes, it truly was a miracle," her daughter replied. She paused for a moment and added, "And I'm wondering if your visit to the cemetery yesterday had anything to do with it."

"Yes, I think it did, Jenny," Jeff replied. "I know you're familiar with your mom's prayer box."

"I am," Jennifer replied, "of course."

"Well, it so happens that my mother had a prayer box, too."

"It was buried with her, Jenny," Susan interjected. She didn't want Jenny to acknowledge that she knew about Jeff's prayer box. "But we thought it could still work on Rachel."

"Oh my God!" Jenny replied. She walked up to Jeff and hugged him. "You saved my daughters life!"

"It wasn't me, Jenny," Jeff responded. "It was your mom who figured out that the prayer box could still work miracles even after it was buried."

David walked into the kitchen, "We owe you both for our daughter's life," he said. "And some day I hope we can do something wonderful for you."

"Thank you, David," Jeff said. "That's very kind. But seeing this happy family and being back together with your mother are the only rewards I need!"

"I'm starving!" Susan said. "We were about to eat at the diner but we realized I left my cell phone here at the house and you wouldn't be able to reach me with the news about Rachel."

"So we came here without eating," Jeff added. "And now I'm starving too!"

As the two headed for the door Jennifer said, with a wink, "Okay, you're both hungry now. Of course you are. You kids behave yourselves!"

CHAPTER 35

Jeff and Susan were back at the diner in a few minutes, sitting at 'their booth'.

After they ordered Jeff said, "Honey, this has been the happiest day of my life!"

Susan loved that he called her 'honey'. As close as she and Steven had been he never called her anything but 'Suze'. From Jeff 'honey' sounded wonderful.

"Jeff," she said softly, "Meeting you was the best thing that has happened to me since Steven died. You saved my granddaughter's life and I will always be grateful."

"Sue, do you remember the movie Pretty Woman?"

"Of course. It's my all time favorite movie!"

"It's in my top ten, too," Jeff replied. "Do you remember the scene at the end when Julia Roberts climbs down the ladder to Richard Gere's limo?'

"Love it!"

"And he says something like 'what does the princess do when she gets rescued by the handsome prince'?"

"She rescues him right back!" Susan shouted.

They laughed together.

"Right!" Jeff said. "And that's what you've done for me, so now we're even!"

Susan pondered what Jeff meant by that. She liked where he was going with this. "So, now you know my favorite movie," she asked. "What's yours?"

"'The Godfather,' of course," was Jeff's quick reply.

"Of course!"

"Followed closely by 'The Godfather, Part 2.'"

"But not 'Part Three,' right?"

"Big letdown," Jeff said. He launched into a bad Al Pacino voice. "Every time I try to get out, they pull me back in!"

"How about TV?" Susan asked."Do you watch?"

"You're gonna laugh at me."

"I won't laugh. What's your favorite TV show?"

Just as Susan took a sip of iced tea Jeff said "The Bachelor."

The iced tea came flying out of her mouth as Susan laughed out loud. "The Bachelor? The Bachelor? I can't believe it!"

"Yeah, I have to admit I'm a sucker for all those shows."

"Wanna know the truth?"

"Yep."

"I like it too! I just never met a man who watches it."

"Hey, remember when the bachelor picked one girl and then dumped her for the number two girl?"

"That was the best!" Susan replied.

"Well, now we can watch it together."

Susan pondered for a moment. "Okay, but it doesn't start until the fall." She sipped her drink again. "And where will we be then?"

"I dunno," Jeff said. "But whoever it is I want us to be together."

"Me too, but where? I need to get back to Florida."

"They say Florida is a nice place to retire," Jeff said.

"Yes, yes it is!" Susan replied. She was excited to think that Jeff might join her in Florida. "Do you play golf?" she asked.

"Do I play golf?" Jeff said in a playful tone. "Why, there was time when I was better than Tiger Woods!"

"Really, when was that?"

"When he was two years old they had him on the Mike Douglas show. I think I was better than him back then," Jeff laughed.

Susan laughed too. She loved Jeff's sense of humor. "And how about tennis?"

Jeff started to reply but Susan quickly interrupted him. "I know, I know!" she said with a grin. "You used to be better than Roger Federer!"

"Absolutely! How'd you guess?"

"We've got a nice country club in my community. Twenty tennis courts and eighteen holes of golf."

"How does this sound?" Jeff offered. "Winters in Florida and summers at Miracle Lake?"

"It sounds wonderful!"

"And here's the best part. If you move into my house with me we can put your prayer box right where mom kept hers!"

"What a great idea! Miracle Lake can still have it's miracles."

"And in the winter we can take the prayer box to Florida and help people there, too."

"Okay" Susan pondered, "but we'll have to find another house. Mine is too toxic. We would forever be dealing with people who want the prayer box."

"I see," Jeff said. "The beauty of my mom's situation is that nobody knew she had the box."

"Jeff?" Susan whispered as she grasped his arm.

"Yes?"

"How would you feel about moving here to Miracle Lake? Both of us, just here, together."

"Just here?"

"This place is like heaven. And yes it gets cold in the winter but we have a fireplace."

"And we have each other to keep us warm, too!" he smiled.

"Maybe in a few years, after all the hubbub about the prayer box has died down, then we can find a place in Florida for the winters."

"I love it, Sue. The truth is wherever you are that's where I want to be."

"So let's do this," Susan said. "Let's fly to Florida and put my house on the market."

"Sounds like a plan," Jeff said. "And while we're down there let's find a way to help Carla."

CHAPTER 36

Susan was excited to tell Jenny about her plans, and Jenny was equally excited that her mom was so happy, and that she would be living so close to her and the kids.

"The kids love their grandma," Jennifer said. "I'm so glad you got to spend so much time with them this summer."

Really, Susan thought, all I did was watch them play video games and whenever I spoke to them they gave me a one word answer. Oh well, she thought, eventually they'll both grow up and realize what a wonderful grandmother they have.

For the next two weeks Susan stayed at Jeff's house. They were living like a married couple and enjoying it immensely. Susan loved the warmth and charm of this man and she especially loved waking up at night and feeling his body next to hers. And no, she thought, his snoring isn't really that bad.

Every day Susan called Carla for an update on the situation at her house. At first she was hoping that it would be safe to return to Florida, but she was enjoying living with Jeff so much that she was happy to hear that there still were people in cars waiting for her. Every day Carla asked about the million dollar offered and Susan put her off.

"That man calls me every day," Carla said. "What should I tell him?"

"Tell him I'll be in Florida next week and I'll make a decision then."

"Don't know if he's gonna wait that long, Suze."

"Well he's just gonna have to, Carla!"

Jeff was pleasantly surprised by how easy Susan was to live with. Often, he thought, people get used to living alone and they have a hard time adjusting to another person in their house, but he found Susan delightful to live with.

Each morning Susan woke to a fresh cup of coffee that Jeff had brewed for them. At nine each day they walked around the lake, hand in hand. Along the way they greeted all of their friends. Only Janice Hanley avoided them, and Jeff was happy for that. He never saw Danielle Mauer again, and that was also a blessing. Some days after the walk they stopped by the tennis courts to hit a few practice balls. Susan could see that Jeff was once a very good player, and each time they played his game got stronger.

They went for lunch most days at the diner. They bought fresh food to cook for dinner, stopped by to see Jenny and the kids, cooked dinner, and ended each day curled up on the sofa together watching television. She loved how Jeff would rub her feet as she lay on the sofa with her feet in his lap.

Some nights were filled with love making and, while she knew the excitement wouldn't last forever, Susan longed for the closeness of Jeff's body and the love he constantly gave her. She was certain that this was real.

The travel plans were made on Southwest Airlines. Sue and Jeff were going to travel to Florida together as a couple. They would avoid her house and stay in a hotel so as not to create a stir in the community. She also wanted to avoid the few remaining people who wanted help from her prayer box. I would love to help them, she thought, but then what would happen next? A flood of more people showing up for help.

Beverly Morton's windowsill plan was looking better and better all the time.

Three days later they were at Manchester Airport ready to fly to Palm Beach. Jeff had ordered the plane tickets for both of them and paid for them as well. Susan had her prayer box safely tucked into her large carry-on handbag, She knew that it would have to go through the x-ray machine but she was hoping that it wouldn't be exposed to the public. The more hidden it remained the better. She couldn't help but recall her most recent harrowing airport experience in Paris, but she felt safe and secure knowing that Jeff was by her side.

They passed though security without incident and boarded the plane for Palm Beach. Once they were seated Jeff said, "I'm really looking forward to this trip, Sue."

"Me too, Jeff."

"I have an old college roommate who lives in Boca and I wanna introduce you to him okay?"

"Absolutely! Any old friend of yours is a new friend of mine."

When they landed in Palm Beach, Jeff rented a car and they made the forty mile ride to Stuart. They pulled up to the Eastern Inn, parked their car and walked into the lobby.

As they moved towards the front desk, Jeff handed the clerk his credit card. He noticed a sign behind the desk that said "This property is owned and operated by the Pantaloni Group."

"Pantaloni?" Jeff said to the young man. "By any chance is that Ernie Pantaloni?'

"Yes, it is," the clerk replied. "Doctor Pantaloni owns several hotels in this area."

Jeff reached for his cell phone and punched in a name from his contact list. In seconds Ernie was on the line.

"Ernie here."

"Ernie Pants!" Jeff shouted, "You'll never guess where I am!"

"Jeff! Where the hell are ya?"

"I'm at the Eastern Inn in Stuart. I had no idea you owned this place."

"Yeah, that's one of my hotels," Ernie replied, "How's the lobby look?"

"Good, Ernie, it looks great. And there's a very nice young man named…"Jeff paused to study the hotel clerk's name tag, "Lawrence, who's taking very good care of us."

"Put Lawrence on the phone with me, will ya?"

Jeff handed the phone to Lawrence and watched as he spoke with his boss. In seconds Lawrence said, "Yes sir, no problem." He handed the phone back to Jeff.

"Your money's no good at my hotels, Jeff." Ernie said firmly. "This one's on me!"

"Hey thanks, Pants," Jeff replied, "I'll call you later so we can get together."

As he hung up the phone Susan was perplexed. "Pants?" She said with a grin. "You know a guy named Pants?"

"He's my old college roommate."

"A dentist?"

"Yes, he was, retired now, but he was always big into real estate. When the rest of us were spending our money on fancy cars and vacations, Pants was saving his money to buy properties in New York, Massachusetts and Florida. It seemed like Ernie Pants knew everybody and everybody knew him."

"Sounds like a smart guy!"

"Smartest guy I know, at least when it comes to making money. He played the game of life like it was a game of Monopoly, and now he's loaded!"

"Hmm," Susan said. "Married?"

"Three times," Jeff responded. "But not now. Not for a few years."

"Wow!" Susan said with a smile. "Have I got a got a girl for him!"

They moved their suitcases into their hotel room and unpacked. Susan called Carla to let her know they had arrived in Stuart and invited her to meet them at the Ale House for dinner.

An hour later, as they walked into the Ale House, Carla was waiting for them. She ran up to Susan and the two friends embraced. Carla pulled away and looked at Jeff.

"And this must be the famous Jeff!" she said as she moved closer to him. "You're even better looking in person than the pictures Susie sent me!"

Carla grabbed Jeff in a tight hug. Susan watched and was taken aback because she thought the hug was a little too tight and lingered a little too long. But that's my Carla, she thought, she'll never change. Jeff was embarrassed and tried to pull away. Finally, Carla released her bear hug and said, "Let's sit down, I'm starving!"

They sat in a booth with Carla on one side of the table facing Susan and Jeff on the other. They ordered drinks.

"Did you go by your house yet, Sue?" Carla asked.

"No, but we will," Susan replied. "What's the latest?"

"Well I think we're almost out of the woods. We're down to only four cars that keep parking there every day. Those people must be really desperate."

"It's so sad," Susan offered. "I really wish I could help them."

"If you do that, honey, we'll be right back where we started!"

"I guess you're right, Carla."

"Sue told me all about you, Jeff," Carla said. "And I guess she told you all about me too."

Jeff smiled.

Susan lowered her voice and said, "Jeff knows all about the box and the offer you had for it."

"Oh, yeah," Carla replied. "The lawyer called me again today. He wants an answer."

Susan paused, took a deep breath. She knew what she was about to say would be devastating to her dear friend. "I'm afraid the answer is no, Carla."

Carla was visibly shaken. "Susie, I can't believe you would let me down like this!"

235

"I know how you feel, Carla, and I'm sorry, but I just can't sell the prayer box. I love you and I hope you'll respect my decision."

"Well, I guess I have no choice now, do I? I'll tell them you said no."

Jeff could see that the conversation between friends was tense. He wanted to say something but he was afraid it might be the wrong thing. He decided to try anyway.

"Carla," he said softly. "You don't know me very well, but Susan has told me so many wonderful things about you. She told me how you were always there for her when she needed you the most."

"Yes, I was." Carla replied. She was beginning to cry.

"And I can see how devastating this is to you right now."

"It is." She was sobbing open now.

"But I want you to know that both Sue and I will do everything in our power to help you through whatever you have to deal with. We will never let you down. I promise you that."

Susan listened carefully to what Jeff was saying. This kind and caring man was giving Carla hope.

"I thank you for that, Jeff. I really do," Carla replied with a sniffle. "But I don't know how you can help me. Things are so bad right now!"

"Well, Sue told me that your son used to work for the Hilton, but he lost that job."

"That's right. He worked in maintenance, but they laid him off. Now he's just doing handyman work."

"Carla, I have a friend who owns a few hotels around here. Perhaps I could talk to him about hiring your son."

Carla's face lit up. "Oh, that would be great!"

"No guarantees of course, but I'll ask him."

"Thank you."

"The guy's name is Ernie Pants," Susan added. "He's an old college roommate of Jeff's. I'd like you to meet him."

"Pants?" Carla said, as the tears subsided. "What kinda name is Pants?"

"It's Pantaloni," Jeff laughed. "But everybody calls him Ernie Pants."

"Italian, hmm…"

"And he's from New York, too!" Jeff said.

"And single!" Jennifer added.

"Let me see, he's Italian, he's from New York, he owns hotels, and he's single, and you want him to meet me?"

Susan and Jeff nodded in unison.

"He must look like a troll!"

Jeff laughed. "No, actually he's a good looking guy."

"As good as you?" Carla asked.

Jeff chuckled. "I'll let you two ladies be the judge of that," he said. "But I can assure you he's not a troll!"

They finished their dinner and as they stood up from the table Susan hugged Carla. "I'll call you tomorrow and let you know if Ernie can meet us for dinner."

"Okay, babe," Carla said. "I love you."

On their way back to the hotel, Jeff said, "She's exactly how you described her, Sue."

"Carla's a little rough around the edges but she really has a heart of gold."

"I think Pants might like her."

"I'll bring the prayer box," Susan said.

CHAPTER 37

As they returned to the hotel Jeff noticed a black SUV following them into the parking lot. They walked out of their car and were startled to hear a man's voice utter the words, "Susan Gold."

Susan turned and saw two men, both dressed in business suits, walking towards her. One of the men was small in stature, had gray hair, and was carrying a brief case. Behind him was a much younger and very large man who looked menacingly at them. The younger man was every bit as tall as Jeff but looked like he weighed at least three hundred pounds.

"My name is Allen Benson," the older man said. He handed her a business card that said that he was an attorney in New York. "And this is my associate, Mr. Green."

Jeff stood between the man and Susan. He thrust his hand out to the man. "My name is Jeffrey Morton," he said. "I am Mrs. Gold's attorney."

Mr. Benson smiled. "Come on now, Doctor Morton, we both know that's not true."

"How do you know us, Mr. Benson?" Susan asked.

"And what do you want?" Jeff said.

"Mrs. Gold, several days ago we made a very generous offer to you through your friend Carla Rintone. Carla just informed me that you have rejected our generous offer. Is that correct?"

"Yes, it is." Susan replied.

Mr. Benson reached into his brief case and removed a check. He handed it to Susan.

Susan stared at the check and was startled by the amount.

"This is for five million dollars!" she said.

"Yes, it is," Mr. Benson replied. "I have now been authorized to increase the offer substantially and I trust that this new amount will be acceptable to you, Mrs. Gold."

"How did you know how to find us?" Jeff asked.

"Ever since we made the offer to Mrs. Rintone we have been following her. We assumed that eventually she would meet with you, Mrs. Gold."

Susan thought for a second and spoke firmly. "Mr. Benson," she said, "there is no amount of money you can offer that will get me to give that prayer box to you!"

Mr. Benson paused for a few seconds and smiled. "Mrs. Gold," he said calmly. "Perhaps I haven't made myself clear enough to you. I represent a very powerful man in New York who wants your prayer box. Now, he has made a very generous offer for the box."

Jeff jumped into the conversation. "And I think she has made herself very clear to you, Mr. Benson. Your client is not getting that box. Not now. Not ever!"

The large, younger man moved forward towards Jeff. He placed his right hand into his breast pocket. Immediately, Mr. Benson held up his right hand, and the younger man froze.

"Let me make sure you both understand," Mr. Benson said. "Giving up the prayer box is not an option for you. Now, you can do it the easy way or the hard way."

"And just what do you mean by 'hard way?'" Jeff said. "Are you threatening us?"

"Sir, I do not make threats," Mr. Benson said. "I simply state facts. My friend and I will be at the Royal Beach Hotel in Jupiter this evening. If you are a smart woman, Mrs. Gold, and I have no doubt you are, you will arrange to deliver the prayer box to me by ten PM. In exchange you will receive your check for five million dollars."

Mr. Benson motioned to his companion. "If we do not receive the prayer box by ten PM then my offer is off the table and I will have no choice but to ask Mr. Green here to take over the transaction."

Mr. Green gave them another menacing look as both men walked back into their black SUV and drove away.

Jeff and Susan walked back towards the hotel.

"I'm scared, Jeff!"

Jeff tried to maintain a calm demeanor but he was also scared. "It sounds like these guys mean business, Sue."

"What are we gonna do?"

Jeff grabbed his cell phone and punched in his friend Ernie Pants.

"Ernie, I need a favor right away."

"Anything, my friend, just name it."

"I'm here with my lady friend, Susan Gold."

"Well, say hello for me."

"Okay, I will. That's why I need you."

"What can I do for you, Jeff, anything."

"Ernie, we were just visited by a man named Allen Benson. He claims to be an attorney in New York who represents a very powerful man."

"Who?"

"Don't know"

"Okay."

"Mr. Benson wants to purchase an old family heirloom from Susan that Susan doesn't want to sell."

"Heirloom, what kind of heirloom?"

"It's a box, Ernie. They call it a prayer box."

"Prayer box? What the hell is that?"

"Not important, Pants. What is important is that he threatened that if Susan didn't bring him the box by ten PM tonight he would send a goon to take it from her."

"What? You're kidding?"

"I wish I was kidding, Pants, but it's true."

"This must be one helluva box, Jeff!"

"It's very special, Ernie. Can you help us?"

"Where is this Mr. Benson now?"

"He said he's staying at the Royal Beach Hotel in Jupiter. He's expecting us to bring him the box by ten PM."

"Okay, Jeff," Ernie said. "Here's what I want you to do. First, get your things and leave the hotel now. You can check into the Sunset Inn on Hutchinson Island. It's one of my hotels. Use the name Julius Irving to check in."

"Okay."

"I'll send a few of my men to talk some sense into this Mr. Benson. I'm certain he'll never bother you or Susan again."

"Are you sure, Ernie?"

"Hey, have I ever let you down?"

"No, Pants, you never have."

"Okay, let's meet tomorrow for dinner at Valentino's," Ernie added. "Seven o'clock, okay?"

"Okay, my friend. Is it okay if Susan brings a friend?"

"Is she a looker?"

"Yep."

"Then I'd be delighted to meet Susan's friend!"

"Good."

"And listen, Jeff, you tell your lady friend not to worry. Pants will take care of everything."

As he ended the call, Jeff turned to Susan. "Nothing to worry about now, Sue. Ernie Pants said he'll take care of everything."

"Really? How is he gonna do that?"

"Honey, I learned a long time ago never to ask how Pants does things. Let's just say Ernie has always been well connected. And I know this, if Ernie Pants says it will be taken care of, then it will be taken care of!"

"From your lips to Gods ears!" Susan replied.

They packed their bags, checked out of the Eastern Inn, and drove twenty minutes to the Sunset Inn on Hutchinson Island. When they arrived they walked up to the front desk. A young lady wearing a blue skirt and jacket greeted them.

"Hello," Jeff said. "My name is Julius Irving."

"Yes, Mr. Irving," the desk clerk said. "We've been expecting you. We have a beautiful ocean front suite waiting for you and Mrs. Irving."

Jeff turned to Susan and winked. "Isn't that nice, Mrs. Irving?" he said.

"Yes, dear it is," was Susan's quick reply.

They settled into their hotel suite to find a bottle of champagne on ice waiting for them. Jeff poured two glasses and they walked out onto the balcony to sit and admire the view of the Atlantic Ocean. They sat and talked for an hour before a knock on the door interrupted them. Jeff looked at his watch, it was ten thirty.

"Oh my God, Jeff!" Susan whispered. "Is that them? How could they find us here?"

"I don't know," Jeff replied, also in a whisper. "Take the prayer box into the bathroom and lock the door. And turn the light off."

Jeff waited until Susan was safely locked in the bathroom before he approached the door. He checked to see that the door was bolted and locked.

"Who is it?" He whispered.

"It's Megan, from the front desk. I have a message for you from Doctor Pantaloni."

Jeff breathed a sigh of relief. He unlocked and opened the door, and was met by the young lady holding an envelope.

"For you, sir," she said as she handed the envelope to Jeff.

"Thank you," he replied. He reached into his pocket and handed her a five dollar bill, walked back into the room, ripped open the envelope, and read the note.

"All set, Jeff," the note said. "Benson and Green have been neutralized. See you tomorrow at seven at Valentino's, Ernie."

Jeff breathed a sigh of relief. "Everything's okay, Sue!" he said proudly. "Ernie Pants took care of it."

Susan came out of the bathroom, hugged Jeff, and they slept well.

CHAPTER 38

The next morning, with the stress of Mr. Benson behind her, Susan called three realtors and arranged for each of them to meet her and Jeff at the Sunset Inn. All three were neighbors. Two were golf friends and one was a tennis partner of Susan's. Susan was not ready to go back to her house, not as long as people were still waiting there for her to return with the prayer box.

"It's gonna be tough to pick one," Susan said to Jeff as they were getting dressed for the day. "Each one is a friend and I might lose two friends no matter what I do!"

"Honey, this is a business decision," Jeff said. "And each of these ladies are professionals. They have to understand that you can only choose one agent."

"Yes, that's true,"she sighed. "But each one thinks I'm gonna choose her!"

"Here's an idea," Jeff offered. "You can make me the bad guy."

"How am I gonna do that?"

"Simple, just tell each of the agents that because you are emotionally attached you're going to let me listen to their presentation and I will choose which one gets the listing."

"So then two of them can hate you!"

"Hate is a pretty strong word, Sue, but you get the idea."

Sue kissed Jeff and said, "You are such a sweet man, but I have to do this."

"And I know you can, honey!"

Jeff and Susan sat in the lobby of the hotel and listened quietly as one by one the agents talked about a listing price and how they planned to market the house. They each also spoke about their experience and success at selling houses. Susan thanked each one and told them she would be making a decision in a few days. After the final one she said to Jeff, "So what do you think?"

Jeff thought for a moment. "I liked them all," he said, "but I would definitely choose the second one."

"Brenda?" Susan asked. "Why Brenda?"

"Because she was the most realistic," Jeff replied. "She was the only one who told you that it might take months to sell your house. Brenda was also very complimentary about her competitors."

"That's true," Susan said quietly, "I liked that too."

"And she was the only one who took the time and expense to have aerial photos taken of your house. I like that."

"Is that what Danielle Mauer did for you at Miracle Lake?"

Jeff was taken aback by the question. He really did not want to discuss Danielle with Susan, or anyone for that matter. She was out of his life as fast as she had entered it and that was just the way he wanted it. He chose not to respond to the question.

"I just felt that Brenda was the most honest and sincere of the three, so that would be my choice."

Susan's cell phone rang and Jeff was relieved to hear the distraction.

"Hi, Carla," Susan answered.

"Are we on for dinner tonight, Susy Q?"

"Yep, seven sharp at Valentino's, okay for you?"

"I'll be there!"

Susan was happy that Ernie had chosen Valentino's restaurant because it was a family owned, small and quiet place. She was hoping that Carla and Ernie Pants would hit it off and she wanted them to have a good place to talk. Valentino's also had great Italian food and she figured Ernie and Carla would both like it.

She and Jeff dressed for dinner and headed to Valentino's. Susan made sure that her prayer box was open inside her handbag.

"Tonight we're gonna see just how powerful this thing is!" she said to Jeff.

The restaurant was only fifteen minutes from the hotel but they left early so Jeff could drive her past her house. She was hoping that by this time of day there would be nobody outside waiting for her.

When they got to the house Susan was relieved to see no cars parked outside. Jeff parked and they went in. Susan quickly moved into her bedroom and grabbed as many of her clothes as she could fit into the one suitcase she had left in the house.

As they scurried back into Jeff's rental car, Susan said, "Sorry, honey, I just don't want to take a chance on those people coming back while I'm here."

"I understand, Sue," he replied. He always understood, Susan thought.

"I mean, some people are a prisoner in their own house and I feel like just the opposite!"

Jeff reached across the car seat and took Susan's hand. "This will all be over soon." he said lovingly. Then he laughed and said "You know, watching you pack that suitcase was like watching that old game show."

"Beat the Clock!" Susan said with a grin.

"Yeah, you remember that show from when we were kids?"

"Tick tock, tick tock!"

They laughed together and reminisced about all of the shows they watched as kids, from Howdy Doody to the old black and white cartoons.

"I still remember the rabbit ears on our tiny little TV!" Jeff said.

"Me too!"

"And then one day my dad told us he had a color TV for us. Michael and I were so excited until we saw our dad with an envelope."

"An envelope?"

"Yeah," Jeff laughed. "He opened the envelope and out came a plastic sheet that he placed over the black and white TV screen."

"No!"

"Yes indeed. It was the most ridiculous thing ever. All it did was make the screen impossible to see!"

Susan laughed as they pulled into the parking lot of Valentino's restaurant. Jeff was happy that she had not mentioned Danielle again.

Ernie was waiting for them at the bar of the restaurant and as they entered he stood up from his bar stool and gave a big hug to his old friend. Susan could see that Ernie was a decent looking man, although it was far too obvious that he was wearing a toupee. If he was so rich, Susan thought, why couldn't he spend the money to get a better rug.

"And you must be Susan!" Ernie said as he hugged her. "Jeff has told me so much about you."

"Only the good stuff, I hope." Susan responded with a smile.

"Absolutely!" Ernie shouted. Susan noticed that his voice was very loud. Who else did she know with a voice like that, she mused.

"Ernie," Jeff whispered. "Thanks for what you did for us last night."

"Ah, it was nothing," Ernie replied.

"But how did you do it, Pants?" Jeff asked, as he ordered drinks for Susan and himself. "How did you get that Benson guy off our backs?"

Ernie sat back down on his bar stool and smiled. "Let's just say I made him an offer he couldn't refuse!"

At that moment Carla walked into the restaurant and came straight to Ernie. She was wearing a skin tight purple dress that looked as though it had been painted on her body. Every curve showed, and Carla had plenty of curves to show.

"I'm Carla Rintone," she said as she held her hand out.

Ernie grasped her hand and said, "Ernie Pantaloni. It's a pleasure to met you Carla."

The maitre d' walked over and said, "Mrs. Gold, your table is ready."

The four sat in a booth. Susan slid in on one side of the table and Carla followed. The two gentlemen sat opposite them. Carla was directly across from Ernie and Susan was hopeful that there would be a connection between them.

They made the obligatory small talk about the weather and ordered their meals. Susan could see that there were no immediate sparks between Ernie and Carla so she tried to break the ice. Just as the main course was served she spoke up.

"So where in Italy is your family from, Ernie?" Susan asked.

"Napoli," he said. "My parents met there and came to the United States together right after the war."

"How about your family, Carla?" Jeff chimed in.

"Palermo," was Carla's response.

The silence from Ernie was deafening.

"Is that anywhere near Napoli, Ernie?" Jeff asked.

"It's not even in Italy," was Ernie's terse response.

"What the hell are you talking about?" Carla yelled.

"She's Sicilian. We don't think of Sicilians as real Italians."

"Why not?' Susan asked.

"Look," Ernie said firmly. "When my mother was alive, God rest her soul, if I brought home a Sicilian girl she would've disowned me!"

"Well, you can kiss my Sicilian ass, you pompous bastard!" Carla shouted. Many of the patrons in the restaurant were watching now.

So much for this evening, Susan thought. What a disaster it was to bring these two together. She opened her handbag gently to see if the prayer box was in there. It was and it was open. At last I found something the prayer box can't do, she thought.

"Okay, okay," Jeff said, trying desperately to salvage the evening. "Let's move on to another topic."

In a flash Carla stood up from her seat in the booth. Susan thought she was going to leave.

But she did not leave. She jumped over to Ernie and grabbed him from behind. It was then that Susan noticed that Ernie was choking. His face had a look of total panic and his skin was turning gray. Carla stood Ernie up and performed the Heimlich maneuver. It took three squeezes before a piece of food was projected from his mouth.

Ernie was stunned. He was breathing again but it was obvious that he was still shaken by what had just happened. Carla calmly walked back and sat down in the booth next to Susan. She causally sipped her drink.

"You saved my life!" Ernie said.

"Yes, I guess I did," was Carla's terse rely. "Not that you deserved it!"

"Look," Ernie said quietly. "I'm sorry if I offended you. You saved my life. And maybe I didn't deserve it but you saved me anyway. How can I ever repay you?"

"You can start by giving her son a job!" Jeff said, seizing the opportunity.

"Sure, ah, what does he do?"

"He's a maintenance man," Carla said. "He worked for the Hilton for a long time but they laid him off a couple months ago. He really needs a job!"

"That's a done deal," Ernie said. He took a napkin from the table and pulled a pen out of his pocket. He wrote down a name and phone number and handed it to Carla.

"You tell your son, what's his name?"

"Danny, err Daniel Rintone."

"Tell Daniel to call this number tomorrow. We'll put him to work right away."

"Thank you." Carla replied. But it was obvious to Susan that her friend still didn't like Ernie and there was no hope of a connection between them. If saving a man's life doesn't do it I don't know what possibly could, she thought.

"But that's not enough to thank you, Carla." Ernie said. "You saved my life. God dammit you saved my frickin' life! You haven't heard the last from me yet."

The dinner finished without any further discussion and they left the restaurant at nine o'clock. As they were leaving, Ernie thanked Carla again. He moved towards her for a hug but it was apparent that she was having none of it.

Jeff and Susan returned to the hotel. They were both amazed by the events that had occurred at the restaurant.

"Can you believe what happened tonight?" Jeff asked.

"Let's start with that line Ernie used," Susan said with a grin. She imitated Ernie's gruff voice. "We made him an offer he couldn't refuse!"

"Straight from The Godfather," Jeff laughed, "my favorite movie!"

"Mine too, now!" Susan replied. She thought for a moment and said, "For a minute I thought Carla was walking out."

"Me too."

"And then I see Ernie choking and Carla saves his life!"

"Definitely a prayer box moment!" Jeff offered with a big smile.

Susan removed the prayer box from her handbag, examined it for a minute, and said, "Danny's gonna have got a good job now, but Ernie said Carla hasn't heard the last from him." She paused for a moment. "Maybe this little box is just getting warmed up!"

In an instant they both had changed into pajamas and curled up on the sofa to watch TV. Susan extended her feet so Jeff could rub them. For the first time in twenty four hours she felt completely safe. And every day they were more and more comfortable together.

"What's on tonight?" Susan asked.

"I don't know," Jeff laughed. "Maybe we can find a rerun of The Bachelor!"

CHAPTER 39

Jeff woke up first the next morning. He dressed and went to the hotel lobby to fix coffee for both of them. When he returned Susan was awake.

"Good morning, merry sunshine!" Jeff sang as he placed the two coffee cups on the table. "Are you awake?"

"Not quite yet, but I will be, soon." Susan said. "I'm still trying to process what happened last night."

"Me too," Jeff said. "And I'm gonna Google why Italians don't like Sicilians."

Jeff's cell phone rang. He answered and walked onto the balcony of the hotel suite. He spoke quietly for several minutes before Susan got out of bed. She walked out to the balcony just as the call finished.

"Who was that?" Susan asked. She was surprised that Jeff had left the room to talk to them.

"That was World Health Teams. They gave me my assignment."

"So where are you going?"

"Haiti."

"Oh, when are you leaving?"

"I leave October first and come back at the end of the month."

"Jeff," she said quietly as she moved towards him. "I know how much this means to you and I would never ask you not to do it, but the thought of being away from you for a whole month is tearing me up inside."

Jeff held Susan tightly. "I feel the same way, Sue, but I gave my word that I would do this and my word is my bond."

"And that's one more thing that I love about you Jeff. So how does it all work?"

"Well, we pay our own travel expenses. I'll fly to Port Au Prince and stay in a hotel there. The village we're going to is two hours away by bus so every morning we'll be bussed in and then bussed back at the end of the day."

"We? Who else is going with you."

"It's a whole team. There'll be several doctors, pediatricians. OB/GYN's, Internists, cardiologists, nurses, the whole gamut."

"And dentists, of course."

"We have three dentists and two dental hygienists going."

Susan thought for a minute. "Three dentists and only two hygienists?" she asked. "Do you think they have room for another one?"

"Honey, that's why I walked out of the room. I asked them that question. I told them who you were and about your experience."

"And what did they say?"

"Well, they said you can join the team if you want to. They just have to check your credentials."

"That's no problem." Susan said. She was excited at the thought of joining Jeff on this mission of mercy.

"Well, honey, there is one problem."

"What's that, Jeff?"

"Susan," Jeff sighed. "World Health Teams is a Christian group. We're like missionaries"

"You know I'm Jewish, right?"

Jeff laughed. "Of course I do, Sue. That doesn't matter at all."

"Then, what's the problem?"

Jeff sighed. "Look, the group is very conservative."

"You want me to convert?"

Once again Jeff laughed. "No! That's not it!"

"Then, what's the problem?"

"The problem is that they allow married couples to stay together but not couples who aren't married."

"You mean they don't want us living in sin?"

"That's it, honey. It's as simple as that."

Susan thought for a few seconds. "Then, let's get married!" she said.

"Are you kidding?" Jeff replied.

"Jeff, I've never been more serious in my life."

"Are you sure you're ready for this?" he asked. "It's only been a few weeks."

"It's been long enough for me, Jeffrey Morton. I think you are the most wonderful, generous, kind, gentle, and handsome man in the world, and I want to spend the rest of my life with you."

"No!" Jeff said.

Susan was shocked. She was certain that Jeff had the same feelings for her as she had for him.

"Are you rejecting me, Jeff?" she asked sheepishly. Her heart was pounding.

"No, of course I'm not rejecting you, Sue. But I am a man of great pride, and I refuse to let you be the one who proposes to me. I want to propose to you!"

Sue was relieved to hear those words. "So, go ahead," she said. "Or, do you want to ask my father's permission first. Sorry, too late for that."

"No, honey, not here, and not now."

"So, when?"

"I will choose the time and the place," he said. "And I will choose the way."

"Okay," Susan said with a smile. "But you better not get me pregnant before the wedding!"

They hugged and laughed, but their celebration was interrupted by Susan's cell phone.

She found the phone in her handbag and answered.

"Hey Carla, that was quite a spectacle last night."

"Did you put him up to this?" Carla yelled through the phone.

"Who up to what, Carla? You're not making any sense."

"A man came to my house today. Said he worked for the Pantaloni Group."

"Oh?"

"He handed me an envelope from Ernie Pantaloni."

"Uhuh."

"It had a note inside."

"Yeah, so what did it say?"

Carla read the note to Susan. "Dear Carla. Words cannot adequately express my gratitude to you for saving my life. And I also cannot find words to tell you how sorry I am for the way I treated you. You not only saved my life but you also taught me a lesson I will never forget."

"That's a nice note, Carla."

"Wait, there's more. 'I've often wondered what my life is worth and you made me think about it again. So please accept this check as my way of telling you how much your saving my life meant to me. You are a wonderful person and I wish you much joy and happiness in your life. Sincerely, Ernie Pants.'"

"He gave you a check? How much?"

"Are you sitting down?"

"Okay."

"Two million dollars!"

"Two million?"

"Two million! I feel like I hit the lottery, Susie!"

"That's great, Carla. Now promise me you'll call an accountant and find out about taxes. Then get somebody to invest the money for you so it's safe."

"That's you, Suzie Q. Always the practical one. And guess what else?"

"There's more?"

"Ernie's taking me out to dinner tonight!"

As she ended the call Susan turned to Jeff, "Two million, Jeff!"

"I heard, Sue. I heard. I told you Ernie Pants was loaded!"

"Jeff, my prayer box came through again."

"Can I do my happy dance again?"

"Sure, but you know where that dance leads us. I can't be held responsible for myself when you do that dance!"

CHAPTER 40

The next morning Susan woke up to her coffee from Jeff. She called all three real estate agents and let them know that she had chosen Brenda Porter to sell her Florida house. As expected Brenda was thrilled and the other two agents were very disappointed. Both were professional and wished Susan well, and both offered to do everything they could to find a buyer for her home.

As she and Jeff sipped their coffee Jeff contacted Southwest Airlines to book their flight back to New Hampshire. When he ended the call Sue told him something she had been thinking about all night.

"Jeff," she said. "I've been thinking about those four people who keep coming back to my house. It's been more than a month now and they all keep sitting there every day, waiting for me to help them with my prayer box"

"I feel sorry for them, Sue. They must really be desperate."

"I know I can help them if I use the prayer box, but how can I keep them from telling everyone what I did?"

"Well, maybe that doesn't matter any more." Jeff said.

"How do you mean?"

"If you go to the house and meet with each of them today they probably won't see results until after we're long gone. If anyone else shows up at the house later there'll be a for sale sign in front of it. I think they'll get the point!"

"I guess we can pull it off."

"And then later today we can pack up your things and get them shipped up to Miracle Lake."

Susan paused and said, "Let's try it, honey!"

They packed their suitcase and checked out of the Sunset Inn. As expected their bill was zero thanks to Ernie. They drove to Susan's house where, as expected, four cars were parked in front.

Jeff pulled up behind the last car in line. Susan exited his car and walked up to the car in front of them. A young woman was sitting in the front seat. In the back seat was a baby that looked to be about nine months old. Susan walked up beside the car and knocked on the window, startling the driver. The woman rolled down the window and Susan spoke. "Hello. I'm Susan Gold. I understand you have been waiting to see me."

The woman broke down in tears. "Oh, *Barukh Hashem*! I sat here and prayed every day that you would one day come home and meet me!"

"Your prayers have been answered. What is your name?"

"My name is Shoshana Barron, and this is my daughter Chaya."

"Chaya. What a beautiful name. Please come into my home."

Shoshana carried her daughter out of her car and followed Susan into the house. While she was going in Jeff stopped at each of the other cars and told them they would get a turn shortly.

Susan, Shoshana and Chaya sat at the kitchen table. When she walked in Susan quickly realized that Shoshana was dressed like the Rabbi's wife she had met a few months ago. She was wearing a long skirt and a blouse that covered her upper body completely. It also looked like she was wearing a wig.

Susan removed the prayer box from her handbag and set it on the table. "How can I help you, Shoshana?"

"You met my daughter, Chaya."

"Yes, she's beautiful."

"Thank you. When she was five months old she began to have serious medical problems. The doctors told me that she had Tay Sachs disease."

"I've heard of that." Susan replied. She remembered that her friend Joy had a daughter who had tested positive as a carrier and that the prayer box had saved the baby.

"They told my husband and me that Chaya would only live four years at the most. "

"I'm so sorry."

"So I went last month to the synagogue in Hobe Sound to pray and I met Rivka Rosenberg."

"The rabbi's wife?"

"Yes. And she told me about you and your prayer box. So I looked up your address and drove to your house. When I got here there were a hundred cars parked here."

"Yes, I know," Susan said.

"But I kept coming back every day. The only day I didn't come was Saturday because that's our Sabbath and we don't drive."

"I'm so sorry for what you've been though."

"So every day I sat here with Chaya, and every day I prayed that you would come home with your prayer box."

Susan and Shoshana were both crying. "I'm here now, dear," Susan said quietly, "and so is the prayer box. I can't guarantee that it will work for you but I can tell you that we have seen many miracles."

"Oh, it will work," Shoshana said. "It will work."

The two women hugged and Shoshana headed out the front door. Susan held the prayer box in her hands and spoke to it. "Please help this little girl just like you helped my Rachel."

Just after Shoshana left the house an elderly black woman entered.

"Hello, I'm Susan Gold," Susan said as she held out her hand. The woman grabbed Susan's hand with both of hers.

"I'm Shirley Johnson. Pleased to meet you, ma'am."

"How can I help you, Shirley?"

"My son, Rodney, is a wonderful dancer. All his life that's all he ever wanted to do was dance. All the kids made fun of him, called him a sissy and even worse names because he was a ballet dancer."

"But he stuck with it? Good for him!"

"Yes he did. He stuck with it and now he is going to perform with the Royal Ballet."

"You must be so proud!"

"Proud as a peacock!"

"So how can I help you.?"

"I'm going blind, ma'am. And you see I ain't asking not to go blind. I just want to be able to see long enough to watch my son perform in three months time when he comes to Miami with the Royal Ballet."

"How did you get here every day?"

"I can't see enough to drive so my other son, Dwayne, drives me here every day."

"And you've waited all this time for me?"

"I heard you had a miracle box ma'am and I figured since the eye doctors gave up on me maybe you wouldn't."

"I have the prayer box right here, Shirley, and I promise you I won't give up on you."

"God bless you, ma'am."

"And you too, Shirley," Susan said, as the two women hugged.

The next person to enter the house was a young man who appeared to be in his early twenties.

"Hello, I'm Susan Gold."

"I'm Ryan Morrisey," the young man said, as he shook hands with Susan.

"And how can I help you, Ryan?"

Ryan took a deep breath. "Two months ago I came out to my parents."

"Came out?"

"I told them I was gay."

"Oh." Susan was embarrassed that she had to be told what 'coming out' meant.

"So, how can I help you?"

"When I came out to my parents they said they would always love me but they never wanted to see me again unless I changed."

"Oh my," Susan said. "So you want me to use the prayer box to make you straight?"

"No," the young man replied. "That's not it at all. What I want from the prayer box is to cure whatever sickness is in my parents' hearts that would allow them to give up their son because of who he loves."

Susan breathed a deep sigh. "I'll be honest with you, Ryan. I've never seen or heard of the prayer box doing such a thing."

"That's what I thought you'd say," Ryan said. "But I was desperate for anything to help me."

"Well, Ryan, you have the prayer box open in front of you. I've seen a lot of miracles come from it. I would never say never when it comes to this box."

"Thank you for seeing me, Mrs. Gold."

"I wish you well, Ryan."

Susan was emotionally drained from these people in need. They were all good people with real needs and she was happy to do what she could to help them, but it was all very exhausting.

Soon after Ryan left the fourth and final visitor came into the house. She was surprised to see that it was someone she knew.

"Jimmy, I'm surprised to see you here," she said with a smile. Jimmy Balfour was the tennis pro at their country club. He was a handsome young man in his mid thirties. Tall, blonde, and in great shape, Jimmy was a heartthrob for all of the ladies in the club. His group and private lessons were booked weeks in advance.

"I'm surprised to see me here too, Mrs. Gold," Jimmy said. "But I'm desperate and I hope you can help me."

"How did you manage to sit out in front of my house every day when you have a job at the country club?"

"Truth?"

"Nothing but the truth."

"I paid someone to take me to work, drop me off at the club, and then come and sit here every day in my car. I was hoping you would eventually come back and see me."

"I'm sorry you had to go through all that, Jimmy. I would have made the time for you if you had called me."

"Well, I'm here now and I'm grateful to you for helping me."

"What can I do, Jimmy?"

"It's pretty embarrassing, Mrs. Gold."

"Don't be embarrassed, Jimmy. I don't judge people. I just try to help"

Jimmy paused. "Mrs. Gold, do you remember when I hurt my back last year?"

"I do."

"Well, I went to an orthopedist and he prescribed pain medication for me."

"Okay."

"It worked for a while but eventually the medicine wasn't strong enough."

"Uh huh."

"So then he gave me a stronger medicine."

Susan could sense where this was heading. "Okay, so then what happened?"

Jimmy took a deep breath. "Eventually I was taking Oxycodone. Five milligrams at first, and then ten. But the pain was still there."

"Did you consider surgery on your back?"

"I went to a surgeon and he wanted to cut me but every one of my friends who ever had back surgery told me it was the biggest mistake they ever made."

"I've heard that too. So you kept taking pills?"

"I kept taking more and more pills. My doctor wouldn't give me more so I went to another doctor, and then another. Eventually I had five different doctors and five different pharmacies. Then everybody cut me off so now I'm buying the drugs from Canada."

"You're obviously addicted, Jimmy."

"I need help, Mrs. Gold. And that's why I'm here. I know I need to stop taking this stuff because eventually it will kill me. But every time I try to stop the pain comes back."

Susan showed Jimmy the box. "Jimmy, I hope the powers in this prayer box work for you."

Jimmy stared at the box. "People told me about Danny Rintone and Bill Scanlon. The prayer box worked for them and I think it can help me too."

"I wish you well, Jimmy. I hope the next time I see you things will be better."

"Thank you, Mrs. Gold."

As Jimmy left the house Susan was happy to see Jeff walking up to the door. He was carrying a supply of cardboard and a roll of tape.

"I brought these so we could make up boxes and pack your things."

"Okay, great," Susan replied. "But right now I'm exhausted. Let's go have a drink somewhere and then we can pack things up, okay?"

"Okay, babe," Jeff replied. "I made us reservations for the ten AM flight on Southwest tomorrow. Can we spend the night here?"

"I think so," she replied. "There's nobody I would rather spend my last night here with than you."

A quick trip to the Ale House found them drinking and eating. Susan talked about each of the four people she had met with.

"That was so wonderful of you to do that." Jeff said.

"I only hope for two things," Susan replied. "I want the prayer box to work for all of them and I want to be left alone after all of this. No more visitors!"

"I'll drink to that," Jeff said as he lifted his glass.

CHAPTER 41

When all of the packing was completed, Jeff and Susan went to bed for the first, and probably last time in her bedroom.

"Shall we?" he mused as he turned towards Susan in the bed. He gently rubbed her leg. He knew she was exhausted from the day but maybe she would want this last night in Florida to be memorable.

He waited patiently for a few seconds and then realized that Susan was sound asleep. He smiled, kissed her on the shoulder, turned to his side, and went to sleep.

The alarm woke them in time to make the drive to Palm Beach International and board their plane for Baltimore. From there they would change planes and complete the journey to Manchester.

They dropped off the rental car, checked their bags, passed though security easily, and boarded the plane. They settled into their seats and waited for takeoff of the Southwest flight to Baltimore.

Once the plane reached altitude the lead flight attendant, an attractive young woman wearing a light blue Southwest shirt, made an announcement. "Ladies and gentlemen, the captain has turned off the seat belt sign and it is now safe to move about the cabin."

Susan was comfortably seated in the center seat of row twelve with Jeff on the aisle next to her. She reached her arm under his arm and leaned against him in a loving way. Then the flight attendant had another announcement. She was holding a bouquet of red roses.

"Ladies and gentlemen, my name is Denise," she said. "You may not know that today is national rose day," she continued. "And the local florist at the airport was nice enough to give us this beautiful bouquet."

Another flight attendant, a tall African American man picked up the microphone. "Hi, I'm Ralph," he said. "And we love our Southwest passengers so much that we want one of you to have these roses. Would anyone like them?"

At that, several passengers raised their hands.

"I'll tell you what," Denise said. "We have a box here with all of the seats and we'll draw one lucky passenger to have these roses."

Many of the passengers began looking to see what seats they were sitting in. Ralph held the box while Denise reached in. She pulled out a small piece of paper and read it aloud. "And the winner is seat twelve B! Please come up here and claim your prize."

Susan did not respond until Jeff nudged her and said. "That's you, Sue. That's your seat!"

With that, Jeff stood up and let Susan out into the aisle. There was a smattering of applause as she walked towards the front of the plane. Denise handed her the roses and asked her name.

"Susan Gold," she replied sheepishly.

As Susan started to walk back to her seat, Denise said, "Wait just one more minute, Susan. We have one more special gift for you."

Susan was puzzled. What more can they be giving me, she thought. And how much more embarrassment can I take?

"Susan, there is a gentleman on this plane who has another gift for you and a question he would like to ask you. Is there a Jeff Morton on the plane?"

Susan covered her face as she watched Jeff walk towards her with a giant smile. Jeff stopped two feet from her, got down on one knee and opened a jewelry box. Inside was a shiny diamond ring.

"Susan," he said. "I am deeply, madly, and wildly in love with you. I want us to spend the rest of our lives together. So, today I am asking if you will do me the honor of accepting my proposal. Will you marry me?"

"Yes!!" Susan shouted, as the entire plane burst out in applause.

Jeff placed the ring on Susan's finger. Tears streamed down her face as she helped him up and kissed him. They walked hand in hand back to their seats as many of the passengers cheered and offered congratulations.

As they returned to their seats, Ralph walked up to them and handed each of them a glass of champagne. "Compliments of Southwest Airlines," he said.

"How on earth did you pull this off, Jeff?" Susan asked, as she stared at the beautiful diamond ring on her finger.

"Well, yesterday while you were busy at the house I called Jenny and told her what I was planning to do."

"Was she happy?"

"Ecstatic. She gave me your ring size and suggested the type of ring you might like."

"You're amazing!" Susan said, staring at her new ring. "And Jenny really got this one right. I love it!"

"I went to three jewelers before I found one that had this ring in stock." Jeff added. "And then I made them replace the center stone with a larger one."

"But how did you get the airline to?"

"Oh, that was easy," he said with a grin. "Southwest loves this kind of stuff. I called them and told them what I planned and they said leave it all to them. It turned out even better than I expected!"

"I love you, Jeff," Susan said. She could not stop staring at her new ring.

"That's what I was going for!" Jeff replied with a smile.

Susan couldn't wait to call Jenny as she stepped off the plane in Baltimore. The second Jenny answered she yelled, "Eeeeeee!"

"Eeeeee!" Came the reply from her daughter.

"I'm the happiest woman in the world right now, Jen."

"We're gonna have a fabulous wedding at the lakefront, mom. I've already started working on it."

"Oh wait, Jenny, I wasn't even thinking about a wedding. I just thought we'd go down to city hall."

"No way, mom. We'll talk about it when you get to the lake."

CHAPTER 42

The wedding took place on September 24th, one week before their departure for Haiti. The sandy beach at the lake was decorated in wedding bells and a large canopy was erected for the ceremony. Reverend Joe Rinds from Hooksett and Rabbi Deborah Levy from Lexington jointly presided. Jennifer was the maid of honor and Michael was the best man. The four grandchildren, Adam, Rachel, and Michael's two kids, were in the procession.

Susan was dressed in a beautiful cream colored lacy gown that she had picked out with her daughter's help. Jeff wore a cream colored suit to match.

Several chairs had been rented and placed in front of the canopy. All of the Miracle Lake friends and neighbors were there to celebrate with the newlyweds. Jeff was pleasantly surprised to see his old pal Ernie Pants arrive, and equally surprised to see Carla on his arm. Susan's two brothers and their families came up from Boston, as did David's parents, Larry and Joyce Cohen.

Jimmy Balfour came from Florida with several of Susan's neighbors, golf, and tennis friends.

"How are you doing, Jimmy?" Susan asked. His big smile and thumbs up gesture was all she needed to know that the prayer box had worked for him. If it had worked for Jimmy, she thought, maybe it had also worked for Shoshana, Ryan, and Shirley.

It was a short wedding service in which the couple exchanged vows, said "I do" and kissed. Then Jeff stomped on a glass and everyone yelled

"Mazel Tov!" All of the guests came back to Jennifer's house for a catered lunch provided by the diner.

The whole month of September had been spent getting ready for their trip to Haiti. Jeff renewed his passport. David administered vaccinations for Hepatitis A, Typhoid, and a tetanus shot to each of them. Susan pulled together all of the documentation the World Health Group needed to accept her on the trip and Jeff sent along a copy of their marriage certificate. Everything was now set for their trip.

One day before they left for Haiti, just after they finished their walk around the lake, Jeff said, "Honey, I'd like to visit mom's grave today. I haven't seen the engraving and I want to make sure that it's right before we go away."

"Of course," Susan replied. "I'll go with you."

"And bring the prayer box."

"Okay, sure," Susan replied. "But why?"

"I want mom to see it," Jeff said as he took his wife's hand, "and I want her to formally meet my wife."

Susan smiled as they left the house and moved into Jeff's Mercedes. They traveled twenty miles to Hooksett, parked the car in the cemetery lot, and made the hundred yard walk to the Morton grave site.

Jeff looked carefully at the tombstone. In the center was the engraving

BEVERLY

November 7, 1925

July 11, 2017

"It's perfect," he said as he held his arm around Susan.

"I'm glad it worked out well."

"Mom?" Jeff said as he moved closer to the tombstone. "I want you to meet my wife, Susan. She was here once before but now we're married and I wanted you to meet your new daughter-in-law."

"Hello, Mrs. Morton," Susan said softly.

"Sue," Jeff said. "I know that she would want you to call her mom."

"Hello, mom."

"And I know she would have loved you, Susie."

"Mom," Susan said, "I have so much to thank you for." She reached out and grabbed Jeff's hand. "First I want to thank you for raising such a wonderful son. He is the kindest most gentle and caring man I have ever met. I am so happy that we met and so happy that he married me."

"And, mom," Jeff added. "Susan is the most amazing woman I have ever met. She makes me happy every day."

"The second thing I want to thank you for, Mrs., er mom, is for saving the life of my granddaughter, Rachel."

"Mom," Jeff interjected. "Rachel is only nine years old. She was going to die until we brought her here to your prayer box."

"You saved her life," Susan said. "And I will forever be grateful to you."

Jeff then reached into Susan's handbag and removed the prayer box. He held it up in front of the stone.

"Mom," he said, opening the box, "Susan has a prayer box just like yours."

"I know it's hard to believe," Susan added, "but I am also one of the thirty-six righteous people who have a box like this."

"Sue and I are going to Haiti next week to take care of some very poor people. We're bringing the prayer box and hopefully it will work many miracles for those poor people."

"The Haitian people have been through so much," Sue added.

"And when we come back we're gonna live in your house at Miracle Lake, and Susan will place her prayer box in the exact same spot that you had yours."

"That way Miracle Lake can have its miracles continue for many years to come," Susan added.

"I love you, mom, and I love you too, dad." Jeff said. He paused before continuing. "Dad, my Mickey has taken over the dental practice now. He's a great man and an even better dentist than I was. I promise he'll make you proud. And Michael, I have missed you for so long. Please take care of mom and dad now. And I want all of you to be proud of us and proud of what we are doing."

"I'm sure they are, Jeff," Susan said as she took his hand in hers. They walked slowly back to the car, knowing that their adventure together had only just begun.

EPILOGUE

Susan and Jeff were excited to be celebrating their twentieth wedding anniversary. Now at eighty-one and eighty-eight they were blessed to have enjoyed so many wonderful years together. For twelve years they had volunteered at World Health Teams until Jeff turned eighty and was too old to serve.

Susan's daughter, Jennifer, and her husband, David, continued to spend their summers at Miracle Lake and, even in her eighties, Susan was still a regular on the tennis courts. The mother and daughter team was almost unbeatable.

Susan's granddaughter, Rachel, was now an intern in Chicago and she planned to join her father's pediatric practice as soon as she completed her residency. Her brother, Adam had experienced a growth spurt and was now as tall as his father. He was married with two beautiful children. Jeff's grandchildren were both married and each had one child. His grandson was in dental school and was almost ready to join Michael in the Morton Dental practice.

Despite their advancing ages, Susan and Jeff both continued to be in relatively good health. Each day they walked around the lake hand in hand. Their pace got a little slower every year but as they walked they often reminisced about their lives and the miracle that had brought them together back in 2017. Three times each week they ate lunch at the diner and, by now, everyone knew their names.

Every winter they visited Carla and Ernie Pants at their spectacular home in Boca Raton. Carla's son, Danny, was now the director of maintenance for all of Ernie's hotels. Bill Scanlon was still going strong with his transplanted liver and Carolyn Johnson's twin granddaughters were sophomores in college.

On their first visit to handle the sale of her Florida house Susan found a plastic bag hanging on the front door. She opened the bag and found a photo of Shirley Johnson and her two sons. The older son was dressed in ballet tights. Susan turned the photo over and read a note that said, "I made it, thanks to your prayer box. With much love, Shirley Johnson."

On a later visit Carla was able to reconnect with Ryan Morrisey and his new husband, Randy. Ryan's parents had finally accepted him and they had walked him down the aisle for his wedding to Randy.

On her most recent trip Susan stopped at the synagogue in Hobe Sound. She was thrilled to see that the synagogue was no longer located in a strip shopping center but now had its own beautiful building. She entered the building and saw Rivka Rosenberg, the Rabbi's wife, busy preparing for an event.

Rivka greeted Susan with a hug. "Do you remember Shoshana Barron, the woman who came to your house with her daughter Chaya many years ago?"

"Of course I do." Susan replied. "How are they?"

"Chaya is getting married here tomorrow."

* * *

Susan's prayer box continued to keep its place of honor in the window sill of their Miracle Lake cottage, and thousands of people came every year to the lake to be helped by its miracles.

One evening as they sat having dinner they were interrupted by a knock on their front door. Jeff opened the door and found a young man standing on the steps. He appeared to be of Indian heritage. He was about five foot seven, dark of hair and complexion, and he looked to be in his early twenties. He was carrying a leather brief case. He is probably selling something, Jeff thought at first glance.

"Can I help you?" Jeff asked.

"Yes, thank you, sir," the young man responded. "My name is Rajesh Asthani. I came here from New Delhi, India and I was hoping to meet Beverly Jean Davis. Does she still live here?"

Jeff was shocked by what he heard. He called to Susan who joined him at the door.

"Come in," Susan said.

The young man followed them into the house and took a seat on their living room sofa.

"Tell me again who you are looking for," Jeff asked quietly.

"Beverly Jean Davis. I was told that she once lived here."

"Well, yes she did," Jeff replied. "Beverly Morton was her name. Davis was her maiden name."

"I see," the young man said. "Is she here?"

Jeff chuckled. "Beverly was my mother. She passed away twenty years ago. Why did you want to see her?"

The young man reached into his leather case and removed a small wooden box. He held it up to show Susan and Jeff.

"This is called a prayer box," he said. "And I was told that Beverly had this box before me."

Jeff was stunned by what he saw. It looked exactly like the prayer box his mother once had. He took the box and examined it closely. Carved on the back were the letters RKA.

"RKA," he asked. "Are these your initials?"

"Yes. My full name is Rajesh Kumar Asthani."

"And how did your initials get here?" Susan asked.

"I have no idea," Rajesh replied. "They were on the box when I found it."

Jeff looked below RKA and saw the initials BJD. There was no doubt that this was the prayer box that he had buried in his mother's grave.

"So, how did you get this box?" he asked the young man.

"I don't know. It just appeared in my apartment in India about two months ago. Since then I have been traveling all over the world trying to find out where it came from and why it came to me."

"Let me ask you something," Susan interjected. "When exactly were you born?"

"I was born on July 11, 2017 in New Delhi."

"Make yourself comfortable young man," Jeff said. "Have we got a story to tell you!"

MY INSPIRATION

The story in the book was inspired by the incredible creativity and kindness of my wife Joanne Caras.

When our dear friend Steve was diagnosed with cancer Joanne purchased a small box. She then asked all of our friends to say a prayer for Steve into the box. After all the prayers were said Joanne closed the box and handed it to Steve.

Steve was so touched by the thoughtfulness of this prayer box that he was moved to tears. He brought the box with him to the hospital as he underwent surgery. Steve survived and now is cancer free and healthy.

Buoyed by the success with Steve, Joanne went on to create prayer boxes for several other ailing friends, and the result for each was the same as for Steve.

Joanne's act of love for our friends inspired me to write this book. She is truly an angel.

CPSIA information can be obtained
at www.ICGtesting.com
Printed in the USA
BVHW030017280620
582476BV00001B/282

9 780578 706375